JAN BALABÁN

WHERE WAS THE ANGEL GOING?

TRANSLATION OF THIS BOOK WAS SUPPORTED BY

MINISTRY OF CULTURE
CZECH REPUBLIC

WHERE WAS THE ANGEL GOING?

by Jan Balabán

Translated from the Czech and introduced by Charles S. Kraszewski

Translation of this book was supported
by the Ministry of Culture of the Czech Republic

KUDY ŠEL ANDĚL by Jan Balabán
Copyright © 2003 Heirs of Jan Balabán

Proofreading by Kevin Bridge

Introduction © 2020, Charles S. Kraszewski

Cover art:
© 2016, Daniel Balabán, 'Pohřeb'

Book cover and layout interior created by Max Mendor

© 2020, Glagoslav Publications

www.glagoslav.com

ISBN: 978-1-912894-27-7

First published in English
by Glagoslav Publications on November 27, 2020

A catalogue record for this book is available from the British Library.

JAN BALABÁN

WHERE WAS THE ANGEL GOING?

Translated from the Czech
and introduced by Charles S. Kraszewski

GLAGOSLAV PUBLICATIONS

CONTENTS

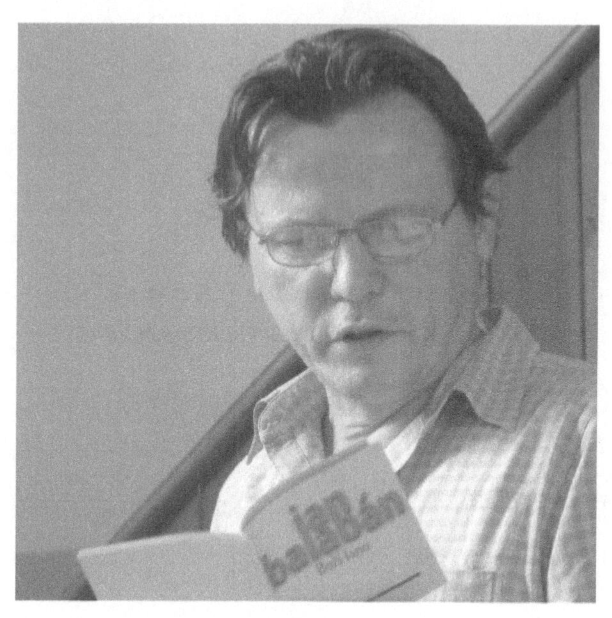

JAN BALABÁN

1961 – 2010

ANY PORT IN A STORM
JAN BALABÁN AND THE RETURN TO EDEN

Charles S. Kraszewski

I once had a friend who was a chef. A real chef; someone who loved the art of eating, preparing food, and knew a lot about both. I remember telling him once, off-hand, about having eaten in a Hungarian restaurant somewhere off Bloor St. in Toronto. 'What did you have?' he asked. 'Fish,' I replied. 'How was it?' 'Horrible.' He laughed. 'What did you expect from a landlocked country, hundreds of miles from the sea in every direction?' I had nothing to reply to that. His logic was impeccable.

Now, in one of the poems that make up his autobiographical cycle *Zvíře dětství* [The Animal of Childhood], Rio Preisner, who was raised in an atheist household, compares himself to the other, Catholic children, as he gazes from afar at the affection they have for the kindly parish priest, their catechist. While they had something he was deprived of, some sort of hope, some love — which he saw, but could not understand — all he was left with was adventure stories of 'happy shipwrecks.' Unsatisfying, but somehow fitting for his situation: alone on a desert island.

Aquatic imagery abounds in Jan Balabán's *Kudy* šel *anděl* [Where Was the Angel Going?] as well. In chapter 29, for example, sitting at the window with a coffee, Martin dreams of great expanses of water which 'should' be found just beyond the tracks:

> There, at the railway line, the city ought to end. The brick hovels and the ramps, the approaches and the bridges and past all that there should be a pier, a strip of dirty harbour water and there, where the blinking red warning lights on the roofs of the prefab blocks emerge

from the mist, there, the horizon, and on the horizon ships, and past the horizon, the measureless expanse of ocean.

The apartment in which Martin grew up is described in terms reminiscent of a sturdy little craft — something like the barque of Peter — breasting the turbulent seas of an inimical world:

> The only light came through the peephole as if it were a window on another world, or the tiny porthole of a boat. Their boat, with which they navigate the adverse waters of that city. That's where they live, where they have their books and their faith, which the people around them can't understand. There, inside the boat, they sing their old songs, the echoes of which sometimes meet their neighbours' ears there in their living rooms full of television (4).

His son always has to have little boats in bed with him 'so he wouldn't drown' (34), and now that he is divorced, when he can only see his children on certain weekends, he dreams of gathering them together in the 'temporary rented haven' of his garret apartment 'as if in a ship's cabin' (29). Even Monika, when reminiscing on her own childhood as the interracial daughter of a single mother, speaks of their home as having been 'as cosy as a boat. A little boat' (36).

Whence all this nautical imagery in the literature of a landlocked country like the Czech Republic, or Czecho-Slovakia, as it was back in those days, which is about as far away from a sea as one can get? Perhaps the answer is to be found in the myth of Noah's ark — which is not so far away from our present reality as we may think. When the spell-checks of our ubiquitous electronic devices (that we take to bed with us?) underscore 'Tri-une' in red as if it were something misspelt, and offer 'Goddess' and 'Gods' as suggestions when we type in 'God,' it is not too far from here to a sense of being surrounded by a rising tide of incredulity and even the enmity of a society, once Christian, that now treats Christianity as a foreign body. A foreign body to be expelled, ignored, or wondered at, like some quaint curio. Fifty years ago, the young atheist (or agnostic; he seems more like someone who has never given a thought to God, rather than someone who rejects Him) who shows up at the chapel Martin is cleaning in chapter 39, oblivious to Christian realities, would be the odd man out. Today — in the UK and France, no less than the Czech Republic — he is the norm. Folk like Martin are the oddballs, the fossils, the trinkets to be picked up, examined, and set back down with a shrug.

Martin Vrána, the protagonist of these stories, is, like the author himself, an evangelical Christian.[1] This puts him at a farther remove from the mainstream, as the member of a minority (Czech Protestants) within a minority (Czech Christians, most of whom are Catholic) in the overwhelmingly a-religious Czech Republic of today. Of course, Moravia, the eastern portion of the Republic, where most of the action takes place, has traditionally held a larger number of committed Christians than Bohemia, the western portion dominated by Prague. Martin, in short, is an outsider — something that becomes apparent from the very first chapter of the book, incongruously numbered 'Chapter 19:'[2]

> O, just don't let me run across any neighbour. He'd never really quarrelled with them, but they still didn't like him for some reason. He had striven to come to terms with this since childhood. The people I've actually done something to like me more. You come across a neighbour, your brother in humanity, in the gloomy light of the stairwell and he gives you a dirty look. Even if you've greeted him nicely, really meaning it.

His being cut off from the main currents of society is not merely a confessional matter — it is an ontological state. After Chapter 19, our first glimpse into the life of adult Martin (divorced, despairing, perhaps even despised) the narrative flow takes a hairpin turn to Chapter 1, in which we meet up with the adolescent Martin during his short-lived erotic idyll with his girlfriend, Eva.

....

[1]   That is, a Protestant — the term in Central Europe has little in common with what the word means in the USA.

[2]   The book begins out of order with chapter 19 so as to underscore the importance of every moment — Eliot's eternal moment. On the other hand, it could underscore futility. 'So this is all there is?' Martin asks himself in that chapter, thus intimating, 'yep' — the preceding 18 Chapters of his life lead to nothing more than a lonely attic flat… Will this change from 19 on? Is this all there is to life — no hope for progression?

Escaping from their prefab estates, they enjoy an innocent frolic on the grounds of an abandoned colliery. Their existence there is typically adolescent — oscillating between the adulthood of heavy petting and the childlike innocence of play:

> One simply lost oneself in that fantastic land, which they regarded as their own. The sunlight flashed and flickered on the aspen leaves, the bindweed curled toward the tree branches and they two curled toward each other as well, just a little frightened. They would kiss and embrace on an iron catwalk stretched between two pipes over a black stream. They would smudge up Eva's blouse, pressing against one another, until they couldn't tell where those snapping sounds were coming from — whether from the pipes below them, or the pipes within their bodies. And then again, a few steps apart from one another, to leap from the concrete pylon — she into his arms, there in the wood that figured on no maps, but all the same was full of birdsong and breathed its cool exhalations; where the ground was covered with nettles and burdock and birches stood naked, like skin suddenly revealed from beneath clothes. There was no end to it. Martin, knackered with standing, couldn't stop; Eva, tousled and manhandled by Martin, would fall on him, again and again. From the elderberry above them protruded an old winch, on the rusty drum of which there remained a few twists of wire rope, its end slithering on the grass like a snake.

It is an Edenic scene — underscored (not overbearingly) by Eva's name — but that cable, 'slithering on the grass like a snake,' seems a foretelling of doom. And indeed, before too long, the couple are to be expelled from Eden — through the agency of 'Eve' no less — who blindsides Martin by suddenly breaking up with him.

Is Martin's tale, like that of Adam himself, the story of us all? It's hard to be certain. Yet Balabán hints at just so much in Chapter 33. There, the two former young lovers find themselves, by coincidence, together in London. When Eva rings up Martin, he sets a rendezvous for Lambeth station, something that makes little sense — is it the proximity of the old Battersea power station, familiar to them from the album cover of Pink Floyd's *Animals*? — until he explains to her:

'You know, there exists this unprovable and yet irrefutable legend, that somewhere in the garden of one of these old houses the Lake poet Wordsworth surprised William Blake and his wife, seated on a garden bench beneath the woodbine, as naked as Adam and Eve. The Lake poet supposedly turned aside his chaste eyes, but then he kept flapping his gums about it so, that it entered into every literary history.'

So, we might say, just as the Blakes' Edenic idyll was sullied and ruined by Wordsworth, so were Martin and Eva expelled from their Eden by the world. You can't escape the surrounding world; it penetrates every little Eden and ruins it. Those little boats of ours, bravely breasting the billows of an inimical world, are listing, punctured and cracked, the waters of the world constantly seeping into our dangerously heavy ballast.

Where Was the Angel Going? is a book about displacement — no Archimedian pun intended. While the main character, Martin, is the eternal outsider, much the same can be said for any of the main characters. Monika, his lover, is a Czech girl with slanted eyes — the fruit of her mother's dalliance with an Oriental colleague while away on a stipend in America. She, as her half-sister puts it, is 'responsible' for the breakup of a family, although she's paid a high price for it — being 'hidden' as much as possible from the outside world by her otherwise loving mother, and constantly having to bear the questioning eyes of those who look upon her as something 'other.' Even Martin cannot withhold his curiosity, a cruel trait in his character that, oddly enough, humanises him for the reader. He is sinner as well as sinned against; whoever the titular 'angel' may be, it is certainly not Martin Vrána.

Martin's eldest brother, Petr Jr, searches for what he lacks in West Germany. Perhaps he alone of all the searchers finds some semblance of his particular lost Eden. Tomáš, the middle brother, a photographer, *must* live in Prague, and even though his mother can't understand why this must be so, she herself idealises her life in the countryside, that period from before she got married and moved to industrialised Ostrava.

As the story plays out in the milieu of a family of committed Evangelicals, it might be that we are dealing with an allegory of the *homo peregrinus*, underscored by St Augustine in his famous dictum 'our heart is restless, until it rests in Thee.' But it must be remembered that the majority of Martin's story, at least those parts of it narrated as recollection, is set in the frustrating years of Communist Czechoslovakia, where Gustav Husák 'gazed at us' from his official portraits with those censorious eyes of his and that somewhat sadistically pursed lip, like a broad pretending to be a guy. He too was a great mystic, of a sort, who knew that his material face, that trembling map of aged liver spots, didn't really exist — that only those silver icons of it glowing everywhere did — those dusty holy pictures of him hung in each and every classroom and office (20).

And so, it is a generational sense of displacement, not merely a confessional one. All of Martin's chums shared it, fantasising in a cheap sci-fi way of a lost world where they 'really' belong, and from which they have been transported to this 'prison planet' for some crime they can't remember having committed:

> We drank ourselves stupid in taverns in Prague, Olomouc and Ostrava; we blushed in shame in our schools on account of all that Marxist idiocy, we goofed off at night, and, half-joking, half-serious, we told one another stories of how somewhere in the cosmos there were happier places — maybe on Jupiter or in the Pleiades — and that people are transported to the planet Earth for punishment. Part of the punishment is their ignorance of the fact. We'd forgotten that we'd forgotten. We're all in a penal colony, though we don't know it. We'd say that somewhere our letters must be hidden, in among the pages of old books, under the tiles in church, in boxes in the pillars of old bridges. Somewhere, the message I wrote to myself before they wiped my memory clean is hidden. Before they brainwashed me. There is my real name; there I could find out what it was I did, and what I'm being punished for. How I got here, and how I might get out (28).

Anyone of Balabán's generation who remembers what the world behind the Iron Curtain was like, during the decade preceding the great upheavals begun in Poland and resulting in the *sametová revoluce* that swept all the Husáks of the old Czechoslovak Socialist Republic away, will comprehend these sentiments perfectly. But the work has a wider resonance, too. Eva Topolská frames her sense of displacement — which began when she was a child, at her parents' divorce — as something we all experience: the exile from the security and bliss of early childhood:

> That's what these mobile phones do. You can be anywhere. That's no advertising slogan, that's the truth. You ring somebody up just because a friend in common gave you his number. Because you have this feeling, or maybe somebody told you, that he'd be in England, or, rather, no, you didn't suppose that; he has to be at home after all. Somewhere in northern Moravia, among the collieries, somewhere in northern Czechia, amidst the exhausted quarries, somewhere in some unreal land, where everything is disappearing. Buried in ash like the shadow of years one recalls with sweetness, because they no longer exist. Because you are no longer a young freckled girl in his embrace, but a damnably independent woman, who does little more these days than ride around in taxis and ring people up. So you pick a number, you can be anywhere. And he's not sitting there amidst the exhausted quarries, he's here, on the other side of the river, and makes a date with you at a train station (34).

And so it seems that those landlocked Czechs know quite a bit about those oceans metaphysical after all. Ask not for whom the ship whistle toots — it toots for thee.

Displacement, disenfranchisement, or exile, however one chooses to term it, is an unnatural state, if universal to all men and women. In chapter 25 Martin meditates on man's unique loneliness and abandonment in all of creation:

> Since the strawy fairy stories of fated encounters of people destined for each other have long ago been ground to dust. Dust that can give rise to nothing except allergies. People are not fated to one another, people are condemned to their fate. They can't belong to one another, they can't belong to themselves, they belong nowhere. Has he not lived through enough already to understand that this not-belonging is the only home left to a person beneath these dangerous heavens? Unlike the unconscious creatures with their safe dens and cosy nests, man alone must stop deluding himself that he belongs somewhere,

that someday he'll discover that other half from whom he was once separated, and that their souls will flow together and re-meld, like it's some kind of romantic movie.

And yet, despite all the divorces and broken families that litter the pages of *Where Was the Angel Going?*, Martin is continually in need of someone. This Leitmotif by itself puts the lie to the bitter words just cited, suggesting that the true nature of humanity is communion, community. Martin's deep-seated need of this, whether we choose to refer to the Judeo-Christian myth of a return to Eden, or the pagan Greek myth of our originally composite nature which he refers to above, does find its fulfilment toward the end of Martin's story.

After Martin's horrific accident, his father, with whom he could find no common ground during the daily grind, sits patiently by his son's bedside, praying for his return, 'ben[ding] down over Martin, strok[ing] his head and [speaking] to him, as if his son were able to hear him' (46). Even more telling is Monika's decision to move into Martin's flat after all. She knows there are good reasons for not aligning her fate with that of this very imperfect man:

> Suddenly, she realised that she was afraid of him. She wanted to be afraid for him, but she was afraid of him. With her eyes closed, she rolled over under his blanket and waited for him. For that dreadful man to come along and wound her. To throw her beneath the wheels of a car and then look on as her blood flowed, and then feel sorry for her and say that things like that can happen. She saw his dreadful hands, so often unwashed and with broken nails, his face, on which his beloved, boyish features gave way to hard, pitiless edges. His stomach, which would only swell larger with time, his sex, that weapon of his, with which he wounded other women, when, faithlessly, he procured himself pleasure and others — pain. He was unfaithful to his wife, unfaithful to that Eva of his, unfaithful to everybody. Ah, Martin, you're the guy who buttons his trousers and goes off on his own roguish way. Right now, in hospital, you have no feelings for anyone. You're a dreadful, dreadful person. What dreadfulness you carry around inside yourself! I can understand each and every woman who

runs off as soon as she catches sight of you. I can understand each and every wife who runs off from her husband, who doesn't want anything to do with him, with that unshaven mug, scratchy beneath the neck, with those sly glances that pierce to the very heart (44).

And yet something, something more than mere sentiment, overrides her reason and impels her to take that very step. And thus, the end of Martin's story is, actually, its beginning.

This may come as a surprise. But 'surprises' are at the very heart of the work. One of the most frequently encountered words in *Where Was the Angel Going?* is *najednou* — 'suddenly.' Suddenly, something happens, and life takes a diametrical turn from its wonted path, setting off in a new direction. The sharpest of these sudden turns happens, of course, when Martin steps off the kerb and is slammed by the car. At any rate, the Leitmotif of sudden shifts is a warning against resignation, or despair, which, as any good Protestant lad should know, is the one unforgivable sin — the sin against the Holy Ghost. That He will in, at any time, as long as one is receptive to His coming, is apparent from Martin's story of spending Pentecost at home. Contemplating a Gothic image of the flames of the Holy Ghost descending upon the Disciples,

> Martin gazed at those motionless flames above the heads of the saints and felt an endless peace in contemplating their ecstasy — just like the arrow ever fixed in its target. Not striving for anything, not twitching and jerking — being, belonging to God.
> And in this way that good son Martin compensated for so impiously refusing to participate in Whitsunday evensong (7).

The painting in question is a relic of the Middle Ages and — like the gold-flaked icons from which it ultimately derives — a window onto a different dimension. An eternal reality, the eloquence of which — it is so difficult to speak here without being misunderstood — is dependent on the receptivity of the beholder. The same picture, purchased (so sacrilegiously) at an antique store liquidating the furnishings of some gutted church, laicised and transformed into a community centre or apartments, perhaps hanging over the liquor cabinet in one of the nooks of just such a flat which had once been a chancel, would be a mute, lifeless composition of colour and volume, easily replaceable by a Petr Lik reproduction of Antelope Canyon, once the lady of the house tired of funky faux-religiosity. For a believer like Martin, it is an unbroken, living continuum of power that links the apostolic age with that of the cosmonauts.

For Christianity is not merely a culture, like a mother tongue or an ethnicity. It is a manner of dealing with existence, which is often so difficult to deal with. 'Honey and dust, that's what life tastes like in this city,' muses Martin at the very beginning of the book (19). As he nears its almost catastrophic end, it seems that there is more grime in the aftertaste than sweetness:

> The bare earth and the bushes along the railway line were covered with litter. So many crumpled plastic wrappers, bottles, cinders, fag-ends and piles of dog shit. What's going on here? Here in this subway beneath the rumbling corpus of the railway — what is this greasy filth, with which the water is clogged, ankle-deep?
> Who makes us live here? Here amidst these bushes, from the bare branches of which tatters of plastic flutter? Here, where iron plates crumble to rust, where even iron is exhausted, handrails sag, tracks are empty, buildings shuttered, windows grim and grimy with poisoned perspectives and retrospectives on the low sky from which this dreadful April drizzle is seeping. Who was it fixed these sights before our eyes? How am I to walk off my despair, how do I get rid of this dreadful hunger? (41)

After meditating on the hopeless reality of neighbouring Poland, 'N.N.,' the anti-hero of Stanisław Barańczak's *Sztuczne oddychanie* [Artificial Respiration], composes a suicide note on an empty cigarette packet before opening the window and climbing out onto the ledge: 'No one is to blame for what has happened. / No one but myself.' The double-entendre is obvious: N.N. is taking responsibility for his own suicidal act and — for what drove him to it, the state of his society. Why is it that Martin does not do the same? Does he not bear some guilt, too? Yes, Christianity answers — but it is the guilt of Adam, who is ultimately responsible for the fallen state of all creation; it is this guilt which Martin, and all of us, have inherited from our parents like a spiritual syphilis, to use St Augustine's colourful term. But that guilt was washed away by the waters of baptism, and, although this fact absolves none of us from the responsibility of doing what we can do ameliorate a bad situation, it prevents despair by pointing at the wider context. Here, we are not merely speaking of the world 'beyond,' which we may be made to enter at any moment, but the renewal of all things at the end of time, in the eternal moment.

It is this attitude that informs the prayer of that ancient happy virgin, Marie, who arrives to help Martin clean the chapel on his free day:

> 'And now, Martinku,' said sister Marie, taking him by the elbow, 'let's lift up a petition to the Lord together.' She knelt down and her gaunt hand, suddenly full of strength, pulled Martin down to his knees as well. They folded their hands and Marie prayed. And that prayer was to remain with Martin for the rest of his life. Amen. (39)

Marie, as Martin points out, is a girl, despite her years, because of her perpetual virginity (no allusion necessarily implied). A girl, and therefore a child, and, as we know, one needs to become like a child in order to enter into the Kingdom of God. It is perhaps for this reason that children are so often mentioned in the pages of *Where Was the Angel Going?* They are not merely symbols of innocence, they are sage emissaries from that other world — the titular angels, perhaps. Children see things in a simple, direct manner, and offer simple, real solutions to complicated problems: love, compassion. 'You told me how your daughter crawled beneath the table in fear when you were quarrelling,' Monika reminds Martin, 'about your son, who ran out into the corridor after you when your wife was screaming that she hated you. How that helpless little fellow wanted to soothe you' (36).

Children are wise with the wisdom of eternity, which is to say: goodness; they can be, in this respect, more mature than their elders. As Martin is leading his son back home after a visit in Chapter 31, he stops at the door and says:

> 'You know, boy, even though we don't live together, that doesn't mean that…'

'I know.' The boy was suddenly older than Martin was. Martin was ashamed of the tears that he somehow fought back (31).

But whereas children can be mentors, calling childish adults back to order, for this very reason they should not be disabused of their innocence, deprived of their simple ideals of right and wrong, by relativising adults. Morality — like it or not! — should be as ironclad as grammar, thinks Eva's professional grandfather, heartbroken at his granddaughter's deprivation of stable development by parents who put their own comfort and pleasure before her good. When his wife objects to his strict moral tutelage of the little girl, our hearts are first on her side. *Let the girl have as normal a childhood as possible. Don't torment her!* we nod. And yet, it is difficult not to see his side of the argument:

> 'You're messing up that little girl's head with adult problems,' his wife would chide him when little Eva didn't know where to rest her eyes, at each mention of her parents.
> 'They've already messed up her head with adult problems,' the old man shot back. 'I'm setting forth examples, you understand, Olinka, examples that someday she'll be able to grasp. So that she'll know that in every sentence there has to be…'
>
> […]
>
> Because it still holds true, even now, that a proper sentence has subject, predicate, and object, right? And each proper family has father, mother, and child. Or not? Maybe that doesn't apply anymore? the old man seethed, then, brimming with love, he looked down at the small curly head of his granddaughter (24).

However much the modern world might want to inveigh against this sort of attitude, it bears fruit in the life of Eva. Having become pregnant by a man who took pleasure in 'demeaning' her, she still, in the end, decides to keep the child, and does so, with a sudden uprush of warmth at the recollection of her grandfather's 'soft heroism […] that whole courageous game with life as its stakes, that game with the suppressed subject.'

We may be surprised at that phrase, 'soft heroism.' In our way of looking at things, the old professor may have subjected his granddaughter to a rather harsh didacticism, but it was not empty pedantry. Even if it hurt her to realise that her parents were acting wrongly, better that pain now, than poisonous servings of sugared moral indifference. This much at least is required by Christian honesty. As we know, or should know, not even Pope or Patriarch can conscience immorality for dubiously pastoral reasons. And in this case — it saves a life.

With man's expulsion from Eden, time begins. The clock starts ticking with the first sin. And yet, Martin's expulsion from Eden fixes him in the moment of his fall:

> As Zeno of Elea proved long ago, the arrow shot from its bow does not fly, but, rather, is stationary in each segment of its route. Because the same arrow can't be in two places at once. No more could Martin, and so he remains there, in that one shattering moment, shirtless at the culm bank, with his stomach lifting and his eyes gazing round at the empty reaches of the surrounding world, which he must, now, take for his own. (6)

'Stunned' is perhaps a better word than 'fixed' — as at the moment of his particular fall, Martin finds himself faced with the new, inimical world that he must enter. From this moment on, Martin is in the position of the first Europeans in California (and of Europeans first in California), gazing at what must now be conquered, since it has been seen, to paraphrase Czesław Miłosz. He must now set off into that land, like it or not. As in the case of old Adam, Eva has made the decision for him.

Still, in a curious sense, Martin will ever remain in that moment, at once Edenic and infernal, standing at the lip of paradise, 'in the subsequent vacuum created by her absence [when] he could still feel the aura of her body on his face, still taste her saliva in his mouth' (2) but facing the imminent exit, in that horrible pause between the nearness of just-passed delight and the rough thump of the angel's hand between the shoulder-blades that will send him packing.

Eva will always remain with him — as Monika notes, referring to her as 'your mysterious Eva, whom you never stopped loving despite your marriage' (36) — to whom he was 'unfaithful' (44), even though it was she who had broken with him. Martin, it seems, is the one who 'betrayed' her the first time his eyes wandered to another woman. Eva is Martin's *donna ideale,* his Beatrice, and while she does not upbraid him in London for his 'infidelity' as the Florentine girl does Dante, when he finally meets her again in Purgatory, Monika does it for her, here.

Now Purgatory is also a place subject, in a certain sense, to time, while more than once, Balabán refers to eternal states in his record of the history of Martin Vrána:

> In a tunnel, time means nothing. The moment when total darkness falls is the last moment, and others such follow, until the greyish mould of light appears in the window frames. The eternity between that moment and this is a slate wiped clean, which has different dimensions and parameters than events in time upon which the light of the sun falls (13).

Hell is eternal; one of the most moving — and frightening — parts of the *Inferno* is in Canto X when Cavalcante de' Cavalcanti explains to the pilgrim that, whereas the damned are aware of both the past and the future, knowledge of the present moment is denied them. Thus, when time ends, when the last soul in Purgatory has been received into Heaven and nothing shall remain but Heaven and Hell, the sufferings of the damned will be augmented by the total eclipse of their rational mind. In that now eternal present moment, no consciousness will remain them but that of their suffering; they will be locked eternally within the sin for which they were condemned.[3]

Such, however, is not the case with Martin. His frequent musings on eternity, reality, and absence tend in an affirmative direction — towards the Christian Neoplatonic idea of the mind of God, in which all things, even those hidden from us, are acknowledged and present. This is the sense of

----

[3]   See *Inferno,* Canto X: 'Noi veggiam, come quei c'ha mala luce, / le cose', disse, 'che ne son lontano; / cotanto ancor ne splende il sommo duce. // Quando s'appressano o son, tutto è vano / nostro intelletto; e s'altri non ci apporta, / nulla sapem di vostro stato umano. // Però comprender puoi che tutta morta / fia nostra conoscenza da quel punto / che del futuro fia chiusa la porta'.

his brother Tomáš's 'broadcasting' of his photographic negatives into the seemingly empty spaces of the galaxies above Ostrava, and Martin's comforting reassurance of the simple cave-paintings of men, with which he, his brother, and their friend covered the interior of an abandoned mine-shaft. Even though the vault collapsed one day, denying them further access, 'the pigments evoking the outlines of people are still there in the darkness, invisible due to the lack of light, but still there all the same. You can believe me or not, as you like. I can't prove it' (20).

This segment of the book inevitably leads us back to the prehistoric fresco, which Martin sketches on the wall of his flat:

> On one side of the wall he drew a man. He was naked, but set in motion in such a way that his private parts were hidden. One of his hands was stretched out before him, as if he wanted to touch something. I'll paint over it in a minute, anyway, Martin reassured himself, and started to work on the woman. She was standing on the other side, looking out from the plane of the wall on which she was painted. She had a beautiful behind and breasts, and her long hair fell about her face. Children were playing between them, building some structures from flat stones. They were naked too, a little boy and a little girl; engrossed in their game, they weren't looking at each other. Just like the office of a child psychologist, Martin chuckled, shading the design and happily planning the background he would carve out behind them. Gigantic trees — not a pine forest, but ancient growth. (18).

This is also a cave-painting of a sort, and the primaeval setting with which he endows it also has an Edenic eloquence. His life with Daniela and the kids seems to have had little of the paradisiacal about it, yet this too is significant in its exposition of Martin's key trait: regret, sadness at the passing of *anything* good; goodness itself, however brief or trifling its appearance here, is always a reflection of prelapsarian bliss. Even as a child he had this trait, as his mother reminisces:

> Martin, Martin the lefty, who always glances aside somewhat, playing with something the other two can't see. He's always got something stashed away somewhere. And won't show anyone. He'd rather stand

there, teeth clenched, with something gripped in his left hand, and should Tomáš try to pry those fingers open, he'll kick and bite in a furious whirl to keep it hidden (14).

This is not some morbidly selfish petulance, it is an image of Adam tenaciously gripping the edge of Eden with his fingernails.

Finally, *Where Was the Angel Going?* is an elegy for the most important thing in the world — not the individual, but the coming together in complete trust and support of two people. Martin and Eva, Adam and Eve, whatever it is that comes between them and breaks them apart indeed precipitates an expulsion from Paradise. Balabán is firmly set in the Biblical tradition, following which Milton correctly shows that the devil was only able to gain his brief victory over humanity by first separating Adam and Eve, to conquer them — a thought reprised by Jan Zahradníček in *Znamení moci* [Sign of Power], where it is the devil's modern helpers who do the same thing in post-war Czechoslovakia by breaking down the bonds between people; and Eliot, who underscores in his great dramas that isolation is the foundational characteristic of Hell, of damnation. However, in the final coming together of Martin and Monika, Balabán brings his little gospel full cycle by intimating a fresh beginning — the renewal of all things at the end of time. Not unlike the vision with which Dante returns to earth after his awe-inspiring journey, Balabán's novel shows us that this world is not an absurdly incomprehensible scattering of Sybil's leaves, but a book, bound together by Love.

ON TRANSLATING JAN BALABÁN

Literary translation is always a curious endeavour leading to curious results. It is both something obvious — for many years, the Anglophone world has been indebted to Constance Garnett for her magnificent translations of Dostoevsky, which have enabled the great Russian to reach, and influence, millions of people who know no Russian at all — and misunderstood, as something mechanical. Now, English speakers may chuckle at the German bon mot: 'Shakespeare is a fantastic poet. It's a shame the English can't read him in German,' but the phrase, as ironic as it may sound, contains more than a kernel of truth. Schlegel's versions of Shakespeare in German are of such high poetic quality that a seemingly heretical statement suggesting that they are even an improvement on the original is, at the very least, theoretically admissible.

The one thing that can be said with certainty is: each translation is an original work, in its own right. That sounds like an unforgivably prideful thing to say, depreciating, if not dismissing, the original and its author. However, my intent is just the opposite. In claiming the present translation as 'my own' writing, I do not mean to blur or downplay its nature as that strangest beast of literary endeavours, translation, which is a 'new' creation that, all the same, would never have seen the light of day without the previous existence of the original work that it represents in English. What I wish to do is accept the blame for all its faults and roughnesses — I am their sole perpetrator; Jan Balabán had nothing to do with them.

Kudy šel anděl is a beautiful and fascinating work of literary art in the original Czech. This is the very reason I wished to recreate it in English. Every act of literary translation should be an act of love, and this, my *Where Was the Angel Going?* is certainly that, if nothing else.

It is, however, not the same book. It cannot be. No translation is; no translation approaches that ideal — if you can call it that — of Borges' fictional translator, who is so concerned with preserving every stylistic nuance and every shade of meaning of Cervantes' masterpiece *Don Quixote*, that he ends up 'translating' it from Spanish… into Spanish.

Translations are meant to entertain their readers — and that is all, or nearly all, that can be expected of them. They stand or fall on their own strengths, and must be judged as satisfactory, or unsatisfactory, on their own merits alone. In the best possible case, the 'ideal' translation will so delight its reader as to motivate him or her to see 'what's behind it,' and learn Czech (in this particular case) so as to read Jan Balabán in his native tongue. If this book of mine adds one more reader of Czech to the world tally, I'll have accomplished my task.

One thing a literary translation cannot, and must not, be used for, is literary criticism. A translation can never stand in the place of the original work for this purpose. Pierre Leyris' French versions of Gerard Manley Hopkins, and those of Rio Preiser and Ivan Slavík in Czech, are magnificent poems. But the French critic attempting an explication de texte on the basis of Leyris, or his Czech counterpart commenting on 'Hopkins' by utilising Preisner and Slavík as his primary text, are simply being disingenuous, if not dishonest. It is not Hopkins' poetry they are explicating, but that of Leyris, Preisner and Slavík. It is false advertising at best; at worst, it can lead to catastrophe. I'm still hoping to find some misguided essay in English on Czesław Miłosz's *Throughout our Lands* in which the poor, gullible critic performs acrobatics of inventiveness, trying to explicate the deep symbolism (one supposes) of those 'clocks woven of tanager and hummingbird feathers' by the natives of California, whereas the English word 'clock' is a mistranslation of *płaszcz* — 'cloak.' I'd also love to be a fly on the wall of the study of a Russian scholar, furiously searching through arcane books on North American botany, for those elusive 'lily bushes' mentioned by Konstanty Belmont in his translation of Walt Whitman's 'When *Lilacs* Last in the Door-yard Bloom'd.' Literary texts are complex things, and they demand to be met on their own ground, in the original, when being critically dissected. Translations are neither agents nor ambassadors — they cannot speak for the unique and irreplaceable original text. Caveat explicator! Reader, I hope you enjoy this translation of mine, and will be delighted if it moves you to learn Czech in order to read your next work by Jan Balabán in the original tongue. Critic, if you picked up this book in order to use it as a primary text to comment upon Balabán's work, put it right back down and get to work learning Czech, so as to be able to deal justly with one of my favourite authors.

Jan Balabán is a challenging artist, a prose writer with an incredible sensitivity to form. At times, his writing approaches the poetic — from his intelligent interweaving of thematic rhymes and Leitmotifs across many and varied narratives, to his colourful verbal expressions in both standard Czech and the jargon of Silesian miners, to his sensitivity to class and regional manners of speech and cadence. There is also the hallucinatory blending of narrative voices — first person to third person and back again — without any grammatical or syntactical distinctions, something that adds to the incantatory feel of his writing. Finally, he often employs an unusual, split-second shifting of tense — and this in a work that places such importance on the idea of time.

In my earlier attempt at recreating Balabán in English, my version of *Maybe We're Leaving*, I departed from the author's style in respect to the blending of narrative voices by introducing italics to set off a character's interior, first-person meditations from the general third-person narrative flow of the story. I came to regret this decision in the final stages of the book's production, but it had already been set for print, and so we let it go as is. I won't say that this intrusion of mine was the worst sort of betrayal of the original, but it is certainly Kraszewski, not Balabán, writing there. I have not dared anything like that in this translation. The reader knowledgeable in Czech may note some differences in my expressions of tense, for example. But in all such cases, it was the nature of the English language that determined my choice; it was no arbitrary whim of my own. In cases like that, leaving the original expression of tense in the English text would sound wrong, or at least unnatural, and by its quirkiness draw attention to something that the author had not intended to highlight. The first rule in the translator's Hippocratic Oath is to have the translation sound like it was a work originally written in the target language. If I have succeeded at least in this, I will be satisfied with the trade-off in form.

———◆———

The text upon which the present translation is based may be found in: Jan Balabán, *Romány a novely* (Brno: Host, 2011).

A glossary of personal names and historical terms is appended to the text. Footnotes have been reduced to the minimum and mainly deal with linguistic matters and Biblical citations.

ACKNOWLEDGEMENTS

Portions of this translation were read by Jan Zikmund of CzechLit, for whose advice and suggested corrections I am deeply indebted. This translation is so much the better in all those places where I have incorporated his expertise, his careful readings of the original, and his sensitivity to both Czech and English. If my translation reproduces Balabán's original flavour, much of the credit is his. Where I have fallen short, or, — God forbid! — mistranslated, the fault is squarely my own.

I wish to thank the Ministry of Culture of the Czech Republic for their support of my translations, as well as Ksenia Papazova, my friend and editor at Glagoslav, for her support and continuing faith in my work.

Miami Beach,
30 October 2020

WHERE WAS THE ANGEL GOING?

THE NINETEENTH

He got off the tram and a shred of wind and rain chased him along the pavement under the blooming linden trees, from which sweet water was running in tiny drops. When linden trees bloom, they get covered entirely in honey, even the surface of their leaves. Honey and dust, that's what life tastes like in this city. He pulled the zipper of his leather jacket right up under his chin. It was an old leather jacket; shiny from wear on its sides, around the pockets, and on the elbows too. It never rested in some safe and secure wardrobe. He had this sort of habit, in common with his father and his brothers — whenever bad times come round, get yourself inside a decent coat, preferably a leather one; something that won't soak through or let the wind in. He snorted with a smile at the sudden recollection of his mother's voice. Then he walked on through that bittersweet rain and said to himself that it'd be nice to toss that jacket into a corner, strip down and get comfortable somewhere, in his soft flannel shirt.

He turned into Zborovská St. This is where I live. Directly across from the entrance to our building is a keg-bar. Guys with bottles in their hands were standing with their backs to the wall beneath the eaves, and though rain was dripping from the tips of their noses and shoes, they kept their cigarettes dry. He squeezed his way in between them and bought himself three bottles of a strong beer — Red Dragon. He'd never drunk it, but he didn't know what might dispel the loneliness of his attic flat better than Red Dragon. Silliness, he admitted to himself, pushing his way back through the humid and greasy odour of the men out into the street with those three bottles in hand. The spring downpour was raising thousands of water bubbles on the asphalt.

He took out his key and opened the door to the place, which he never really thought of as his own, even after the passage of a year. That place didn't really belong to him; only the key did. The main thing is not to lose the key. The corridor was clean, well-kept and dark, like the virtues of a bourgeois life. Wearily, he plodded up the stairs to the fifth floor. O, just don't let me run across any neighbour. He'd never really quarrelled with them, but they still didn't like him for some reason. He had striven to come to terms with this since childhood. The people I've actually done something to like me more. You come across a neighbour, your brother in humanity, in the gloomy light of the stairwell and he gives you a dirty look. Even if you've greeted him nicely, really meaning it. Or, should he hear the sound of your feet on the stairs near his door, he'd rather wait with his hand on the knob until he hears your footfalls die away past the turnings — even if he were already dressed to go out, with his parasol and keys in his other hand, breathing heavily there at the door, pissed off with impatience. Just *humph, humph*, pissed off like that, he thought to himself, as he passed by the door that stared at him with the evil glare of its peephole. He arrived at the door of his flat in the attic, which hadn't been hoisted off its hinges, and entered the room, which hadn't been robbed. This always made him breathe a little easier; at least there was that. Hello, he said aloud,[4] hanging his coat on the nail, cracking open one of the Red Dragons and heading for his bed.

So this is all there is? The little mirror, which was still standing on his writing desk ever since his morning shave, reflected back his worn out, but somewhat astonished, face. His eyes seemed to have moved farther apart from one another than they had been. That's what a computer does to you. Pretty soon I'm going to look like a horse, or a jackass. A person who has stared at the computer screen for so long as to finally become an ass, like the one in the ancient fable, who can't decide if he's supposed to eat from the bushel on the left or the bushel on the right, until he ends up starving to death, while his eyes keep helplessly growing farther and farther apart.

Sitting in front of a screen producing hundreds of senseless translations of senseless texts all in order to settle the accounts, pay the bills, pay the rent, pay the alimony, the child support for the kids though the devil only knows what's up with them…

....

4   In Czech, *Dobrý den*, literally 'good day' — the possible irony of which is absent from the English word.

For an alcoholic beverage, Red Dragon is weak, but for a beer, it's quite high octane. Again he glanced in the mirror. It might have been a movie: just after lovemaking, a woman might still be lying beside him on this empty bed, stretching out her leg over his in a voluptuous movement. And he would make a properly existential grin, squint his eyes closed and ask: So this is all there is? And She would get up, get dressed, and go away without a word, and it wouldn't move him in the least. He'd much rather have his kids here anyway. He only saw them here and there from time to time, and didn't have anywhere to take them, really. Here, to this shoebox? Sometimes. Sometimes even for an evening, but without a bath, without sleeping over… he didn't dare draw the adventure out too long, so that it should become torture.

Outside it stopped raining. Above the roofs of the workshops and warehouses the colours of twilight began to seep from the inky clouds. Views like this were the best you could come across on Zborovská St. *When the twilight breathes above the Zborovský* heaths… That's what he sang — one of his father's patients, and friends, who'd lost a foot, not in the trenches, but quite simply because of a train tearing off a piece. He was a somewhat clownish railway watchman. The wound stretching athwart his instep, from big toe to heel, was covered by a skin graft taken from his stomach, and all his life long it suppurated, try what they might: silver nitrate, ointments, tinctures. At last, in '67 it was cancer that did him in. You might say that he bore up for a long time. When they'd have cleaned up the wound as nice as could be, dressed it, bound it, and he'd jammed it into a hideous shoe that looked like the foot of an elephant, he extracted from his railwayman's satchel a bottle of drink that he called somersault sauce, and both of them went at it, Dad and he. Quite often, under the influence of the somersault sauce, they galloped away with memories: childhood, the war years, Christmas carols, the songs of Karel Hašler. With tears in his eyes, my father's friend would sing of *rows of crosses pale, which stand about the vale, over which the moon's pale light keeps its watch throughout the night…* This was perhaps the only occasion when, in their family, one drank slivovitz openly, and sang profane songs… *You will never return home again. You're never, ever, ever, coming back! Never to see your homeland, my friend!* Yes, yes, said the man sitting on the bed. You'll be staying on Zborovská St. forever and ever amen.

The memory of the old railway man warmed his heart, still unused to loneliness. He told himself that loneliness was really what he wanted now, after all those horrors, which people inflict upon themselves and one another in the name of love, but as it is written: it is not good for man to be alone. At the very least, to sit around in some signal box or another with a railway woman, during the night shift, having a pull of somersault sauce and bawling about the fact that you're never, ever, ever coming back. That would be cosy. He had to laugh. He laughed, and then he brayed a bit, just like a jackass drinking Red Dragon.

A blow to the window woke him up. It was a rock, or a brick. And then another, and another, until finally he heard shattered glass. He opened his eyes. His window was white, and untouched. Then he heard a clatter from far away, as if somebody were treading over shards. He looked out his window onto the street and that's when he saw it. The shopwindow of that computer place, that something-or-other-COM place slantwise across the intersection, had been smashed. Some fellow was picking his way through the dangerous, sharp-toothed hole in the window, carrying out a computer. After him came another, with a monitor, while a third was returning from the corner, where their car had probably been parked.

You motherfuckers, he whispered, blowing off a little steam, and fumbling about his bag for his mobile phone. Son of a bitch, the battery's dead, and I didn't set it to recharge. He opened the window. It was far away, that store. They couldn't hear him, even if he shouted helplessly at them, with one leg in his pants already. By the time I run over there, they'll be gone. It's all useless anyway. Out of breath, he watched as the three chums slipped through the smashed window once again, stooped beneath the weight of their plunder. Then he heard car doors slam shut, and it was pedal to the metal. The shopwindow somehow reminded him of a mouth that had endured a thrashing. He couldn't get over it. He slipped on the other pants leg and reached for his jacket.

When he went out into the street, he realised how quiet and cool the city was. Now, at the start of the summer, the start of the day. How beautiful it was at this hour, just before dawn, when even the birds haven't begun to sing, when the colours have just begun to be recognisable, in this sunless light. Then the siren of a police car was heard. Well then. Now you're here.

Late as usual. From afar he saw the police car drive near, and some rudely awakened tenant or other lean out the window to see what's going on. All of this suddenly rubbed him the wrong way. What am I going to say, now? You can all go to hell. Then those spunky fellows crossed his mind, who at that very moment were dashing through the sleeping city to some pawnshop or other that was open at all hours. You're as likeable to me as anybody. Who am I that I should open my mouth? Who am I, after all? You don't ask such questions at four o'clock in the morning; at least you won't get an answer to them from anybody.

So he made his way to a non-stop bar. Walking over to a little table right next to the large, as yet unsmashed, window panes, he ordered himself a beer. Then he looked around for the first time. The bar was dirty and gilded; the wind made the curtains move, and the foam on his beer, which just at that moment was brought to him by an unbelievably fat waitress, took on a rosy colour in the sudden dawn. Prostitutes, hustlers and taxi drivers going off their shifts were congregated here, none of them with any clue as to what to do next.

Aside from the exhausted females and their indifferent bodyguards, there also was a public telephone in the non-stop, which dejected him even more than the whole little world that spun about him as he sat there. He had his card with him, but… nothing matters after all. How many hours over the past few months had he spent with his ear glued to a telephone receiver? How many misunderstandings, how many reproaches had seeped through the twisted cables and in the end — silence, a silence into which you're not going to jam that card of yours. He lit up a cigarette and cloaked himself in the bitter smoke of memory.

THE FIRST

They regarded that place as their own. That place, which would not have been but for the blind horses and the lads and the machines underground. The hills that would not have risen up were it not for the mining industry, which in the old days became the obsession of this land. Cages on cables were pulled up to the towers, trolleys. The iron pouches tilted out coal to the left, and slate-rubbish to the right. Coal went to the furnaces and the refuse to the culm banks near the shafts. What diminished down below accumulated up top. The culm banks grew and nobody gave them a second thought. Even if they resembled pyramids, they were not raised as monuments to anyone. They signified nothing. They were not heaped up so as to reach the stars or the gods; they simply remain, enduring, out of bounds. And when a mine has run its final course, when fits of coughing and other dramas down below cease for good, the culm banks are orphaned. And then the rails and the gates begin to be covered over by mosses, grasses, orache and birches and everything that is able to grow from grime and dust. No one wastes a second thought on these useless woods or wonders who the trees belong to that grow there, or thinks of the animals that hide among them, escaping the plains now built over with prefab tower blocks. Life crowds in there only in a very subdued fashion. Nothing stands in the way of the vegetation running riot, becoming overgrown. Someday, the whole world will be like this. The primaeval forests and beasts of prey will return, and maybe even some primitive people will too, retreating in ever smaller bands into the thickening, intertwining vegetation. What would the world be like without man, asked the poet Voznesensky. Beautiful, replies the man destroyed by punitive shifts in the mines. The Lord God created neither these mines nor those shifts, nor the ox, that castrated power, which through the ages has pulled the human wagon along the ruts of slavery…

It could be beautiful there — like a desert island — when Martin Vrána and Eva Topolská would go there on a date. Right from the tram stop the path dipped into bush and scrub. Martin always walked on ahead, parting the branches and looking back to Eva, as if he were afraid that she might suddenly disappear. One simply lost oneself in that fantastic land, which they regarded as their own. The sunlight flashed and flickered on the aspen leaves, the bindweed curled toward the tree branches and they two curled toward each other as well, just a little frightened. They would kiss and embrace on an iron catwalk stretched between two pipes over a black stream. They would smudge up Eva's blouse, pressing against one another, until they couldn't tell where those snapping sounds were coming from — whether from the pipes below them, or the pipes within their bodies. And then again, a few steps apart from one another, to leap from the concrete pylon — she into his arms, there in the wood that figured on no maps, but all the same was full of birdsong and breathed its cool exhalations; where the ground was covered with nettles and burdock and birches stood naked, like skin suddenly revealed from beneath clothes. There was no end to it. Martin, knackered with standing, couldn't stop; Eva, tousled and manhandled by Martin, would fall on him, again and again. From the elderberry above them protruded an old winch, on the rusty drum of which there remained a few twists of wire rope, its end slithering on the grass like a snake. On the banks of a little pond of rainwater some small yellow irises were blooming.

THE SECOND

'Give it to 'im, right in the mug!' came the jolly cry from the group of metallurgical apprentices swarming onto the bus at the main stop near the gates of the Klement Gottwald New Foundry. The petty conflict ended with a brutal closing of the folding doors, which separated the surging queue just like on the feed-line of the meat processing plant when a sausage or a ring of brawn is choked off. But then another bus rolled up, and the mob who'd just finished their morning shift pressed their way into it; and so it went on, as the stream progressed homewards.

That cry remained in Martin's memory, as did the view of those butts crammed into coarse Rifle jeans, from the back pockets of which comb-handles protruded, along with ID cards and trade certificates. The zest for rowdiness, with which you squeeze into buses head over heels, with which you give it to somebody, offhand-like, 'right in the mug!' That said it all for him, about the lived-in moment, that hail-fellow, cheery, 'Give it to 'im!' How sweet it is to give someone a boot in the arse on the trot from the gym to the lockers. Just a little kick between mates. Just don't stumble, you jackass! Give a loud chuckle and then… Martin was waiting along with the last of those standing at the main gate when, suddenly, he felt on his tongue the astringent taste of emptiness — just like after masturbating. Politely, he got on the last, half-empty bus, and set his satchel upon his lap. He felt the painful blackheads on his face and the nape of his neck. He wasn't really quite sure what this feeling, this sickness for something, this sad yearning, was all about. If he wasn't ashamed to do so, he'd pull his book out of his satchel and read. But of course you can't just pull out a book and read it like you can read the sports on the back page of the *Nová svoboda,* that is, *New Freedom,* newspaper.

Nová svoboda was black and yellow. In those days, it seemed like some new, stricter safety rules had just come into effect, for sedulous painters had begun smearing all first and last steps, all tricky passages and lowered soffits in public buildings with yellow and black stripes. They cared for people. So that nobody'd trip or whack their heads, and if after all something like that did happen, well then, you only had yourself to blame, for the dangerous place had been properly marked. In the end, just about everything, everywhere was marked up. That's how brigade-worker Martin saw it, as engulfed in the roar of the bus he gazed out at the world through drooping eyelids, and saw nothing but black and yellow smudges.

And yet there still existed gaps in the system outside of the school and the workplace. In grammar school, for instance, when the pupils were taken to the cinema, or when one of them had to go to the dentist, the teachers always had to lead the child right back to the school building. Then and only then could they permit them to go their own way, by themselves. Even in such cases when the road back to school passed directly past the front door of this or that pupil. The teachers in question wouldn't dare let the child simply go home — for the paedagogue's responsibility for the welfare of the child entrusted to him or her ended only at the very threshold of the school. As one of the teachers once put it: I let you go home early, you get run over and I get locked up. On the faces of some of the more diligent girls — who were later to become teachers themselves — one could read a profound understanding of that logic; in such cases, Martin was sure that what would give them the greatest pain as they were writhing beneath the wheels of that van would be the thought that now Comrade Teacher would be locked up for all this… Nothing of the sort ever happened, of course, and those girls continued to diligently cram their way through high school. By now, they'd sent their applications in to the Paedagogical Faculty, and it was more than probable that they would spend the entirety of their lives in school and common room. Granted, of course, that they don't get run over by a car, or that the flies, as the saying went, shouldn't shit on them. In the jargon of the housing estates, that phrase was used in reference to the sort of bad luck that turns a boy into a jailbird and a girl into a whore. No, the flies would keep their crap off them. The bigger risk was that they might have shat all over Martin, who took up smoking and drinking beer at such an early age, and vulgar speech, and the habit of knocking about unmarked terrain.

They tried to find somewhere to hole up beyond the confines of the new freedom. The park, at night, near the river so venomous that gulls scorned to alight upon it, was one of those places. Not that long ago, Martin would meet here with his mates for some nips of applejack, and now — Eva. Dating means waiting. The tension of impatience, the torsion and the rising of all that one has within oneself (which some people know how to describe so fittingly, that it can make you hurl). One night, after endlessly wandering the dark paths, after all those whispers and touches which precede the knowledge that expectation is much better than fulfilment, they arrived at Eva's bus stop. And Eva's bus was taking a long time in coming. They were standing beneath a nearby buckeye and there they went on with that touching and feeling, which perhaps was to have no end. They had no idea that they were being observed by an old fellow in an army coat — some former militia man or old brass hat who had been pensioned off. When at last Martin accompanied Eva to the very doors of the night bus and while in the subsequent vacuum created by her absence he could still feel the aura of her body on his face, still taste her saliva in his mouth, the old man shuffled up to him and asked him, off-hand like, if perhaps he didn't cream his boxers? The sliminess of the old creep's comment struck Martin only after a few moments. It arrived with the sad realisation that the old jerk had him, as it were, by the short hairs, and that if he laid into him with all the invectives that at that moment rushed to his tongue, if he buried his fist into the mug of that snoop, it would all be in vain, because the world belongs to him, that creep; this is his new freedom of army coats, and the might and the right are always on that side.

THE THIRD

Thus they went out together; thus they had to go about among the tiger stripes of their school years. Yellow and black sparkles amidst the parched desert? You were high-and-dry romantics, Martin, Eva… In school, on the street, everywhere around you there was that odour of locker room and gym. The intimacy of group showers and comradely fingers, which knew how to transform your secrets into a slimy fretboard, which a person was soon ashamed to possess. There were busloads of them; they pushed in everywhere: loud-mouthed, occupying the whole city. They were called the 'collective' and from afar they sounded like cattle being readied for transport to the market on trains. In order to belong to the collective, an individual had to lose himself in it. Learn how to be yellowblack in that thicket of hatred and rage. Where was there room for people to enjoy themselves, here? Only in secret places, painful and embarrassing like a concealed disease. For that sickly pallor and attachment to toxins constituted a remarkable oddness that, by nature, couldn't escape the notice of the well-fed stoolie of the state, who sits in every class, every tavern. We know them and rub up against them; we know how to like them between those tiger stripes and we are ashamed of it.

This won't get us anywhere. Eva knew that long before Martin did; Martin, who cawed along like a ruffled crow and secretly declaimed Ginsberg's 'Sunflower Sutra': 'We're not our skin of grime [...] we're golden sunflowers inside.' Inside where? There, where that beautiful triangle forms, when the wind presses my dress against my body? There, maybe, there's nothing at all, nothing else, Martin. There's only that dress and that wind, an intangible wave racing across the surface of the plain. Your gaze and my chills. The rest is a lie, a skin of grime. The less we touch it, the less grimy it'll be.

But they continued touching each other. They stole away from the ti-grified world to their deserted island among the brows of the culm banks and continued to consider that place their own, even if it grew smaller with each repeated visit. They preferred to sit there amidst the vines, conversing awkwardly. They kissed each other with hungry lips, and the water irises became more and more of an awkward burden. The water spread out over the sand and had nowhere farther to go. For they still wanted to go to their striped high school, and after the maturity exam to enter the yellow and black world. And it was then that Eva thought up the lie. For a long while she couldn't force it through her lips in this snug nest set amidst the weedy vegetation. She preferred to allow him to take off her blouse, to let his hands wander over her body, without any initiative of her own following his erotic movements, all in despair as he was at her submissive indifference — and then she wouldn't let him. No and no. Then he would sit on his haunches, smoking one cigarette after another, defeated. He was really good looking. She dressed herself up in his shirt. It was cosy. And then, off-hand like, she pronounced the phrase that flicked open in her like a switchblade.

'I'm afraid I'm going to have a baby.'

'With me —' he didn't know whether there ought to be an exclamation point, or a question mark, at the end of that sentence.

'No,' she said, looking at him from the distance of a life that had not yet begun, and he's already jealous. Just as he was then, constantly turning around to make sure she hadn't disappeared.

'You're sleeping with somebody else?' he asked, knocked back at the sound of his own words.

'With anybody and everybody,' she repeated harshly, surprised at the area that spread wide before her at that moment; surprised at how she had suddenly changed so. But she didn't blink; she was, actually, no longer there in that horrid anxiety. She really was afraid that she might get pregnant.

And he, a child, could conceive that she might be lying, yet he felt that she was speaking sincerely.

'And so it's over,' he said — again, not knowing what sort of punctuation with which to end that statement.

'Yes.'

He arose, like the first man after having sinned. The world around him was empty, but extraordinarily wide-spreading. He picked his jacket up off the ground and looked at his shirt, which Eva had on, then at Eva, then at his shirt again, and through his head tumbled the stupid cliché of the shirt being closer than the coat.[5] He felt everything inside him surge precipitously upward, as if he were a kid.

'You're not coming with me?'

'No, I'm fine here.'

'I'm not.'

And off he went, between the birches, into the yellowblack world. His old, second-hand woolen jacket on his naked flesh, his long unruly hair in his eyes, he looked just like an Indian, or the member of some hard rock band.

----

[5] In Czech: *Košile bližší kabátu.* The old saw is somewhat similar to the English 'blood is thicker than water.' It has little to do with what is going on here, except for the manner in which Martin, stunned by the sudden turn of events, senses his sudden alienation, his sudden loneliness.

THE FOURTH

And now, no Eva, summer, the work brigade in Nová huť, steel blocks, furnaces, crane cables, petroleum jelly and oakum. But now, without that rambunctious brouhaha of apprentices. He felt himself growing poorly and thin. Stepping off the bus he didn't want to go home — so soon to be abed, barricaded in half-slumber. From the time he started going out with Eva, the pleasure of home as a concealed retreat from the blackyellow world had paled somewhat. She had given him a sort of seclusion that he carried home with himself. A solitude which was dearer to him than security.

His mother saw it in his eyes, reading in each of his movements that the boy was, somehow, alone. The way he put on his jacket, the way he tied his boots. His tall, boyish frame, which until recently still moved about clumsily, uncertainly, suddenly found its plumb-line, so to speak, straightening solidly in a way that was impossible not to notice — just like the way he'd suddenly grown silent, and the assertive jutting of his chin.

It vexed his father. The boy got on his nerves with that mysterious aloofness of his. He'd never had any problems with him before — now he had. He didn't want to belong to him. He'd have to put some pressure on him — let him come out with it, let him spill it like an overturned tumbler on the table during Sunday dinner — so as at last to give him a good dressing-down and then forgive him. Put him in his place. While his mother liked the manliness that shone through Martin's eyes, despite all the unease it caused her, to his father it seemed an overgrown branch that someone mistakenly took for the vine itself. There can be only one vine, the real vine, and you others are the branches. The family is like a little church and, what's more, a church in diaspora amidst the new freedom. There must be order to the faith, and the families of those who do not bend the knee before Baal — at least not too often — must be the sure, load-bearing points of the Church invisible.

Thus only is the faith of our fathers and their values carried forward, faith and values persecuted by the blackyellow plague. Here, all must be safe and good; you can't drag in here your own private solitude, especially if you've gotten it from some girl.

Martin's two older brothers were more to their father's taste. They gave him problems, but such as were dealt with in quarrels and animated conversations. Every place was full of them and everyone was in his element. They cawed like crows worthy of the name.[6] Martin himself stopped cawing the day he sensed the shakiness of that security.

There was that moment, years ago, but it felt like yesterday to Martin... With eyes ablaze and holding his breath deep in his lungs, Martin stood stock still in the corridor, at the door; the only light came through the peephole as if it were a window on another world, or the tiny porthole of a boat. Their boat, with which they navigate the adverse waters of that city. That's where they live, where they have their books and their faith, which the people around them can't understand. There, inside the boat, they sing their old songs, the echoes of which sometimes meet their neighbours' ears there in their living rooms full of television. As soon as he walked through the door, he sensed that something wasn't right. It was as if he had to fight his way through a heavy invisible curtain. And he was in a hurry to tell them about what he'd just experienced. He started speaking before he'd even taken off his coat, and then, suddenly, he noticed that nobody was listening to him. They'd just glanced up at him and then took up again, right where they'd left off speaking. And in his head he had such a dreadful thing to get out...

Why are they not with me? Suddenly he felt the same sort of alienation that he felt back then in class, when he picked a fight with that good for nothing Mirek Fridrich, who egged on his weaker classmates to address him with Your humble servant, Factory owner, sir. Nobody was with him then, either. Let'm have it, Mirku, Let'm have it! they all shouted. And even when he'd smashed the mug of that beloved tyrant of theirs, so that his mouth was bleeding, and he was bawling, the whole class still looked upon him, Martin, as if he were some sort of bully murderer. He couldn't figure it out. But then he said, Well, whatever. That's them.

....

[6]   An untranslatable pun. The common last name *Vrána* also means 'crow' in Czech.

                                                       JAN BALABÁN

Or that time when the teacher belittled Tonda Gona… Martin could still see him: a twelve-year-old boy who came to school in gym suits darned in places, whose mother was an alcoholic with legs swollen like water jugs, who smelled funny and didn't learn well. And the teacher, she pulled him by the hair and mocked him in front of the rest of the children: Look at him! Take a look at him! she said. At that sweater — at those elbows — at those dirty hands! A disaster! What a disaster! she hollered, pulling his tattered schoolbooks out of his satchel one by one and flinging them about, along with all the other trash he carried about with him. And he struggled to get out of her grip, while she swatted him on the behind, and he was panting in a way that everyone found funny. And as the others were laughing at him, she went on: Laugh at him, that's right, laugh at him, because he's so messy and stupid! They ought to expel him from school! He's hardly here anyway, and probably a thief on top of it all! And because the others began laughing even more, Piskalová, the teacher, was in her element. She really erupted, grunting with righteous indignation — Something like this is impossible, after all — intolerable!!! Martin couldn't hold back any longer. He tossed some vulgar expressions the teacher's way, and the result was that he caught it from her too. She slapped him and wrote him up. And in the end the whole class, along with the teacher, started laughing at him, too, even that Tonda Gona, who was, finally, relieved, glad that somebody else was being pilloried — if even for a while. Martin was alone again. And again he said, That's what they're like.

Well, that was there, in school. But what was going on in the kitchen? Suddenly, he saw his father and his brothers, as it were, from a great distance. They began to hover in the yellow light like strange fish. They were eating and talking, frightfully loudly, with their mouths full of food, about politics of some sort, about some fellow or other who'd set himself on fire in protest against the Russians. All of them were roaring for all they were worth, his brothers with their sonorous voices of young men, and his father, in a voice stronger than them all. Only his mother Marta sat there in the background of it all, with her greyish-green eyes addressing Martin, it seemed… But what, exactly, was she trying to say? That's how it is, I guess, when someone's head is on fire, him screaming, Rescue me, and no one comes to the rescue. Even now he didn't know what she was saying then, about the life that was waiting for him. He pushed his way through them and threw himself onto his bed, burying his face in his pillow so as not to have to see that first crack, through which his security was starting to seep away. So that he wouldn't have to scream Rescue me! Since nothing really happened to him, after all. But what happened to them, that they'd become so horrid, all of sudden? Maybe we all, in protest against those Russians, those classmates, those teachers, ought to set ourselves on fire?

THE FIFTH

From then on, Martin met up with Tonda Gona only as a grown man. But they talked together only once. It was in the Stalingrad Restaurant — to which the local hooligans referred only as At Hitler's, and despite the fact that the history teachers of the time did their level best to hide from their charges all parallels between the two colossal figures, as much as possible. This was perhaps intuition — or just one of those sarcastic reversals, which sometimes contain more truth than one knows at the moment. In short, Martin Vrána and Tonda Gona drank their beer in At Hitler's, and nowhere else. Tonda turned out to be a big fellow — a whole head taller than Martin, broad-shouldered, with hands like shovels, and black miner's glasses framing his eyes. These days, that human wrecking ball could wallop the life out of the sadistic teacher Piskalová with one flick of his wrist. But she was already safe and secure in the fogs of oblivion. Evil teachers are fortunate in this, that children nudge the cruel moments of their abasement into the darker recesses of their souls. Nobody ever returns, as a grown man, to give an evil schoolteacher from the first grade a healthy slap in repayment for wounds inflicted, which remain as scars on the spirit. Nobody ever settles accounts with those perverse bastards of our childhood, man — as it were — to man. They bully children, and parents, with impunity, and even those decent teachers, who find themselves amongst them like the proverbial wheat among the cockle of the collectivised fields. How rough it is in school, in those prefab villages, which have no sooner arisen on the fields beyond town than they are chock-full of all sorts of new arrivals, eager to accomplish the factory-retooling of new people. As punishment! That's what the teachers would say: Here, one is assigned as punishment, so the employees of blackyellow surveillance sighed, while they themselves were the worst punishment imaginable for the children who, quite simply, had no choice as to where they were to live… But all of this has already been forgotten, just like the great deeds of *Batyushka* Stalin.

When Martin asked Tonda if he still remembered Piskalová, the young miner didn't. As a matter of fact, he confused her with a certain blonde who, in the later years of their youth, would give it to anyone and everyone in the housing estate. But no — her name was Pilonská; Piskalová was our teacher in the first grade, Martin reminded him.

'O, that cunt,' Tonda recalled, but had no desire to set out on any sentimental journey. Martin gazed at his glum face, stiffened with the years, somehow reminiscent of the early humans from the illustrations in the book *Hunters of Mammoths*, searching it in vain for the wide-eyed expression of the lonely boy for whom no one cared at home, who wandered the streets, his only possessions whatever he could steal, and who at the same time looked like some child poet waiting on something that would never come to fulfilment. He looked around at the guys drinking down their daily shift. Hair still damp from the shower, cigarettes fixed between their lips, beer resting between their elbows. When they were six years old, all of them were open, like windows to the skies, tiny men, who with tiny hands grasped their first handles, levers and toys so new, and so quickly ageing.

'How's it going at work?' Martin asked.

'Nobody dreams of mine shafts,' Tonda said, curtly. He drank down his beer and returned to his mates, from whom he'd slipped away for a moment to see his old classmate from grammar school. Not even knowing why. Not really giving it a thought.

But Martin did. He ordered another beer and made his way back through time, slowly. Up the corridor to the classroom where the portrait of Antonín Novotný hung on the wall, to the teacher who taught them that fossils were formed by magma seeping into the shells of ammonites and other prehistoric creatures before cooling and hardening. I suppose they were made of asbestos, he thought, pushing on to the days when the portrait of General Ludvík Svoboda was hanging above the podium, and the teacher, who told the pupils that the Soviet Army was here to rescue us from the ravings of the hooligans in Prague. It was all so black and yellow that he had to close his eyes. From afar, Tonda Gona seemed like the slate rubbish extracted from the mines and piled up in culm banks. A sort of stony grey fellow, with elbows that hump down on the table in the unbearable yellow light of At Hitler's.

Eva wasn't far away — she was right there in the darkness when he closed his eyes, springing up like a slender stalk, a girlish figure at the banks of a black lake. A pale horse, a girl, a naked man. An unfamiliar Šumava landscape. That's what he wanted, and that's what he had, behind his eyelids. He shivered slightly. He should tell her all that, but if he tried, it would only be a mistake. He couldn't open up to the girl as he used to open up to his mother. Futile attempts, and everything futile is dangerous; futility puts pressure on you and makes you bend and breaks you before you mature. He saw it all clearly now, in those borderlands between the blackyellow world and the little church — and that's where he'd like to be, alone with Eva. She didn't even have to be real — just that slender stalk of a girl. Martin cleared out. It was impalpable, impossible. He swept the bar with his eyes — that thick cloud of smoke, those chunks of pink meat. Tonda staggered out of the gents and waved affably at somebody else. Two busty females at a nearby table had the look of a young Pilonská and an old Piskalová.

THE SIXTH

As Zeno of Elea proved long ago, the arrow shot from its bow does not fly, but, rather, is stationary in each segment of its route. Because the same arrow can't be in two places at once. No more could Martin, and so he remains there, in that one shattering moment, shirtless at the culm bank, with his stomach lifting and his eyes gazing round at the empty reaches of the surrounding world, which he must, now, take for his own. The inhabited world is small, contained in the hands of two people. The desert world is gigantic, spreading widely all around the borders of the inhabited world. If he hadn't just split up with Eva, chances are he'd never have noticed this. He would have continued to move about happily, secure on the safety lines of all those telephones, messages and insistent words. He'd have flown along like that arrow toward its target, missing it, perhaps, never realising that he had been standing still all the while. And thus, there he was, fixed above the earth, as only birds are capable of being. Everything was alien, yet real. The rust on the abandoned train tracks, over which he passed on his way into town, the football pitch, the green shed, the gardens alongside the workers' houses, the weak plants set in jars in the black flowerbeds, beneath a sky with a yellowish-green streak along the horizon. The bright depths of sky with its Baroque drapery of clouds, iron pylons, chimneys, towers, swifts flying off somewhere in the direction of Cape Town. The yellow and black streaks had paled. Everything was clean, washed clean by the alcohol of a bright perspective, with which he suddenly knew how to come to terms, or at least he thought he did. He didn't know anything at all, really — he sensed everything.

Where should he return to now? Where will he have to return to? Back to those tracks over which the blackyellow life rolls, the new freedom, that great family of the Church, his family and the family he doesn't yet have.

No, you don't return to something like that. You have to move forward to get there. Rather, he'll be returning here, to that moment, where the arrow stands still.

Eva had left him at last. This was something he'd begun to fear from the very moment he first took her by the hand. Suddenly she's with him here, again. Her lips, those very soft lips, half-open, searching for kisses in the air before her face. Eva spread out on the ground like a hunter's prey, Eva ajar, her lips searching the air before her face for the kisses of someone else. That triangle on her skirt, her breasts freed of all confining fabric, that certain movement she makes, when she brushes her hair back from her brow. Martin… the slight tilt, a sort of inconspicuous yes, the slope of neck and chin, the hand with its narrow wrist, and then — nothing. She still has his shirt. What will she do with it, when she gets home? Maybe she'll toss it in a rubbish bin along the way? Or will she launder it, iron it, and put it among her own blouses?

He still felt her with him and in him, as they say people go on feeling their amputated limbs. To the tips of the fingers and toes. The solitude remained with him, the solitude she gave him, which they'd found together. Eva, he said, gazing off into the far distances that stretched before him all the way to the Beskid mountains — pure and blue above all the industrial smog. But we'll never go there together, not now.

THE SEVENTH

'God save at least the Siberian tiger,' he repeated the line of the Vlastimil Třešňák song. No, he couldn't put it on. The cassette was fixed in the recorder, firmly, so bakelitedly fast. He couldn't bear the idea of depressing the button, setting the magnetic heads, the whole dry mechanism, in motion, which from the dark, poorly recorded tape would wring out the berserk despair of the singer, speaking to him from his very soul, the singer with the name that sounds like cheap wine. Once again, Martin could drink him up in the park along with his friends on those lazy June evenings, which would come along for sure, as sure as that abominable sweet dessert wine would be opened. It's horrid, when the sun is shining on the dusty cassette player and you don't dare press Play, so as not to start bawling… so as not to fall into fucking despair, you say, pushing out your chin like a hooligan. But who are you playing to now, Martin? Here in the flat alone, with no one to see you, as everybody's left for evensong? It's Whitsunday. You should have gone with them, but no one could do anything with you. You lied so stubbornly about not feeling well, until, at last, your mother intervened and convinced your father to let you stay home. So here you are, ill at Pentecost, that day when the tongues of fire appeared above the apostles' heads.

Martin had an image of that in his head. An icon maybe, or perhaps the work of some Czech Gothic painter. Or maybe something of his own invention, the sort of memory that sticks with a person, though he can't place it, where it came from. Twelve old men in heavy robes without a crease, as if those clothes they had on were made of wooden planks, shields with faces above them, all of them nearly identical and all of them looking straight at him, each with the different urgencies of their attributes. And yet their eyes and mouths were nothing more than holes leading to plumbless depths. Their halos make them look a little like cosmonauts, and above each of them hovered a quite palpable flame, like that of a cigarette lighter, a drop of light. All of them so perfectly unified that you couldn't tell which of them is the newcomer, the replacement for Judas the betrayer. You enter the circle of the twelve as a good, blessed by fate, chosen apostle and today, along with them at Pentecost you become a new man. Now, at last, something'll happen; now those wooden figures will start moving. We're gonna write Gospels and Epistles and found churches in Asia Minor and Europe. You'll carry the good news to pagans north and south. Only now, with that flame sparkling above your head like St Elmo's fire do you make a step in the proper direction. Without that flame you can go hang yourself on an aspen, like Judas, or go extinct like the Siberian tiger, on behalf of whom Třešňák pleads so despairingly.

Martin gazed at those motionless flames above the heads of the saints and felt an endless peace in contemplating their ecstasy — just like the arrow ever fixed in its target. Not striving for anything, not twitching and jerking — being, belonging to God.

And in this way that good son Martin compensated for so impiously refusing to participate in Whitsunday evensong. He should call Eva and tell her about it; he should confess it to his mother, mention it in passing to his father and brothers. But he kept it hidden from everyone. And so, what, after all? That blabbering about cosmonauts! He burst out of the house. He gripped his lighter and inhaled the cheap smoke of a Startka. At which he realised that under his bed he still had a box full of Indians. He smoked, and felt sorry for Indians. Truly sorry. His steps led him in among the new prefab buildings. On the roofs of the towering flats, warning lights were blinking. From time to time a supersonic Russian MiG thundered over the city.

THE EIGHTH

'That your Dad's shirt?'

'Maybe not,' Eva replied in a quiet voice to the tall man.

'It's just that it's a little big on you,' he laughed, smugly, and took a drag on his cigarette. His name was Ivan. He was a strapping fellow, brawny and pretty strong, probably, yet all the same his movements and his manners were sort of soft. The coach of his volleyball team once told him, You've got a good figure there. A well-built body. You just need to do something with it. And that good figure of his, that *dobrá figura,* stuck to him. Ivan Figura, that's what his teammates started to call him, then his schoolmates in general, and finally, everybody except his parents. It stuck with him, even though he hadn't played volleyball for years.

He looked at Eva with that soft, half-mocking, half-interested gaze of his and felt, with relief, that the girl was shivering a bit, from nerves. The unfolded cuffs of the washed-out flannel shirt revealed her thin little wrists, and the shirt front, open to the third button, tempted the eye.

'And it'd be a little small for a figure like yours, no?' was Eva's attempt at humour; she upturned the corner of her mouth.

'God only knows who you pulled it off of,' Ivan joked in turn, ironically.

'You just let that be!' she responded sharply, even though she knew she was losing the battle.

'Sorry, sorry… I didn't mean to insult you,' he said, placing his hand on her forearm.

He thinks he's got me like a fish on a frying pan, she thought, feeling the pressure of his fingers on her skin increase a bit.

They were sitting in a café. Past the large, uncurtained window, Stage 4 was slowly decomposing. 'Stage 4' was the name of the housing estate where they both lived. In Stage 4, in prefabs that sprang some twenty years previous from a green meadow amidst a couple villages. Instead of districts or neighbourhoods, that city had stages, and in the stages, blocks of flats and shopping centres and cultural centres and cafés for the working class. There they were at home, in flats 3 + 1, 2 + 1, 1 + 1 and even 0 + 1. These figures had nothing to do with a numeration of sexual partners; rather, they described the parameters of the otherwise identical apartments they called home. Little paths trod bare through the muddy lawns led to these homes, and one of the first vital skills mastered by the children born here was to come to recognise, amongst all the identical towers, their proper entrance, their floor, their flat. Up there, past the door painted a uniform ivory like all of the other doors, on the beige carpet covered in plastic from the very threshold to the place where all the muddy shoes were set aside, there at the mirror between the doors to the toilet and the bath I'll look at myself, like every other day, in Martin's shirt, washed-out Rifle jeans and my hair, on purpose and out of spite clipped short after I broke up with that crazy boy. I'll check my face, my lipstick, my makeup and the impenetrable touch of Ivan Figura. I'll drop my canvas bag on the floor, and I'll be home.

If only I were there right now, Eva sighed, accepting the two more gills of wine that Ivan ordered without even consulting her first. And I'll take it. Taking it is not the same thing as putting up with it. I like the self-confidence of that tall boy. I like how he believes in himself. Perhaps he's dangerous. He went into the army, and afterwards immediately got into uni. When he talks about it, he laughs: 'Economy, International Trade — piece of cake, right?'

'No. Not everyone can do that.'

'What does that mean "everyone"?' Ivan raised his eyebrow while simultaneously turning down the corners of his mouth.

'"Everyone?" You mean the people who live in the prefabs here? I don't give a crap about them. It's all about you. You've got to know what it is you want.' His voice was at the same time dry and persuasive. Where did he learn that, and that eyebrow thing? She felt a shiver run down her spine.

'Like when I was in the army,' Ivan went on. 'There was this boy blew himself up with a grenade. And everybody, you know, they're rolling their eyes, wringing their hands, Horror! Alas, a life cut short…! And I say, bullshit. He fucked up the throw and that's that.'

'What if that had happened to you?'

'Then I'd be dead. But it didn't happen to me. What am I supposed to do about it? Was it me thought up armies? The Warsaw Pact? NATO? Please! Me, I bank up the manure around my own bed, and don't give the others a second thought.'

And in that manure-ringed bed of yours is where you'd like to see me. She wanted to cut him off right then and there, but she couldn't. She let it be.

'And no pangs of remorse at all?' she asked instead.

'Words, big words, higher principle and all that,' he said, lighting up another cigarette. He leaned back in his chair, blew out some smoke, raised that eyebrow again (lowering the corners of his mouth, too), and shot at her:

'Do you believe in God?'

'No, but…'

'But what?'

'But I know someone who does.'

'Well then, say hi to him for me.'

'No need,' she clipped, in irritation.

'Is that the one who gave you that shirt? I once heard of this saint who shared his cloak with a beggar and then rode off on a white horse.'

'Cut it out, Ivan!'

'Sure. We don't give a crap about saints, either.'

So they chucked the saints, too. When she returned home in the morning from Ivan's, she scrutinised her face in the mirror a long while. I look different. Like I lost something of my own. I look like someone else. Her mother emerged from her bedroom — a smartly dressed bank official. Her father didn't live with them.

'Where were you all night long?'

'At Petra's. I went over to her place after that dance.'

'I suppose you know what you're doing!?' her mother riposted sharply, casting a critical eye upon her again.

'What sort of rags are you wearing? I hope you're not going to school dressed like that.'

'No. I'm not going to school at all. I don't feel well,' Eva tossed back before plunging into her room — the second one in their 2 + 1. She listened while her mother closed the front door. Then she crawled into bed just as she was and stared at the ceiling above her, a concrete slab that just hung there over her, covered in white plaster, just like that.

THE NINTH

Ivan, a.k.a. Figura, had been stripped of his usual loquaciousness. That there Eva Topolská, son of a — What an idiot you were, to talk about that grenade… That I allowed myself to say such stupid… for fuck's sake! Seventeen, eighteen years old she is, no more than that — Where'd she learn all those things? He had to admit it: that little girl with the brutally cropped blonde hair terrified him. 'So, do it if you've got a mind to,' she told him when they entered his room, after which, with a wink and a nod, he'd gone off to the kitchen to fetch something to drink. She lay on the pillows as naked as a finger. The finger of a flabby hand, for sure. When, before, they were just petting, he felt in control. And then, 'go ahead and do it, if you've a mind to.' Each movement, each step he had to manage on his own. He had to undress himself before her, touch her with his hands, his mouth… and the expression on her face was completely empty. She didn't move a milimetre in his direction. And it's not like… This wasn't her first, or last, time. He even had to spread her legs. He couldn't even tell if she felt him. From time to time she opened her mouth, as if in pain, but even then she didn't really change her expression. It was like he was masturbating. She was white and smooth, but, what's up? He's Figura; women throw themselves at him, but this one — not a bit of it. He wondered if she were drunk; that maybe he'd overdone it, pushing drinks on her. And that was a helpful thought — after all, that had been his plan. But he got off on her somehow, anyway.

However, she wasn't drunk. When he rolled off her, he didn't even hear her sigh. She got herself together and went off to the bathroom, from which she emerged fully dressed and so damn normal and OK and prepared to have a conversation about his school and her plan to study languages… his dearest desire at that moment was to shove her out the door. And then he sensed that it was only now, with those clothes on her, with those relaxed movements of hers, with her neck tenderly rising from the open shirt front of that idiot, some Martin or other, with whom she'd just broken up, only now, in that frosty solitude, that she was so terribly seductive and exciting, but what to do with her now? Fuck her again? Toss her out? He began stammering, he lost the thread of the conversation, he started to become ridiculous. Then she helped him out. Told him that she had to go, and she went. He watched her still from his window. She grew distant beneath the streetlamps, but so damn slowly, as if she really had nowhere to go, and was toying with that lonely, slow gait.

He didn't know, nor would he ever learn, that as soon as she was out of sight of his window, she lifted the floodgates of weeping and horror, which up until then she'd kept stopped up deep inside — not in her throat, but deep in her stomach — deeper than where sobbing begins. She walked toward the bus station and the tears flowed over her and within. Everything disappeared, somewhere. Where? She felt an empty space within her, a bottomless pit, into which everything can be thrown.

Ivan Figura left his flat on a sudden impulse and went across the road to a green bar called Smaragd, that is, The Emerald. This was a dance hall that stayed open late — but no one was dancing already. The fine, slender, tall fellow parked himself at the bar and poured dram after dram down his throat, gazing at the white bow in the hair of the girl behind the bar. He didn't have the urge, somehow, to chat, as usual. He just drank and drank, getting green at the Emerald. Then someone leaned up against the bar next to him. Ivan glanced over in that direction, annoyed. He saw a round, sweaty face with thick-lensed glances, a protruding lower lip, and broad shoulders. He glanced at that face only a moment and then, thunderstruck, peered at his shaven nape. That's… that's Kosinský. Jesus Mary and Joseph! His blood froze — it wouldn't flow at that moment if you cut him deep. Kosinský, here? They couldn't have let him out already, for Pete's sake! Instinctively, he turned away so that the other wouldn't recognise him immediately. But all the same, he couldn't get rid of the image of Kosinský in that green army shirt, his thumbs behind his braces, his eyes shining behind those thick lenses: Listen lads, we can't just let this go! That won't do. He was one of us, after all. They kill a man and they call it a freak accident? That just won't do. We have to tell it like it is; make a complaint, submit a grievance — they just can't get away with something like that!

Speeches and gossip, the head's aswim, the whole company in barracks… a strike. We don't go out for roll call. Speeches and bullshit, grievance, a complaint, let's write a letter. And then the interrogations begin. Counter-intelligence creeps. Who wrote this? Who's behind it? And suddenly it's as silent as the grave. Nobody knows what anybody else said. You know what people are like. And the brass, foaming like mad dogs.

Figura slid the corner of his eye toward his barmate. That can't be him — that just can't be Kos…

'What're you glommin' at?' snarled the fat guy, who now didn't look like Kosinský at all, whom they'd locked up in the military prison at Sabinov for subversion.

'Well? What're you after, eh?' the guy insisted, who now only seemed to have been kind of like Kosinský.

'Nothing, friend, nothing,' mumbled Figura, with a shiver.

'That's all right then, matey,' the hideous bloke hissed at him. Ivan almost had the urge to kiss him for not being the person he took him for.

'I'll have one more. And have one yourself, too, on me,' he said to the girl serving the drinks, the sparkle having returned to his eye.

'What're we drinking to?' she asked.

The bus station was soaked in cold light. Eva sat down on a bench in the waiting room, curled up, and waited. She had arrived during the long pause between bus routes. The buses from the afternoon shift had already carried away the last groups of workers, and those who were on morning shift still had a good three hours to go. There's time enough, she said to herself, and thought about the little boy in the English novel, the boy hastening through the morning drizzle over muddy fields, the puddles of which shone like mercury. Beyond the dunes the sea, and on it, afar, against the horizon, the ships awaiting the morning, when they would be able to draw near the shore. The village is asleep, the lady of the house has set aside her beige apron and with an arm as course as a grater embraces her husband. She was sleeping with her mouth open, as if she were screaming silently, while the boy snuck past her outside, bearing in a bundle some food for the prisoner bedded outside on the muddy ground; he'd also stolen a file, with which to work on the man's fetters. It has to be this way, otherwise that frightful fellow would send someone after him to rip out his guts at night. And so the boy hurries through the waterlogged fields, while the dawn begins to split the horizon. Hopeful prospects and great expectations draw near, but for the time being, these are like those boats: somewhere out there in the mist that lies upon the sea, just like Eva, who at last has disappeared, slipping free of the night, unbinding herself from Figura, from all people hereabout. She's with her granddad, a retired teacher in a main district town near the border. They're reading the English novel while outside it's raining and nobody's dying now, nor will anyone be dying for a long while yet. There's time enough.

When the ships begin to near the shore, the first buses of the morning shift begin to roll up as well. Eva got up and numb and fragile set out on the familiar road leading home.

THE TENTH

Ivan Figura wasn't sure if he was doing the right thing, but it thrilled him, that's for sure. He called that boy, that St Martin of hers, on the phone. What do I want from him, really? He asked himself, as he searched out his father's name in the telephone book. He was poking his nose into somebody's private business, and this excited him, too. He has no idea of my existence, yet I know who his father is, and where he works. So he rang up the Vrána house. He persuaded his older brother Tomáš that it was a friend calling, Martin's friend Ivan.

'Hey, Martin. I need to talk with you.'

'About what? Who is this?'

'About Eva! What else?' He'd played the scene out so many times in his head, and now when he launched into the line, it sounded like a recording. Martin was disconcerted — and angry. Who is this guy, and what does he want? Well, a friend — a friend of Eva's. But why? And just like that? But I have nothing to do with her anymore. So, you know, no big deal… So then, all right, six o'clock this evening. At the Na Společenstvu Gardens. You know the place, right? Great, then. Till six.

He didn't know if he was doing the right thing, what he was doing, but it entertained him, greatly. He drove off from his housing estate to the city where Martin lived, in his blue Soviet Fiat, feeling high in the saddle. A man on a high horse. Ever since his father died, Ivan could drive wherever he wished, and that suited him just fine. He always said of himself that speed was his element; speed, speed. It's what he always said, and what he told himself. When he floored it, it gave him a good 140. What did he have, Martin, that Ivan didn't have, as far as Eva was concerned? What sort of a bloke was he? Well, let's find out.

He drove through the village and, suddenly, on the road in front of him, he saw a cat that had been run over. Instinctively, he swerved, but at the same moment, he had had enough time to notice that it wasn't dead. Strangely, crippled, it still moved that half of its body that had not been crushed. It waved its paw, as if it were trying to flag down a car. The despairing and painful slowness of that gesture suddenly moved something inside Ivan Bereza, a.k.a. Figura. Thoughts that had been pushed out of the way with effort now began to leap out, one after another. Suddenly, Ivan saw himself writhing horridly on some smooth floor while everything was seeping out of him, uncontrollably. And he also thought of his mother, impotently limping out of the kitchen after his father'd given her a thrashing. That's how she went, or you might say crawled,[7] from the kitchen, holding onto the hip that had been battered when she fell to the floor. His father knew how to wallop back then, so that you'd 'cop another one from the ground,' as he would say with relish. And she, instinctively, like an animal, distanced herself from the spot where her drubbing had taken place, as if the rest of the flat, the building, the city, or the world could provide her with some safety. But even that boy, so small yet, back then, could not stand between her and the punishing paw of paternal authority. As red as a tomato, he asserted his right to wallop the bitch who *slips off* him somewhere. In the jargon hereabouts 'to slip off someone' meant to go wandering, to start something with somebody else, to cadge, to squeeze through a hole in the fence like a hen. Everything his mother never did, but perhaps might have wanted to do, if it wasn't for how afraid she was of her man, who was feared at home, at work, and in the Party, who only observed law where the Citizens' Militia was concerned. With somebody like that to deal with, she stood even less of a chance than that poor, unlucky cat, who at least might have skipped between the tyres had she been nimble. But with Ivan's mother, it wasn't about nimbleness, but endurance. To hold on and not ask, What've you been doing on all those Party retreats and integration outings of an evening? There's women at them too after all and dancing and… That's enough, not a word more! And so she held on knowing that she'd hold on to the end, enduring more, holding on longer, than he could.

....

[7]   The original Czech reads: *Tak šla, chtělo by se říct lezla.* Czech uses two verbs to signify movement, one proper to humans, the other to animals. *Jít*, feminine past tense *šla*, is used for men and women; *lézt*, feminine past tense *lezla*, is used almost exclusively for animals. The connection between his mother and the cat, and her dehumanisation at the hands of his brutal father, is made immediately apparent to the Czech reader.

                                                         JAN BALABÁN

Her man was tough, sure, but he wasn't sharp enough to know from which way the wind was blowing, let alone survive the transformation in Party legitimacy. When that happened, first, he bellowed like a stuck bull thrashing out on all sides, dealing blows, We fought, fuck your mothers! We built it all, for fuck's sake! But when he saw it in black in white — *Expelled* — he crumpled, as if beneath a nightstick blow. How could they do that to me? And suddenly he was the one tottering, completely naked, stripped of function and position — just a petty warehouse official was all that remained of him — a warehouse man! He preferred to remain home now, and there he spoke in a low voice, whispering and wheezing, afraid to curse and swear, believing all the while that They would take him back. As if that wasn't enough, an unhealthy bile began to seep from his liver, a cirrhosis that was quickly to bring his life to an end. Expelled and ill, he was unable to defend himself, unable to live on in the world, the walls of which were closing in around his sickbed more and more. No one came to visit him except his wife and his son, to whom he bequeathed nothing but political discredit and that Soviet Fiat. Just before the end, he would come home from the hospital now and then, and when he did he would make his wife take him to church. Earlier, she went there only in secret, when he was away on Party business. She'd bless herself swiftly, say a prayer and be off. She didn't even dare approach the Sacraments. But they went now, both of them — him all grey with red splotches, and her with a scarf covering her head, just like long ago back home in Slovakia. There was no church at Stage 4, but a little one stood amongst some lindens in the village close by, where a decrepit old reverend celebrated the Mass, despite the regime's enmity, for a few old women. That's where they'd go. His father in a sheepskin coat, as stiffly upright as a pole — otherwise he couldn't move at all — passing through the doors of the church with precious little hope in his eyes, just the way his wife used to pass in through the doors to the kitchen. And so he crawled, as the saying goes, toward his cross. Ivan understood none of this. Stubbornly, he remained outside, walking around the car that would soon belong to him, smoking his Dad's cigarettes. It all seemed embarrassing, so embarrassing, to him.

After his father's death, his mother evicted all memory of him completely, liquidating all that had belonged to him. It was as if she'd always calculated on the role of a widow. Old Bereza disappeared, and Young Bereza got his own room. They arranged everything well. Almost wordlessly, they agreed on everything, from that chestnut rinse that her mother treated herself to, at the hands of her neighbour-hairdresser, to the determination of signing the car over to her boy, once he'd finished with his military service.

THE ELEVENTH

When the blue Soviet Fiat pulled up at the fence of the Na společenstvu garden restaurant, Martin Vrána had been sitting there a good half hour, cursing himself for not getting up already and leaving, as he should. Figura spotted him immediately, picking him out at once from among all the other long-hairs and regulars of the tavern, which was the supposed asylum for those who, in their imprecise thoughts, oscillated around the concept of an Underground. Besides this, it was a fertile hunting zone for all types of informers, panhandlers, thugs and grungy hippies, long in the tooth, slithering around after girls and drinks. And yet if a person were young and stupid enough, he might get the sense that all this here was kind of anti-Communist. The police had an eye on the place, but unlike these young enthusiasts, they knew that nothing of that sort was really going on there. Martin himself was beginning to sense this, and Ivan Figura, who now walked up to him and greeted him by his first name, also knew what he knew.

'I'm not going out with her no more,' Martin pushed through his teeth, feeling somehow entrapped by the good-buddy familiarity of this man, who wants to just, you know, shoot the breeze about Eva. It looked like… the usual sort of muscular joviality, with which people like him push themselves on you. He seemed somewhat bigger than he actually was; that grimace of greedy interest made him lean in a little closer than was proper. He's sniffing around me, that's it. A sort of eternal card-carrying member of the Union of Socialist Youth with the virility of a deflowerer of little girls. If this is the dude that Eva's sleeping with, well, God bless her. 'I'm not going out with her anymore, like…'

'Of course!' Figura leapt on his painful phrase as if upon a horse. This here long-haired boy with the inferiority complex turned out to be quite, quite legible.

'So it's no big deal then. It's OK. I've known Eva, Evička, a long time and —
you know, I care about her.'

'That's your business,' Martin grumbled.

'Mine, yeah, mine of course. I mean, you don't have to give me any of
your precious time if you don't want to.'

'Great, then. I don't.'

'But, Martin…' Figura sensed that he had him now, as he liked to say,
like a fish in a barrel. 'If you really didn't, you wouldn't have come here in
the first place. You wanted to talk about Eva with me — you're interested
in her still, after all; you want to know what's going on with her. You're
angry with me; you think that I'm to blame for what happened between
you, but you're wrong there. I'm on the sidelines. I've known Evička since
grammar school. To me she's like… like a little sister. I see that she's acting stupid, so I try to help her. She doesn't have it all together, you know
what I mean?'

'What's that to me, if she's like a little sister to you?' Martin tried to give
his words a sharp edge, but he felt that it was futile to try to get anywhere
with this guy. He simply couldn't, he wasn't up to the task; he couldn't be-
tray Eva in that way. Once more he felt as if he had been thrust into some
strange game. Again somebody was forcing words to his lips which were
not his own.

Once, when he was twelve years old, during his civics lesson, Headmistress Mikesková asked him if he believed in God. Back then he didn't know
that the one correct answer was to tell that evil women to go to Hell. He
reckoned that he had to answer, clearly, just like it's written in the Bible: say
yes when you mean yes, no when you mean no, anything more than that
comes from the devil. And that headmistress was of the devil, for sure. So he
said yes, he believes in God, for which he earned the nickname Holyroller,
but that was better than denying Jesus before men, so that Jesus would deny
him before the throne of the heavenly Father on the Day of Judgement.
She had him prone on the plate and his schoolmates could jeer at him: The
pious Vrána! Vrána the pious crow! Caw, caw! But what he was supposed
to do with all that, no, he didn't know, he couldn't see. He could still see
the blackyellow eyes of Headmistress Mikesková behind the thick lenses
of her glasses, and the complexion of her face, as brown as Clea cigarettes,
sixty of which she smoked each day, like General Secretary Husák. She lit

them instead of candles on an altar; she wolfed down their manurish smoke instead of incense, that there activist of the Communist Women's League. And he did sin against his God at that very moment, when he stood to her game; he sinned with his flaming hatred of her person, who, when she was twelve years old, still the daughter of a kulak, had certainly been a pious believer herself. Who knows what she whispered to her parish priest back then in the confessional.

And now he was gazing into the blackyellow eyes of Ivan Figura. Was he supposed to tell this meaty fellow in the snow-white T-shirt and skin-tight trousers about the sad love that broke into pieces in their hands, of nights spent wandering, wandering around, peering through lit windows, of words and of sudden silences and chiefly of how they still played like children on a wagon once pulled by blind horses, of how they could still sense the worlds they really came from, those old solidly-built houses now rubble in the depths beneath the housing estate, somewhere in the woods past the horizon? Was he supposed to tell him about those dream-buildings, leaning out of the night, as black as one huge pile of soot in a landscape where a distant light burns, where the wells are, in the woods? Their real home-lands, from which they were cut off forever by layers of tar and asphalt with yellow stripes? Here there were only barracks in which they, lost children, must live. Must he express to him what he and Eva never once expressed to themselves? That it was a miracle that they ever met — those two, who weren't from around here; those two the only ones that still carried within them memories of those now-vanished lands? He's supposed to tell these things to that guy, who's jabbering here about Evita unbalanced, and about that sex, that prolonged suicide of hers?

'It's possible, Martin, that you wanted more with her than you can get, and now she…' Figura raised his eyebrow and gazed closely at Martin, with interest, again, unmannerly close.

'There's something to that,' Martin replied. All at once he felt perfectly calm, as if he'd just walked a long way. He drew away from the radiating mug of Ivan Figura. On the table between them there was some sloshed beer and glowing cigarettes; around them swirled tatters of conversations. An autumn sun, the buckeyes, the air sharp, like a shot of vodka. And the old familiar stupefaction — how did I wind up here? So now they might have a shot or two of that vodka, break the ice and shoot the shit about Eva,

Evička, Evita, like a couple of concerned blokes who actually have something to say to one another.

'Whatever was between me and Eva has nothing, thank God, to do with you, Ivan. You've nothing in common with it. Don't even try to understand it. I myself don't understand it all that well.'

Martin got up. Sitting there felt so unreal.

'Wait,' said Figura, grabbing him by the jacket. 'You don't understand me. I respect you, really...'

'But I don't respect you.'

'Wait — I've got a car. I can drop you somewhere.'

'Drop yourself somewhere.'

THE TWELFTH

'Chuck it! Chuck it, stupid!' shouted the other grunts in the trench.

'Throw it away! Throw it away!' bawled the officer from the carrier turret, and the little soldier on the front line dutifully braced his hands to tear the pin out of the grenade. Then, he raised his tommy gun, with the bayonet, before his face with his left hand, stretching his right behind him, so that he could chuck that goddamn tin can as far away as he could before falling flat on the ground. But that last bit wasn't to happen. The soldiers in the trench and the officer in the turret saw how his right hand, stretched backwards, suddenly burst with a bright flash, the horrid power of which lifted the soldier high above the front line. At just such a camber, with such a sweeping stroke, with his gun and his bayonet, he ascended into the heavens without a cry. Only then did the percussion boom, and Private Závadský fell to earth, where he lay in a pool of blood, his arm torn off, his back broken, his pelvis shattered.

'"A fatal dud," it's called. Such things have to happen from time to time in the army.' The expressionless man in the lieutenant's uniform smiled in the direction of Ivan Figura. He had small, almost childish lips, and a little nose like that of a girl. It was this that made him terrifying. Especially when he smiled. Ivan, who still felt as if he had a mouthful of dirt, couldn't comprehend it — how that little miss from counter-espionage could smile at him like that. When he saw what had happened, he had instinctively sunk his teeth into a lump of clay at the breastworks of the trench before him. This is why, from then on, the sight of someone dying would always be accompanied, for him, by the taste of yellow clay.

'And yet it seems to me, Comrade Lieutenant, that that grenade was…'

'It seems to you? How it seems to you, who don't know the slightest thing about grenades, is not the subject of this investigation.' The little girlish face of the powerful man set him straight.

'I want names. Who it was that organised it all, who it was who wrote the complaint. You know. We know that you know, and we also know it wasn't you. So this is your chance.' And he smiled at Ivan again.

So we still have a chance. We can still blow the whistle, right? Here everybody's smiling, like we're in a whorehouse or something. Ivan couldn't tear his eyes away from the lieutenant. Like a whorehouse, when they bring a fourteen year old girl there. Nothing's gonna happen, nobody's gonna hurt you, as long as you'll be a good girl. Martina, Martina! He suddenly thought about his older step-sister, his dad's daughter. How she sobbed there on those stairs after being slapped. How could anybody wallop her like that, father or no father? Just yesterday, you were running around the prefabs in your tracksuit, and now the police, now the police are leading you off. And then they never saw her again, never spoke of her; Dad advised us to forget about her, and you listened to him, you know, and now…

'So, now you've had some time to consider the matter carefully. So let's move on,' the lieutenant encouraged him.

'But still, I mean, that grenade…'

'I'm not interested in grenades,' the lieutenant interrupted him, sharply. 'We have our own grenade specialists. But I'm getting quite interested in you, because you're not cooperating. This is the intelligence service, it's not some discussion club. Heads roll around here, and roll they will. Your little head won't even be noticed, when it does.'

The girlish dimples on the lieutenant's face smoothed out, and suddenly, he looked like nobody. That nobody, as in Nobody's gonna give you a second thought, Nobody's gonna help you, Nobody's gonna stick up for you, Ivan. At once, Figura felt like all the faces in the company, in the barracks, in all of Czechoslovakia, were glaring at him like his dad when he turned Martina over to the cops.

'Well?' the lieutenant spoke up again, not personably now, but drily, quite officially.

Shit on him, Ivan thought. This one's interested in facts; he's doing his job; this isn't about me, after all.

'Kosinský,' Ivan tossed out the name, just as drily, just as if it didn't interest him at all. 'He's the one who organised everything. He wrote the complaint, took it from the barracks, and mailed it to the president's office.'

'Was he a friend of Závadský's?'

'Not exactly.'

'What does that mean, "not exactly"?!'

'No, he wasn't,' Ivan said, speaking more precisely, amidst the clatter of the typewriter. And he smiled so coyly and acidly as if to say — buddies, friendship, they're nothing but games anyway. But nobody was interested in his smiles, so he stopped smiling.

THE THIRTEENTH

From the Na Společenstvu tavern, where he left Figura with two unfinished beers, Martin went off to the Družba bar, which, despite its actual name meaning 'The Groomsman,' was popularly known as Medvídek, i.e. 'The Teddy Bear.' Why, no one knew. Perhaps, someone was there once who looked like a teddy bear. Say, Eva Topolská, when she would snuggle up in the halflight on a well-worn chaise, she could be that teddy bear, to stroke, to whisper secrets to. She probably still has one somewhere. Grown up girls don't throw them away; although they might forget them in an old apartment when moving. The more idiotic of them never do; they drag them around everywhere with them. A love of shaggy things and plush animals remains strong even among downright whores, who again and again arrange their cute little stuffed pets around their colourful and shiny bedclothes. But I'm just a little bitty girl, they lisp naughtily to their backdoor boys, toying with their flies. No, Eva doesn't have any such plush corner. Eva's by herself; Eva doesn't lisp, she doesn't play around like that — things happen to her, and she just looks on at them with those big eyes of hers. Right now, that Figura's what's happening to her.

Martin rested his elbows on the bar and ordered himself a vodka. This was one of the first he ever ordered and consumed alone. It was the first wagon of a train plummeting into a tunnel, dragging in after it a myriad of passenger cars and freight cars, into a darkness that doesn't thin out even a little bit for long hours that just don't move. In a tunnel, time means nothing. The moment when total darkness falls is the last moment, and others such follow, until the greyish mould of light appears in the window frames. The eternity between that moment and this is a slate wiped clean, which has different dimensions and parameters than events in time upon which the light of the sun falls.

Martin ordered another. Underneath all of this fluster, as humid as a wrestling match, as humid as someone panting into your mug in the centre of the mat, underneath all this humid flesh he sensed something as calm and cool as stone. He realised that he was completely uninterested in any future. Neither the school to which he'd applied, nor that 'Someday, we'll be farther on,' sung half-conspiratorially in the evangelical church, nor the fact that he'd get married and have kids, nor that truth, which shall be victorious, nor what it will be like after death. Everything's going to be just the same, and even that doesn't interest him. And now, with the Russian spirits on his palate, on his tongue, it came to him, why he was here — only to be destroyed. On the River Ussuri, or somewhere else, in some foreign war, all of us will be trampled into the earth under horses' hooves or burnt to a crisp by lasers. It's not for us to live to forty, fifty. To become respected, reverend elders, or at least granddads, tattered old men. That's not in store for us. For us, there'll be a war.

A nuclear war?

Sure — nuclear war!

Thus, Martin's brother Tomáš held forth in impassioned tones at the U Eliáše tavern — prophesying just like the eponymous Elijah a scorched earth and concentration camps everywhere. It's not heading in any other direction. Humanity has nothing in front of it, no future. God is silent. All we can do is write our journals, sketching little pictures in the hope that someday, somebody will find them. Dig them up from the rubble.

A soft rain was falling on the prefab estate. Rain was falling on the old colony, on the race-track, over which glowing metal speeds past kitchen windows in the form of torpedo-like vehicles known as veronicas. Rain was falling on Veronica, the beautiful gypsy girl who used to attend the people's art school with them, until she got pregnant and scandalised all her little worshippers with her growing belly. Rain was falling on the stars made of lightbulbs affixed to the roofs of the factories, and water, dirty water, was flowing through the tram-track grooves. Up in the stratosphere, supersonic MiGs were booming and everything, everything, was tending to war. You didn't need to be a wise man from the East to understand that now was the time for a flight into Egypt. But road and pathway were barbwired shut to Veronica and her child, as well as all the rest of the innocents.

Later on, when Tomáš took her picture in her dirty kitchen, with her child at her breast, a black madonna, the black Mother of God from Mariánské Hory, the print was angrily torn from its place in a photo club exhibition by some ideological Herod or other, who bellowed at Tomáš that such things do not exist in our country. At the time, the Vrána brothers reckoned that that comrade, Švanda was his name, our man from Strakonice, who wasn't able to climb on top of his old lady without first covering her face with a copy of Rudé Právo, that bloated old piper of the party tune from the orchestra of the Ministry of the Interior, only wished to cover up the societal problems of real socialism. Only later, when Veronica's photo with its torn corners had become nothing more than one more yellowed document among other journals and pictures that no one will ever dig out of the rubble, only then did they realise that Švanda was doing his bit to create a new reality, in which there was no room for any black or even purple Mother of God!

No room for her, but plenty of space for a whore's stuffed zoo and for songs from the radio, spun for you by an adept disk jockey. No help for him was in the offing, either from Veronica or his brother. The stone was still deep inside him.

He called for a fourth vodka, and cynically studied the couple, both nearing their freshness-expiration date, seated at a nearby table. Maybe that's the future we'll never see. That's no future at all, Eva. The word 'no' used in this combination with 'future,' with the addition of 'at all' was capable of echoing so mournfully and sadly in Martin's soul, that he sniffled back a tear. Sentimental boozer! He wiped his nose with his hand, then with the back of his hand, and finally, his hand on his trousers beneath the bar. He kept staring at the bald guy in the black shirt sitting at the table next to the plump female with the hairsprayed topknot and tasteless plastic earrings. And so they're drinking that foul white wine and the guy's giving it a go. He keeps on touching her one way or another, like a faggot, you might say, if she weren't a woman. His face was brushing up against her face, his hand was on her mighty leg in that tight dress. He keeps on talking and she, she keeps looking around and smiling, smiling, constantly adjusting that dress, pulling down the hem. And he's pulling his chair closer to hers; he keeps on doing it even when their chairs are already touching, as if he wanted to push them somewhere farther away from all this weariness here, where he's got to keep on telling her something, all red in the face from that white wine, snuggling up ever closer, pressing himself ever more tightly upon her. He's gaping at those large tits of hers, how they sway in that tight dress with the plunging neckline, and he keeps on talking and she keeps on fretting with that dress and smiling and now and then she screeches loudly with laughter, kind of how she'd screech later, if everything fell into place. They're probably coworkers from some office testing out an affair. That can't be too pleasant for him, sitting like that so long with his legs crossed. He's rubbing up against her side, rubbing until he starts trembling even, and she's trembling along with him, running her tongue along the lower edge of her upper lip. And that wine, more of that wine from that gal o' mine and from that other one fine, white, just white, vinegar-yellow — Templar, Three Graces, poetry, maiden dreams and romance… Even Martin was aroused now at the sight of that powerful overhang of hers, that fleshy gorge, those predatory smiles, as she feigned that she's nothing more than a peaceful little herbivore, a little sheep, whereas she might also be a shaggy old swine, and all the while she's squirming on her chair with that behind of hers, and while the guy's already adrift, not knowing what or how, she dips beneath the table, where she has a bag with her shopping; soon she'll be on her way, hurrying home to her family… She rummages with her hand in that bag and pulls out something wrapped in paper. It seems as if she'd had that in mind for a while now. They're low-calorie franks in artificial casings. She gives a guilty smile and helps herself to one. She holds it at the end of her fingers, her polished nails elegantly peeling off the artificial skin before she takes a greedy bite. The guy, elbows on the table before him, capitulates. Martin orders himself a fifth and wonders whether it'd be worth living to forty, even if such a thing were possible.

THE FOURTEENTH

When the train rolled onto the viaduct, a flotilla of stormy clouds was sailing through the heavens, while in the spaces between them oblique rays of afternoon sunlight were shooting down, with a splendid, Baroque sublimity upon the green fields of grain with a brilliance so penetrating, that each and every one of the green stalks cast its individual black shadow upon the buxom earth of the fields swelling to the horizon. Slowly, carefully, the train slid over the old arches, and Mrs Vránová, the mother of Martin and his brothers, looked upon these heavenly acts with breathless delight, swept up from the mundane present moment. Look at those ships up there — just look at them! If they collide, there'll be a storm, but if they scatter, we'll gather home the sheaves of hay, nice and dry. It was her father taught her to read the clouds like that. Even though she's been a city dweller for thirty years now, and the windows of her lab look out directly upon the steel guts of Nová huť, she's never ceased being a little country girl. The sweet green of well-plotted fields were still capable of convincing her that all was not yet lost on this horrid earth. Not when the rye spreads and grows so beautifully.

The train rose almost soundlessly above a valley in which a stream was spilling into a deep pool, over the smooth surface of which a few children were swimming. They were literally frolicking amidst the first drops of a coming storm, the winds of which were causing the crowns of the alders above their heads to swing. And suddenly they were gone. Ah, to leap out like that and tumble down over the railroad embankment covered in nettles and goosefoot between the thin groups of acacias and come to a halt down below there, at the deep and bright water, deep and bright as only a river that flows out of forests can be. To be all of a sudden in the sharp wind, with goosepimples on one's white flesh like those little boys and girls, those wild children, who will certainly get soaked to the bone. To escape to the shelter of the viaduct with your clothes in a bundle under your arm, inside the dry stone arch beyond which shimmer the drapes of the downpour. The lightning flashes there, and there again, and the thunder that follows hard upon just makes that heavenly waterfall rage all the more strongly, as we gaze upon it with wonder, shyly, like little birds sheltering under a ledge.

Just like my boys. How grown up they are becoming now, growing away. Mrs Vránová sees once again three little bare bottoms in one great cast-iron tub, back in the old place, before they moved to the housing estate. They're like three refugees, skinny as rods, that I scrub with a washcloth from tip to toe — back then they still let me. Petr, the eldest, so serious even as a child, scratching his soaped-up head thoroughly, and not even letting a peep escape his mouth when the suds get in his eyes. He got that from Petr Senior — bearing all pain patiently, all his life long, stifling his emotions. The middle one, Tomáš, that poacher and setter of traps; he's the one who secretly takes a pee in the water where all of them are bathing, and then bursts out in laughter about what they were washing themselves with, laughing at Petr especially, who awkwardly thumps him in the belly with his fist before rinsing off again, seriously, using only the tepid water that remains in the iron barrel. And Martin, Martin the lefty, who always glances aside somewhat, playing with something the other two can't see. He's always got something stashed away somewhere. And won't show anyone. He'd rather stand there, teeth clenched, with something gripped in his left hand, and should Tomáš try to pry those fingers open, he'll kick and bite in a furious whirl to keep it hidden. Not long ago, he got drunk as a lord and then clammed up about something. That'll pass, hopefully.

Her husband Petr Vrána is standing out in the corridor, straightening his aching back. Mrs Vránová admits, silently, that she's happy at this moment, when she's alone in the compartment, the train passing through the woods, and she senses that when they return from the funeral of their aunt in Prague this might be the last time that the flat that's awaiting her will be full of her boys.

It's a small flat, there's not much room, they're crawling over one another — but we're all together there. The next time we return from Prague, there will be waiting for us a wretchedly tidy and wretchedly empty place. So many rooms, so much room in the closets, so much silence. I'm not looking forward to that. That'll be our funeral, then. The burial of our walks, hand in hand, with our little boys, the end of notebooks and school-books, of snacks, of 'be a good boy and behave.' Petr said that he'd take advantage of the first opportunity and go to Germany, never to return. He wants to leap the barbed wire and try his luck there. Tomáš will go off to Prague, and we'll lose him there. He's got to be there; that's where he must be. Even if he has to become a stagehand or work in a warehouse, it's only there, supposedly, that he can be a photographer. How does he know, since he's never lived there? And Martin, O, he'll leave us. He doesn't say anything, but I can see it in him: he's changed, he's not sheepish any more, he's not afraid of anything — actually, he's gone already.

Suddenly, the compartment door slid open and big Petr, a man with a barrel chest, a high forehead and a thatch of stiff grey hair, sat down next to Mrs Vránová. He glanced at her and noticed immediately that she'd been crying.

'What is it? Thinking of Auntie? At eighty-two, a person's got every right to die. That's already the grace of God, if we…'

But she'd stopped listening. She covered her mouth with her handker-chief so as not to blurt out, I don't give a rap about Auntie. She could've died even earlier, for all that I care. I'm the one dying here. We're dying in this horrid Ostrava and we're not even fifty yet — but you don't see anything!

'Well, it's hard,' Petr Vrána went on with his commentary. 'Old, good people depart, and nothing all that good is awaiting the young in this sty. And it has an effect on them all, the swinishness all around. O, that Martin tied one on, he did! Had he ever seen anything like that at home? And it wasn't the first time. Can you ever imagine me coming home drunk like that at eighteen?'

'No,' laughed Mrs Vránová. 'I can't even imagine you coming home drunk now.'

'Well then. And am I any less the man? What's going on with these boys?'

'Perhaps they're going through some things that we don't know anything about.'

'Nonsense. They've got to start working hard and watching out, so that they'll make something of themselves. I…'

The train rolled down from the hills onto the lowlands of marshy fields and lazy rivers. Horizontals set a person's soul at ease. People from the flatlands are slow, firmly set on a broad basis, mostly rich and tight-fisted.

The rich treat well only those they can make a profit from. That's what Mrs Vránová's father used to say to her. In the mountains, people pull stone from their fields and are delighted if anything at all grows there. They're closer to heaven, but they're hard on themselves and others. She stole a sidewise glance at her husband. That's us, too, hoisting stone after stone out of the field. But the field doesn't belong to us anymore. Only the stones do.

'A while ago I was looking at the river under the bridge, and at those storm clouds, and it got to me. I used to spend a lot of time at the river when I was a little girl.'

'I know,' he said, looking at her. She sensed that he understood her, but in his own way — the way she herself never wanted to understand.

'I remember that you could be a real Viktorka, before we got married.'

THE FIFTEENTH

It's all so simple, after all. Eva finished making her face. As always, she was only partially pleased with her looks. She wondered if Martin wasn't right after all, that in each person there is somebody else, planted inside them, living his own life. Martin, that little warrior, called this being his enemy. Your enemy, who is always with you. She coloured her eyelids a bold black and said to herself: There. Now I can recognise my inner enemy perfectly. Especially when she was making herself up, striving for that ideal face. But yeah, you're right, Martin. There's somebody there. Somebody, standing right there. But you're the only one who calls him an enemy, boyo. She closed her one eye and, holding down the lid with her finger, inspected it with the other. The artificial shadow was exact. Exactly what? Well, exactly for this, that I should look pleasing to my enemy, my self. Not that she'd trust me. We don't trust our enemies. We seek to please them. I don't trust myself, nor am I pleased with myself, so I've got to do something about that. I can't comprehend why you loving husbands — and one day you will be one of them, Martin — say to the wives you care for that, as far as you're concerned, they don't have to make themselves up at all; that they'd be just as pleasing to you even if they just washed their faces — let me try to imagine it! — just washed themselves with regular soap and the water from a stream. Because it's not for you that women make up their faces anyway. I bet your mother never used much makeup. Women paint their faces for their enemies. You used to mumble about truth shimmering somewhere on the edge, of reality shining through at far boundaries — and it's those very boundaries that are dangerous; that's why we need our makeup. Even when we're not yet using it to cover up ageing, which one day is going to steal in here, after all.

She felt that it was all starting to lose its simplicity, that there was a danger here that it would all fall to pieces and she would smear her makeup over her face and somehow disfigure herself. I could disfigure myself just as easily as I'm making myself up right now, but no, my enemy won't stand for that. I'm not with her out of love, but because she showed me how simple it is to be like water, which overcomes everything and fights with nothing.

Figura makes speeches similar to yours, my enemy, about fighting. He's much, much stupider than you, and at the same time, he's unable to be even half so stupid. Maybe you both think that Eva, Evita, is the stupidest of the lot, but that Eva there knows what she knows about all this.

Having now brought her makeup to a conclusion, she gazed at the reflection in the mirror. Success. As she was descending the stairs, her mind made up about taking the step that would help her escape from this all, from Stage 4 and all further stages in this deaf and dumb life in a corner of northern Moravia, she wasn't at peace with herself, but she wasn't worried either, or euphoric… she simply wasn't. Was not. For the first time in her life she'd succeeded in ceasing to be here. Not to participate, and yet to act. The world was now just as she'd always imagined it to be.

She exited her building and got into the expensive car, within which waited the man whom she'd learned to forget about since childhood. A well situated man, who had still never done her any good. Her father.

THE SIXTEENTH

Martin's world ceased being blackyellow. He'd sensed for a long time now that those warning signs were fading away, that the whole childish game, which was to divide the world into mine and yours, would run out of steam. Eva went off to Prague to study languages. His brother Petr got his longed-for pink slip (that's what the stamped insert permitting travel to the West was called. It actually was pink). He showed the stamp of the Interior Ministry to Martin — he didn't let him take it in hand; he only showed it to him. 'So it's only good for two weeks: to Hannover for the expo. Then what?'

'I hope it won't be fourteen years before we see one another again,' his brother said in a voice husky with emotion.

And so it happened that Petr, whom Martin didn't understand anyway, disappeared into that void, which stretched out from the western slopes of the Šumava mountains. Martin imagined the western border like this: a broad region from which mountains arose, and between them a black lake, like in a painting by Preisler. From there, one goes on over brown meadows, through unreal forests and moors toward a hill, until one reaches the barbed wire and the trench-cut open spaces beyond which was — fog. Nothing. The earth breaks off there, as sharp as the edge of a table. One doesn't live there; there one falls into the unknown. All the rest of that German good and German bad is, presumably, far away from the border. There can't be any free movement across out there. Out there is the Zone. The emigration Zone. There you jump, as if over the railing of the steamship General Nachymov — into Turkey, into Germany, it's all the same.

And there, in the deep woods of the border regions one finds a hotel named West Germany. The people who get the pink insert are taken to that hotel after showing up at the border, and that's where they spend their time until the date on their slip expires. They're given all sorts of things there — pictures of their relations, jeans, photos from the seashore — just about anything you can imagine. The regimen at the hotel is relaxed; many people enjoy it. Fleeting affairs are a common occurrence there, because the republic (the Czech authorities, that is) generally don't let couples out together. At first, people have a hard time realising that there's nothing at all past the hill, but the atmosphere in the hotel is so suggestive that they come to terms with it and, in the end, they're happy that they didn't tumble into the void. Should some person out on a random stroll come upon the hotel by chance (which is impossible, given the security measures in place out there), he'd most likely take it for some well-concealed psychiatric sanatorium. The sky is still obscured there with the fog of the frontier and beyond the fence one can see some silent people; people who must have somehow inexplicably come to experience — by osmosis — the real edge of the world, so ghostlike they seem. The stay gets a little unpleasant toward the end, when the travellers learn where they have actually been all this while and what it is they've experienced; and then they sign a binding document. The might of this document is such that, even later, the people have no difficulty to keep their promise.

That's how the Vrána brothers understood it all, until the oldest and most serious of them decided to have a go at it. Petr, that serious chap, an excellent technical draughtsman, technician, philosopher and pianist, the fellow who went around in shirts buttoned up to the chin, will make his way through the wire, never to return until the war is over. The missile war… because nothing less than a missile can pierce that void on the border. Only the splitting of elementary particles is stronger than nothingness.

Martin went off to work at the Triumphant February coke ovens, so as to earn some money. He fed the coke-side of Furnace Nr. 9, where four times an hour he'd see the tiger. He had to open the door, lift the hot cotter-pins, draw the drainage apparatus from the trough, and then mount trough and tunnel in the glowing mouth of the chamber. Then he would wave in the direction of the foreman, who in turn would make a sign to the man on the other side, who was to insert the heavy plunger into the same chamber. The hydraulics started up and the tiger was on his way. His red and white form darted forward through that tunnel, and below, through the trough, onto the sloping ramp, where with crackling and hissing it sprawled and expired. Then, flat on the slope, it was carried off to the cooling tower, where it turned black amidst the yellow benzene fumes that scratched at the bronchial tubes and lungs of the workers. *Tyger, tyger, burning bright.* A snowy curtain of steam poured from the cooling tower, and it was impossible to see the doors of the chamber, closed again, through which the furnace was fed. Little red cubes poured into the yellow gloom, until the rails were clear, and the process was repeated four times an hour, all night long until morning.

In the mornings, passing through the factory gate in that pleasant buzzy mood when the soul has been cheered by a couple of golden morning beers, and the body, showered clean and rubbed down with cream, clamours for bed, it would occur to him that he would never get over his weariness. That nothing would ever change, even if by chance he went off to university. The world began to pale like the windows of the locker room at 5 am. With dread, Martin began to intimate what, probably, his older brother already knew all too well. That nothing was ever going to happen; everything would just continue its slow burn, its smouldering. No one would precipitate the breakdown of elementary particles, and thus our life would roll on. The war, which the pregnant world bore about in her belly so near term, would never be born; it would be aborted behind the atomic shield of the great powers, and all of us, without putting up a fight, would just grow old.

Petr was getting on well. He applied for asylum at the emigrant camp and wrote long, reasonable letters to his parents. Eva was getting on invisibly, in that Somewhere, where no one was with her, not even herself, it seems, as she would often say. Again and again she would forget about the horrid hangovers, which slaughtered her whenever she slipped out of her role. Such a good girl she was, to at least be smart enough to collapse from time to time. His brother Tomáš was in a state of permanent collapse, like everyone in Prague. He drank and drank, and dreamed of photographing what he'd photographed back in Ostrava, that black Mother of God, but he clung to that Holešovice of his like shit to a shirt. Not many people wasted a thought on Ivan Figura, but he often thought about them. And Tonda Gona died.

THE SEVENTEENTH

It was too late to attend the funeral of Antonín Gonda, that Antigona, to whom Martin wandered so often in thought. There had been something between them. They didn't know what it was, and now they never will. There was no funeral anyway. Who buries stuff, right? You use up the stuff you have and then you recycle it.

'How did it happen?' Martin asked the friend-in-common who brought him the news.

'He drank a lot.'

'Always did.'

'But lately, even more than before. He shacked up with some broad; they had a kid, but it wasn't what you might call a happy union. The last time he was seen it was in the tavern, the Kotelna. You know, "The Boiler Room," where the boiler used to be, the heating plant of the building? There's a bar there now, because the apartment blocks have been hooked up to the municipal heating system. So, a bar, or maybe a still's a better term — the tunnellers from the area frequent it. That's where they saw him last. He left sometime after midnight, and they found him lying just a couple steps from his old lodgings, where he'd lived before he'd hooked up with that chick.'

'Fallen in a ditch, with his skull smashed in.'

'What? You heard already?'

'No. That's Bezruč.'

'Well, whether he fell, or had been fighting with somebody… they say he was messed up enough.'

Martin took himself to The Boiler Room. The door was a sheet metal grate, and the bar was of planks sprayed with liquid wallpaper. It was sour, heavy; the windows of wired glass stretched up somewhere near the ceiling. A bare cement floor, raw, knocked-down partitions, posters of naked girls and a beery travesty of the Lord's Prayer: 'Our Lager, which art froth-heady…' First you hit the barrel, then you hit the head. Martin was pissed off enough to start writing verse like Petr Bezruč. What am I looking for here? What are any of you looking for?

Culm banks and housing estates on the meadows, prefab blocks in the villages, hostels, barracks and garrisons. What the hell did I drag myself here for? What do all of you want here? Who drove you all here? Drag your arses back to your narrow river valleys, your untillable fields strewn with rocks, back to Slovakia, Moravia, Poland, back where you all belong, home! Who made you migrate here? Here to the boiler room to get shit-faced. See, Tonda Antigone? You see the scam now, that shitty German, Austrian, Jewish, capitalist, Russian, Communist fraud? Get yourself to Ostrava, with bells on! Leave the old woman and the brat at home and hop on the train! From the main station to Hauling and up to the mines, grab yourself a sledge everybody and off to the mines! Three thousand clear, build the fatherland, shore up world peace and make babies stupid from your booz-ing. Shit on sentiment, go — off to Ostrava. There you'll get a company flat, a bathroom with hot and cold, a tub, sausages and bacon and a little red booklet and a savings booklet and a steel pipe to the head. We're all together here; here we all live together, this gang of ours. Here we're building a new world; here everybody fucks everybody else over, everybody fucks every-one. Here it's a thousand tonnes an hour, get it? A hundred thousand tonnes a second flying out the chimney. Here nobody gives a shit, nobody gives a second glance, here it's all hammer, hammer, here the mob hammers on like a predatory river, fuck your mother, old Gona thumps old Mrs Gona across the head and then little Tonda across the arse with a strop and out! toss your little son out on the steps, bitch, a little rock 'n' roll and fuck a bargirl's eyes out, the buffet slut, dirty banged-up whore, and then off for some skin, you know, belly up for some skin, bacon, ground meat, with big sacks of beer, knapsack, bread bag, grab yourself a Lahváč or two, kisser to the jerrycan and don't be a fuckhead take what's on offer stuff yer sausage motherfucker wherever you please, eat up and don't be pushy… Everybody's got a kid don't get all fucked up over kids kids'er so many round here you can't shake a fuckin' stick at'er go buy'im a soda an' a Tatranka it won't kill'im an' send him home to sleep the sooner the better to sleep wit' Mama put the fuckin' TV on for'im bedtime cartoon or whodafucknose what who got time f'r dat shit. Here we've come from homelands many, one big clusterfuck Czechs an' Moravians Silesians Slovaks Poles Magyars Gypsies, Olaši Vlaši Laši from Hukvaldy and dat Janáček who wrote that Jenůfa here you know with the hair like that? Stepdaughter, stepdaughter take it all fuck y'r mother. The Cubans'll be here soon, Koreans, Vietnammers, tailorbirds Saigon US army Brezhnev's first line and the whole team train fat cats wit' heads like dat — you never seen such a big bloke in all yer life packin' crates o' Stoli what you drink at parties up at Vlčina. Unimaginable amounts they are, and wid' artists and athletes and cosmonauts! O, they got innards, they do, of iron, of Vitkovice stainless steel. Top line quality for the space programme.

Nobody gives a shit round here for any orphan halfwit Antigone. He did his bit, drank his share an' no more drinkin' f'r'im now, there's more o' his sort round here, who needs'm, others'll come, others'er waitin' on flats, there's waitin' lists, get it? A three plus one at Dubin, a thousand interested parties, get it? What do their job an' don't go sprawlin' on the road like fuck knows who. You just wait, the Mongols'll be here, real life Mongols, Djingischchanies wit' red stars, they're already here the Mongols, reformatories full o' Mongols n' Tatars what'll grind you beneath their heel like a mole, asshole, what the fuck you comin' round here asking about Toníček, we cart Toníčeks like him off to the motherfuckin' crematories by the baker's dozen. Go there an' cry yer eyes out if ya wanna an' say yer prayers along wit' the rest o' the old ladies lightin' candles. Go get yourself a grand ol' sirloin, motherfucker, with sour cream if they'll broil it up for ya, go ask'er, task'er, smack'er right across the chops. Where's the schnitzel, cunt, a chop's what we're after, your gonna have ter try better'n that here, nobody's gonna cheat me wit' lettuce, you c'n write letters to your girl from the worl' war, get it, shitass? Here there's gotta be a good tuck-in, fuckin' decent pay for a decent job, corn on the cob, cunt, get what I say? Fuckin-a!

Yer gonna bawl about Antigone? — he soused himself, his business. I don't give a rat's ass, go sob if the spirit moves ya, scream and sob but shut yer gob at home, grab some ol' crockery and smash'em fuck-all on the floor, let'er have somethin' to gather, just don't you go lightin' no votive candles there — you hear how that old hag lit a votive candle and boom! the methane blew from beneath'er hut and see what that got'er? now she's a squatter in a flat without water. Could you be any dumber? Fuckin' spun'er like a top across the floor — whop! candle in'er hand fuck it ain't safe round here. You wanna be safe you shoulda stayed in Slovakia there in that fuckin' hole of a village where you say Night Neighbour to the devil hisself an' all the dogs bark through their arseholes. There you can sing your head off about the buns o' fuckin' nuns up in a tower. But here we got different towers, what stand over coal shafts up an' fuckin' down you go on the crane beneath the crane your mate's a watin' on ya in the co-op flat, he set the bitch cross the laundry winch and then he was lord o' all creation, unnerstan'? Lord o' all creation an' so he stays on top until they tie his body to the caisson till that time he'll be stiff as iron.

Martin spun himself out of The Boiler Room. I can't even cry for you, Antigona, such a shambles it all is. Sour and dark; when you go outside you see the drops on the pavement and the cosy lights in the windows. It's good that you're where you are, it's good that you are as you are. Have a rest, have a nice rest, you've got your jacket, button it up. Don't wait any longer, waiting won't do you no good. Everything here that was to be, already was. It's all winding down now, wheels, motors, everything shoddy, running down. It's time to go, but there's nowhere to go. This is it, last stop, there will be no other. Only that silver one, like steam from your mug, like tinfoil. She gets off the tram and you're not lying here like some wretch, you're waiting for her here, she came to pull you out of the tavern in her fake fur, her boots, her blonde wash. She's been through a thing or two in her life, with you too, you impossible bloke, you idiot foster-child. But you don't have to wriggle and make excuses now, dodging with your eyes any evil teacher. Antonín, you're not wearing patchy trousers any more. Nobody's gonna make fun of you any more. Now the fun starts…

THE EIGHTEENTH

'Once I have my own room…'

'When you get married, that is.' With these words Martin's father settled the question.

'But I'm thinking, for instance, if we should move into a larger flat, then once I have my own room, I…'

'A flat big enough for each young man to have his own room — we'll probably never get. So, really, when you get married.'

Martin plummeted into despair. Not so much because they had a tiny flat, like everybody else, but because he was being prohibited from expressing the amazing thing that had just occurred to him. Why couldn't his father let himself be carried away for once? Why can't he play along a bit, fantasise a tad, just supposing that, what if everybody had his own room? But his father never 'what-ifed.' His father must derive some sort of pleasure from bringing a young fantasist back down to terra firma — and so twelve-year-old Martin would never be able to express his plan. And so that plan's still locked up inside him, now, well into his forties — he's still never said it aloud. It still lies there inside him, undisclosed, even though he's already had his own room along with his wife, even though his own children are now as old as he was back then, even though he's already been deprived of that room he shared with his wife, even though he'd experienced things of which his father had no idea — still he remains subdued and stifled by the inexorable facts of tight living spaces, which cause him to constantly swallow the phrase which still echoes in him since those days long ago. He'd almost forgotten what it was like for five people to live together in a two room prefab flat, almost forgotten those strange sounds at night: the rustling in the pipes, the creaking of a bed and the strange sighs and whispers, which the insufficiently dark, thin gloom was unable to fully cover and stifle. Then the walls vanished and dreams seeped in, spreading wide through glazed doors from room to room, from flat to flat. The rattle of toilets and the whining of spigots when a person couldn't sleep; suffering it all till he was quite worn out with the ceaseless movement between the walls. Martin snuggled up to his wall beneath the window and it seemed to him that something was going on inside that wall, something streaming inside it there, something restlessly rushing. The wall tasted good.

He hadn't yet sampled the walls here on Zborovská. That means he's really grown up now, since he hasn't scraped away a bit of the plaster with his fingernail and popped it in his mouth — he'd forgotten the taste, forgotten himself with his index finger between his teeth. He set his rucksack and his trunk on the floor and went over to his chair. At the moment, the chair was the only piece of furniture in the studio flat he was renting on Zborovská St. Here he'll have some peace.[8] He sat down on the chair at the window, and gazed out at the roofs of the houses across the way. A mighty scream was resounding in his ears. It wasn't from outside, or from the flats beneath him; it was coming at him from behind, from the back of his head, from years past. It was his wife's scream. I hate you! How horrid, when something like that has to be screamed, and heard. Worse yet, when it becomes reality. Soon, that scream grew in strength into a mighty current, without words. He let his chin fall upon his chest and waited until it died away, but it just kept growing stronger, he had to go with it, he had no chance against it. The ten years he lived through with Daniela he'd refused to erase, refused to let disappear, like an old unfinished phrase.

'It wasn't what you might call a happy union,' he tried to say aloud to the empty spaces. And immediately he had to remember all the happiness beneath the weeping willow at the maternity hospital, when a boy was born to them, and just the same two years later, when their daughter was born. There was no anxiety except in the leaves of that willow, which whispered to his, at the time, deaf ears, that this wouldn't turn out happily. Who are you, he asked the little human cradled in Daniela's arms back then, who are you

....

[8] There is a pun here in the original Czech: *pokoj* can mean either 'chamber' or 'peace.' This takes on meaning from his earlier-mentioned dreams of having his own room, in which, presumably, he'd have peace. The reader should keep this in mind at every mention of the word 'room' in this chapter.

he asked the little girl and her mother. The tiny little hand protruding from the downy coverlet groped about the dangerous spaces outside. A mitten of yarn without fingers. This was happiness, won at the cost of horrific sadness. Happiness sprouting from quarrels, that little glove bobbing like a flower, like a blossoming leaf above a dark level surface. Who could not love the mother of that child? Even if all the weeping willows at the windows of all the maternity hospitals in the world should hiss with the tongues of prophets of evil, still and all — this here was happiness. Even if you all can't understand it. Even if you all can't understand it and never will be able to, you will be, all the same, witnesses to happiness. They grew silent, with a bottle of spirits near the unlit Christmas tree, after the children had already gone off to bed. You'll have pity along with your happiness. Endangered, even before birth. No, not everyone knew such happiness blossoming like a tiny little white glove above a dark level surface.

A person has to be crazy in order to be a man, in order to be a new man, that tiny little white glove in your hand, to blubber in tears all the night long, to caterwaul through the night and coo soothingly through the day, to wallow in the muck of lies and futile vows; a person has to be crazy. Crazy beneath a weeping willow. To vow happiness. I hate you. To slam doors. To roll one's eyes in rage. To recall godknowswhy tiny details at moments of the greatest horror, details of bliss that fade, that pale like your face, Daniela. I wanted to find peace at your side. To have that damned peace with my wife. A person has to be crazy to believe something like that. Now I see how great you are, how you can enter into no room in peace; you are like a white cliff — a white cliff of anger. I crawl off from your foot at low tide and into the open sea. I repeat to myself the names of our children and I hear that scream. And suddenly it's quiet here. Just as it is when, at last, the little ones have fallen asleep, and the big ones crash, at last, worn out.

His eyes roved about the four undecorated walls and gazed at the stains on the ceiling, left behind by leaks. Such maps will never lead us to one another. He grew as sentimental as Mowgli leaving the jungle behind for civilisation. From henceforth we shall run along different paths, the wolves yelped, disappearing into the trees. In his rucksack there was a large canister of white paint, but what's the sense of just moving in and getting down to whitewashing? It was quite good just to sit there on the chair in that garret, the ceiling of which was nothing more than the backside of the roof, and so low that he could touch it with the brush by raising himself up on tip-toe. It was good to sit there like that — and the scream died away.

'I hate you too,' said Martin. And he pulled a pencil from his pocket and began to draw something on the wall. He got on with it fairly well. There was a time when he wanted to become a painter, but he had a fear of empty planes, of freely-spreading spaces — he didn't know where to begin, or why. Now he wasn't afraid of anything. On one side of the wall he drew a man. He was naked, but set in motion in such a way that his private parts were hidden. One of his hands was stretched out before him, as if he wanted to touch something. I'll paint over it in a minute, anyway, Martin reassured himself, and started to work on the woman. She was standing on the other side, looking out from the plane of the wall on which she was painted. She had a beautiful behind and breasts, and her long hair fell about her face. Children were playing between them, building some structures from flat stones. They were naked too, a little boy and a little girl; engrossed in their game, they weren't looking at each other. Just like the office of a child psychologist, Martin chuckled, shading the design and happily planning the background he would carve out behind them. Gigantic trees — not a pine forest, but ancient growth. He didn't take too much care with it, knowing that he'd be painting over a minute later.

'You know, once I have my own room, I'll draw some prehistoric hunters on the wall,' he said aloud, and — at last — no one's voice cut him off in mid-speech.

THE TWENTIETH

'The main thing to realise is that matter does not exist. The material world is a function of spirit, and spirit is the vital power which temporarily assumes the appearance of matter — you understand, merely the appearance. Everything around us is illusory,' stated the mystic with the drooping moustache.

'As illusory as a dream,' added the mystic with the shaved head.

'No, dreams are more real than the material world,' the mystic with the drooping moustache enlightened him, 'the greatest error, indeed, is to believe that one actually sees anything.'

'The question is' (here the mystical adept with the big mouth shouldered his way into the exchange), 'why is this material world here in the first place?'

Droopy and Baldy both swivelled their heads *no*, in rejection of the question.

'Well then, why?' insisted Big Mouth.

'You state that the material world "is here",' Droopy set him straight.

'Your path has obviously not led you very far,' Baldy clarified with insight, 'yet still you sense that there must be something beneath the surface — and that's correct, that's a good question you pose, but you must progress further.'

'But,' Big Mouth retreated a bit, 'I know that the material world will disappear, and then…'

'And then?' prompted Droopy.

'And then it's going to depend on how far you've got. How many veils you've parted by then, understand?'

'Sure. I've read that the fourth chakra is the important one. If you don't have the fourth one open, then when matter disappears, so do you.'

'You read that? You read books?'

'You don't?'

'No.'

'So how then…' Big Mouth asked, confused.

'He gets it directly,' the bald head explained, speaking of the drooping 'stache's situation. 'He's gone quite a long ways already.'

'What does that mean? Directly from where?'

'You can't understand until you've experienced it yourself.'

The mystics grew silent and Martin rested his head in his hands. He pondered a while on his fourth chakra. Was it open, or not? But then it occurred to him that he'd be quite happy to disappear along with the material world. He was even bothered by the idiotic sense that there might even be something to these things. Despite the fact that this sort of esoteric literature pops up on every corner. Everywhere, indeed, anywhere — at the train station, in a subway, in every kiosk and at any hour of day or night you could always buy the basics: alcohol, cigarettes, pornography and esoteric writings. There's democracy for you. Which presumably exists in the same fashion as this material world.

He looked around the dark, smoke-filled club full of eccentric youth and it made him think of Husák, Dr Husák, who wanted to keep us from all this. He gazed at us from his official portraits with those censorious eyes of his and that somewhat sadistically pursed lip, like a broad pretending to be a guy. He too was a great mystic, of a sort, who knew that his material face, that trembling map of aged liver spots, didn't really exist — that only those silver icons of it glowing everywhere did — those dusty holy pictures of him hung in each and every classroom and office. Who knows what these wise men here were up to during the Husák era — they're old enough, after all — they had to be busied with something a couple decades ago. Back then, most likely, they were still lost in the material world; back then you couldn't buy porno and spiritual enlightenment in every public bog.

We made our share of mistakes, we didn't know that the material world doesn't really exist; on the contrary, we thought that the Husáks and the Rusáks would be here forever. We got married and we made babies in whom we saw ourselves. We hid ourselves in each other's embrace, in bed, on cots, in one-room flats; we ignored our spiritual development, our path, amidst the fairy lights. I myself got married kind of out of despair and from fear of being alone. Absolve me, wise men, for having forgotten that a royal cloak is awaiting me in the house of my father. I squandered my vigour in marital and extramarital sex, instead of concentrating it in my heart and loving my soul as a bride loves her bridegroom. I wallowed in matter, in money, neither of which I had. I served myself in self-serves. I wanted to create safety, an asylum in the midst of all the swinishness round about. I believed that faith was the foundation of things promised, having no idea that the divine principle is found directly in me, that I could get it, as you say, directly.

'When California slides into the ocean, then the world will see that the age of America is over and done with,' Big Mouth pronounced.

'What about the Age of Russia?' Baldy asked.

'The Age of Russia — I don't know anything about that.'

'The Star named Wormwood, which we call Chernobyl?' Droopy uttered mysteriously.

'But that was twenty years ago.'

'Twenty years isn't even a cosmic second, not even one thousandth of a cosmic second, and the Soviet Empire has disappeared, just as all empires shall disappear. Everything that a man could rely on, from the greatest things, to the least.'

'They won't disappear. It will only become evident that they never actually existed. Was there even such a thing as a Soviet Union around here? Is there anything called America? They're illusions.'

And us? Were we really here at all, ourselves? Reality is maybe like that time when, once, with my brother Tomáš and a painter friend of ours we went down an old shale mineshaft in Silesia, and there, in the gallery buttressed with old blackened beams, where water trickled over the floor and dripped from the vault above us, we began to paint a picture on the shale walls by the light of oil lamps. Silhouettes of people, nothing more. The simplest white outlines such as you couldn't even tell if they were women or men, their bodies filled out with the stony black. We couldn't stop painting them. We painted a whole mob of them and still we kept painting more and more. The old shaft gave out strange sounds, tonnes of shale might have buried us alive at any moment, our rapturous voices echoed dreadfully through the underground spaces and the picture was never complete. We couldn't finish it, because it was always possible to add more and more figures — it was a constant continuum. But still we had to leave it, after deciding that we'd be returning to it later, to keep it going, gallery after gallery. But that wasn't to be. Sometime during the winter the old props gave way and the vault collapsed — and so our picture was finished at last. The pigments evoking the outlines of people are still there in the darkness, invisible due to the lack of light, but still there all the same. You can believe me or not, as you like. I can't prove it.

'They're only signs. Even little children can understand that,' Droopy tossed out.

'Especially little children,' Baldy added conclusively.

'But what about you?' Droopy said, turning to Big Mouth. 'You talk about California, but how are things with your own ego?'

'Well, I only understand that a person must avoid desire.'

'It's not enough to understand. You've got to experience it.'

That's how it is, it's not enough to understand, Martin nodded in his soul there at the end of the table. We've understood things too, without experiencing them. We've constantly desired something or other. But my brother Tomáš, who was always better than me, he understood what was going on with all those paintings. He understood, but he didn't experience it, he didn't experience anything at all. He only said that those bright pictures at which we toiled away in that dark chamber, and about which nobody really cares, are not meant for human eyes — those wet corneas and vitreous humours of those dangerously intelligent apes. They're meant for other eyes. For eyes free of all opacity, for eyes that see right through our physics to the solitary being that is beyond all our structures. And so once, in the dead of night, he took his negatives out on the balcony of the seventh floor prefab flat and, grabbing the best of them, only the very best of the good ones, between his thumb and forefinger, with a spotlight he projected them onto the galaxies, aiming squarely towards the plane of the Milky Way, as much as the position of the balcony permitted. He sent them out on an endless journey, and then went off to get drunk somewhere, because things weren't quite settled with that ego of his.

'That's your responsibility, really — you've got to free your own self of desire,' Baldy explained.

'Sexual desire?'

'Sexual desire too!'

'Unless we're talking about a mystical union.'

'What might that be?' Big Mouth asked.

'Later,' Droopy brushed him off.

'You've got to part the veils of that which is illusory, and pass on further.'

'Ascend Mount Carmel,' Droopy added.

'And with each veil parted, you leave behind a piece of yourself.'

'As if you were stripping yourself of the old man and…'

Yes, exactly. It's just as you say, Martin thought to himself. You've got to strip away all the rags, undo all of the clasps and sit your bare arse down on the hot stove, and then you'll have your experience for you. Then the chariot of fire will descend to you, from the skies.

And he went away. He still looked around him, because things weren't quite settled with that ego of his. It was a lucky glance, because past the heads of the wisemen he caught sight of a girl's face. She looked like an Asian Père David's deer. Her dark eyes were somewhat slanted, her mouth was voluptuous, she had a thick clump of black hair. Their eyes met for a fraction of a second and they exchanged a heartfelt smile. She was sitting alone at a table and seemed as if she were all alone in the world, too.

THE TWENTY-FIRST

From past the office windows a scream is heard. It sounds from the void of the broken lamp near the roof of the ten-story building. In the round hole, among the dead electric wires, some white, downy little predators are screaming their heads off for their mother — who is returning to them with a dead mouse in her talons. The little tail flops in the wind like a piece of string. She brakes her flight with outstretched wings just before she reaches the large tilting window pane. For a moment, it's as if she were hovering in the air. The feathers on the edge of her wings bristle menacingly. Mrs Tomská lifts her eyes from the computer to see that little wide-spread raptor just past her monitor. A flash in the black beady eyes; the mouse is hanging from the yellow claws like a rag. Then the mighty wings pull at the sky again and the breadwinner disappears from her field of vision, striking aloft toward the unseen nest. Nothing remains of her presence except the immense depths of the evening sky, the prefab towers and, beyond them, in the ashen distance, the greyish-green mountains on the horizon. What sort of world is this, where cliff hawks nest in the cavities of broken light fixtures? What sort of security can there be among shards of plexiglass?

'It's dreadful, the way those birds scream,' her co-worker sighs, already dressed in her coat, standing in the doorframe. 'They ought to do something about it.'

Anything but that! Mrs Tomská thinks, but she says nothing. She never says anything. Again she fixes her eyes upon the monitor, sliding down the columns of numbers and words on the endless table — item number, item name, numbers of plans, numbers of norms, order numbers, notes…

'You're not going to the meeting?' her co-worker asks.

'No. I've still got work to do. I've already made my apologies,' Mrs Tomská says, as inexpressively as possible.

'Well, just as you think best,' her co-worker replies, significantly.

'Bye,' Mrs Tomská bids her farewell, with a polite smile, which perhaps only partially covers the irritation that steals into her voice. And the door closes.

It's best like this, when everyone goes away and nothing remains save work and those birds just beneath the roof. Definitely the nicest denizens of the whole building. Right now, irritated, with half-witted grins, the workers that do all the work are sitting down to tables in the large hall on the ground floor, spread with state-provided rolls with salami, state-provided mineral water, while some big shot at the speaker's podium tells them by what percent we've exceeded the sales plan for subsidised manufactures, which we sell at a higher price than their production costs us. This sort of thing is known as a public meeting, voluntary attendance mandatory. You might skip a meeting like this once; if you do it twice, that's suspicious. That's when this or that co-worker will say to you Well, do as you think best. If only dear Madame Comrade, you knew what I was thinking, I wouldn't be sitting here translating *šroub, matice, nýt, ojnice, ložisko, ložiskové těleso, ložiskový skříň, převodový skříň* and *píst* into Screw, Nut, Rivet, Con-rod, Bearing, Bearing Unit, Bearing Housing, Cable Housing and Piston. I'd already be transferring such articles from one place to another in the warehouse, my aching hands in worker's gloves. I'd be like those birds up there. She's always so distraught, Mrs Tomská is, each and every evening. For then it comes to her, the realisation that she deserves everything that happens to her. Even those much worse times that she lived through when she returned from emigration. Back then, she worked as an auxiliary labourer in a wet colliery, where her foreman had the custom of addressing his subordinates per 'you cunts,' and the filth penetrated everywhere, beneath one's clothes and into the most intimate places. When, after the shift was over, three hundred women disrobed to the nude in one locker room, they didn't seem to be human beings at all, with those coal-stains on the inner sides of their thighs and beneath their breasts. Some of them would be having their period and it just dripped down their legs and they — paid no mind at all, just puffed on their smokes and exchanged vulgar jokes. The tattoos there on display! But they weren't bad, those ladies, some of them were even really beautiful, after they came out the other side of the showers, clean, rosy and red; they shaded their eyelids and painted their lips, as did Mrs Tomská. She didn't feel wronged in the least. How much can people wrong a person anyway? Life itself is a wrong. That's how it seemed to her sometimes. By the very fact that we're alive we are wronging something holy, something better, which might have been here instead of us.

Mrs Tomská cuts off her train of thought and plunges back into her work. Her eyes infallibly catch each and every mistake, each inaccuracy. She's had that since she was young — this marvellous ability to catch mistakes. She sees them as if they were written in red, she'd say to her daughter while she was correcting her grade school dictations. They jump out, like something that doesn't belong there. This here though is all red, she sighs, not thinking at all about the red rags with which the large hall on the ground floor is decorated when the fat cats sit upon the dais and the workers who do all the work eat their state-provided rolls with salami. She's thinking about the red letters jumping out of the story of her life, page after page, paragraph after paragraph. She thinks of her daughter and says to herself: 'Well then, Nika, what's gonna become of us, and what's gonna become of you, you predatory chicks in the smashed lantern?'

Someone knocks on the door. But so lightly, with knuckles brushing up against the surface as if in passing. Mrs Tomská well knows who that is.

'Come in!' she calls out. It's Marie. A good soul. A fifty-year-old lassie, as pale as office paper. She dyes her hair and, at her temples, where it is probably actually grey, it's an unnatural shade of red. I ought to buy her a better quality dye, Mrs Tomská says to herself. But then I should have to tell her that what she's using now isn't flattering, and you don't say such things to good souls.

'Didn't you go to the meeting, Maruška?'

'Of course, Madame Doctor — we were all there. It's over now.'

'I wasn't. I'm still tinkering with these quotes.'

'But of course you were there, Madame Doctor,' Marie laughs foxily. 'I'm a very important person today, you know. Just imagine — I was the one they entrusted with keeping the attendance sheet. And I kept it so properly, Madame Doctor — you can rest assured that nobody was marked absent.'

'But Maruška — I'd never ask you to do that.'

'You wouldn't, you wouldn't, I know. But tell me why a lady like you should have to look upon such… you know. Let's just let them have a good time, you know, as they say — birds of a feather. We needn't vex ourselves with them.' Marie crosses the room to the shelves, where the folders are kept, saying all the while: 'In the present situation, it's best that nobody has a reason to come visit us — and after all, everybody's exemplary and politically conscious, Madame Doctor, conscious and politically engaged.' Marie reaches behind the folders and extracts a bottle. 'And now, at last, it's time for us to cheer you up a little bit.'

It was getting dark outside — the sky was as blue as a puddle of spilled ink. The two women were sitting at the window, lit up only by the computer screen, drinking the warm white wine and talking. It occurs to Mrs Tomská that sometimes it can be quite nice too, this old world, as she listens to the hodgepodge of Marie's words.

THE TWENTY-SECOND

'Just imagine, Madame Doctor, what happened, right outside our front door…' Mrs Tomská calls to mind the squat little building in the village on the pilgrimage route in Silesia; she sees the church with its rounded tower, the little park, the fire hall, the inn and the beautiful buildings with their burgeoning gardens. It was this village that, some twenty-five years ago, Marie Sněhová left on the bus for her first job in the offices of the Klement Gottwald metalworks, armed with her knowledge of German, which everybody up there in Silesia knows from childhood, and French, which the good parish priest taught her in the free hours after all the Masses had been said. He taught her so well that she passed the state exams at the language school in Ostrava and could boldly fill out the rubric on the questionnaire dealing with foreign language abilities. That was the first time for her, a slender maiden, with her curly hair spilling halfway down her back, in a beret and a beautiful get-up thrown together according to the styles presented by a ten-year-old French fashion magazine.

'So, lying there on the lawn by the side of the road, right before our house was this beautiful tomcat. But that cat, Madame Doctor, was this gorgeous brown colour; he had this shiny coat and his tail, his tail was bushy like that of a a lynx. Marie poured some more wine and it seemed to Mrs Tomská that her eyes were shining with enthusiasm, as they always did when she was talking about beautiful animals with long fur — she even dreams of them. They had placed her, this country sand martin, in the hands of that old hag Materná, a sour old hardboiled StB witch from the foreign delegations department. Everything's clean to those who are clean themselves, and that girl who grew up between the rectory and the village garden looked up to her boss as if to an idol. She was happy to be able to apply her foreign language skills to her job. It goes without saying that Materná checked her out, just like everyone else in the building — just like everyone else, with whom she was acquainted — and to her hidden catalogue she added a little sheet entitled Marie (Hedvika) Sněhová. Hedvika in parentheses, because Marie never used her second name, or even mentioned it — it was only to be found on her parish baptismal certificate. And so it floored her when, one day, her boss tossed out in her direction, So how'd you spend Holy Wednesday, Hedvika? What's new with Citizen Priest? It was a truly ugly Holy Thursday when Marie Sněhová, as white as her last name,[9] had a look into the very eyes of evil. That Mrs Materná isn't evil, but the one inside her — I mean, I don't dare hate anyone, she whispered to 'Citizen Priest' through the confessional screen inside the pilgrimage church in Silesia. You're right, you don't dare hate — but you must be on your guard. Just as the Lord says: 'Be ye therefore as simple as doves and as wise as serpents.'[10] And Marie Hedvika took that to heart. The heart of the Citizen Priest was well-schooled in such simplicity and wisdom, used to prevaricating in the presence of the agent assigned to church matters; here he had to give up a little something, and there the agent discretely turned his eyes away. And thus we lived — like winged serpents, or like doves crawling in the dust. There remained us that one comfort from the sublime antiphon: 'Lord, I am not worthy, that Thou shouldst come under my roof, but speak the word only…' So Marie Hedvika will forget about Holy Wednesday, and Holy Thursday, and about her all boss's comments on how even the way she she holds her ballpoint, book, ID card, or whatever screams virginity. And even that virginity of hers, which Materná also checked out, just wouldn't give the old witch any peace. How she'd like to tear it right out of her lap and devour it, frying it up in oil…

'And just imagine, Madame Doctor, that that tomcat, poor thing, was dead. So beautiful and brown, and dead. So I go find my brother and tell him, Go get the spade, we've got to bury it. And my brother, that brother of mine, O he's a treasure of a soul, he is, something like you, Madame Doctor, always up to his ears in books, always studying something, didn't even have time to get married, so much work he's got on his hands. So under the pear

....

[9]   *Sněhová* contains the adjectival root of the word *sníh* — snow.

[10]   Matthew 10:16.

tree in the garden we buried him, may the earth, as they say, cover him lightly. You know, even an animal wants to rest in peace.'

O Marie Hedvika Sněhatová, as white as snow, blue bloodless lips and dark shadows beneath your eyes, and all around — wolfskin. Soon they will pump your stomach and transfuse your blood — only your heart will they let be as it was, broken in the hotel called Wolfskin — Vlčina. In this swinish resort, where the old bitch Materná and her boys arrange orgies for foreign guests and fat cats and Russian officials. A virgin intact, like the day she was born. I'll chew her up and spit her out; let the girl grow up already and learn a thing or two! They're paying in hard currency after all. And life is hard as it is. How you gonna whisper this through the screen and into Citizen Priest's ear? A woman cashes in and changes money, buys jewels and wigs with per diems and watches, watches carefully. The kid gloves were brought across from Austria. You can't buy gloves like that here, so soft. You don't even have to take anything off and already you're in charge of everything. Hard to soft, that's how the world goes, stop playing at being a nun. Go ahead, trot off to church, give your confession to whomever you want, we've got our eyes on you. They're the best, those Christians — they've got to tell the truth and nothing but the truth, but they'll come up with something too — Marks for eighteen and Schillings for five, I'll write up the report myself.

'And we're just done with burying the poor thing, my brother's still washing his hands, and the doorbell rings. And here's this little fellow standing there with a hat on his head, this kind of pacy-fidgety little chap, as swarthy as the devil himself, and as soon as we open the door he says: There was something here that I need, something laying here, and you took it. And my brother says: What exactly is it you have in mind, sir? And this nervous one says: The thing that was laying out in front of your house — and he keeps pacing, you know, two steps this way, two steps that, Give it to me now. What are you talking about? says my brother. It was a cat, a dead cat laying there. Exactly says the fidgety man, and doesn't he jump at that! Where's the cat? Buried. Who buried it? Well, I did. Who asked you to do that? What? Look here, sir — I see a dead cat in front of my house, I bury it. Who wants the crows pulling it all over the yard? That's unhygienic. What's all this about? What all this is about is, that was my cat, and I need it. Madame Doctor, the guy seemed nuts.'

And then, Maruška, they took you off to the sanatorium in Opava, where the director himself, what a splendid fellow, heart of gold, took care of you; O how beautiful it was to sleep there! You slept there as if you were in Paradise. A Soviet paradise, as your brother used to say, considering the shambles that our comrades from the east introduced into our midst. And those pills, doctor, please, write me a prescription for those pills, so that I'll have a decent supply in reserve. I need to get my sleep, I need to be able to get my sleep. And my brother — he can't find out anything, all right? Tell him it's nerves, a problem with my nerves, that's all. And nerves they were — every day cost you a few years. You worked it out fine, Marie Hedvika, you were lost to them, you hid yourself inside yourself. Nothing remained of the pigeon you had been but a handful of feathers, nothing worth shooting at any more. Forty kilos of living flesh and a complexion as yellowy-white as office paper. You made it; you escaped. Those deep wrinkles about the eyes, hair like oakum. You became untouchable. You began speaking loudly and laughing even louder — you laughed right in the bitch's face, told her so many stories, so much nonsense that she didn't have anywhere to put it already. She hated you, but she couldn't do anything with you. Blessed are the poor, for they will have nothing that may be taken away from them. You beat them to the finish line — that wasn't supposed to happen until the very end. But you put the end at the beginning. Dear girl, who was it gave you such good advice? The priest, the sanatorium director, St Francis of Assisi, or Our Lady of the Seven Dolours? Now you don't have to play the nun anymore, now you have your own order in the Communist paradise. A joke to everyone and everyone so glad to confide in you.

'And so I say to my brother: Listen, go get the shovel and we'll go dig up the cat, because who knows what this fellow'll do otherwise. And so my brother, the poor fellow, took mattock and shovel and we went over to the pear tree, there by the fence, and the fidgety guy went along with us. My brother began to dig, and the fidgety guy, well, when he caught sight of the dark fur there in the clay, well, what does he do Madame Doctor, but leap down into the pit and tear away, literally tear away, the cat from the earth. He grabbed it by the tail and wham, wham, beat the clay out of it against the pear tree like it was a doormat. And then he puts it in the sack and starts to go away. And I ask him, What does he want that for, a dead cat? And he says, That's my business and off he goes, right quick. And me and my brother are left standing there flummoxed. Even after death he has no peace, the poor cat. Our neighbour lady told us that hunters use dead cats like that as bait for rabid foxes; they cut them up and poison them and toss these pieces all over the woods. And I'm thinking, Madame Doctor, you know, he seemed so strange he did, that maybe he took it and… a person never knows, and there's all sorts of people in the world.'

'But, Maryša, he was probably just a hunter…'

'Exactly, Madame Doctor — but you know who disguises himself as a hunter, you know that from folk tales…' Marie's face became one huge mysterious smile — an old woman and a girl, Babička and Barunka in one and the same person, and that hunter began to smell of brimstone.

If only they used devils of that sort to scare us, thought Mrs Tomská. Then they were silent for a while, sipping a little more wine until the meeting was completely over down there; watching the lights of the prefab apartment blocks begin to sparkle in the inky night. It's been a while since Mrs Tomská felt so good. Something began to move, deep inside her. She says, I'll give her that hair colour as a Christmas present. But then she'll just give it to someone else — that's how it always goes. She gazes with tenderness at the modest little smile on those bloodless lips and next to that scrawny little person, five years her junior, she seems so grown up and so shamelessly female that it's even unpleasant. And so she does something she's never done before. Look, Marie, she says, extracting a little leather case with a notebook from her bag, and from that case a photo. She hands the photo to Marie. It shows a young girl with a high forehead, black hair and slightly slanted eyes, like those of a Japanese, but so similar is she to her, to Mrs Tomská. Marie holds that photo in her hands like a holy relic.

'She's beautiful,' she says. 'Such a beautiful girl, and completely, totally you, Madame Doctor.' She can't tear her eyes away from the photo; nor can Mrs Tomská hers, from Marie. She's never before shown that photo to anyone, never said a word about her daughter Monika to anyone. A hot flash suddenly washes over her. That'll be the wine. Marie hands the photograph back to her.

'What's her name?'

'Monika. I call her Nika.'

'Nika. In Czech that means 'niche.' Like for the statue of some saint.'

'We're going to have to go, Marie. It's getting late.'

THE TWENTY-THIRD

Petr Vrána senior awoke fully dressed in the chair in front of the television, on the hissing screen of which it was snowing something sinister. He coughed, wiped the saliva from the corners of his mouth, and then became aware of the fact that Marta still hadn't returned. So he was alone — nobody there but him. The boys used to all go off on their own, but Marta? That's never happened before. When he came home, she was already gone — and there was no message left for him, either. Everything was orderly, clean — and empty. At first, he determined to ignore it. As if nothing whatever had happened. He wanted to continue on in the groove — warm up something for supper, get undressed, take a bath, grab his book and sit down for a peaceful read — I mean, she'll be coming back. But he couldn't. Not even for a second. He began pacing the flat so quickly, so confused… he wouldn't have believed it if someone had told him. Even if someone had up and told him. He soiled a cuff on some cold dill sauce. But he couldn't take off his shirt. He couldn't even breathe properly. The thought that this would go on even a few minutes more was unbearable. He wouldn't survive it.

Where did she go? Where was she? He looked out the window; he even took a few turns around the building. He rang up acquaintances. Marta's not at your place, by any chance? He couldn't understand their calmness, or their amused, reassuring voices. She must have stopped off somewhere. You don't know Marta. Marta never stops off anywhere. Something terrible must have happened to her. I mean, she's always home! She's a proper woman, she doesn't just wander about afternoons and evenings like just anyone. And when she does go somewhere, she always leaves a note on the kitchen table… I checked it fifty times… There was no note. How is it even possible?

He stopped calling everybody so as not to make a fool of himself. But his pacing from window to window only became more frenzied, and besides that, he would go over and listen at the door. Whenever he heard some steps in the corridor he would fling it open, only to abashedly greet his neighbours with a careworn smile and ask, with a sad longing in his voice, You wouldn't know, would you, where my wife is? You see, she's not at home. She hasn't returned home. She went away. It crossed his mind to ring up his eldest son Petr in Germany; he had his number — Petr alone of his three boys had a telephone. But what would he say to him, really? And it cost so much… He dismissed the idea, even though it was the only practical thing that came to him, and forced himself to sit down and think things through. It had never, never ever occurred to him that Marta might do such a thing. Sure, they had their quarrels. Sometimes it even seemed that he didn't understand her. But for God's sake people aren't angels, and people like he and she are faithful to one another. No, something must have happened to her. It was a little too early to call around the hospitals, or the police. Not until tomorrow. But what to do in the meantime? Marta, come home! He repeated this, both in a whisper, and aloud. And again he was pacing from window to window — and he saw her in every passer-by. If only the boys were home. What boys? They have their own lives — God only knows what they're up to — except really for Petr. But Marta? Calm down, Petr, it's only six, six-thirty for heaven's sake, it doesn't mean a thing. Dear God, it's six-thirty — pretty soon it'll be eight!

Then a saving idea came into his head. He'd go for a walk. Just like that, a normal stroll around the development, and she'd be back in the meantime. When I'll be on my way back, the light in the kitchen will already be on. He grabbed his coat and hat and left. The walk in the evening air did him good. Tattered sounds of industry floated on the breeze, with the clatter of trains past the nearby culm banks. The distant rattle of jackhammers striking hardened slag from the moulds sounded like monstrous woodpeckers at work. He glanced through the lit windows of ground-floor flats. At those credenzas in kitchens, at those bottles of Cinzano that the primitives set up there, like trophies. But at least they're together. Even if they do reminisce about the time they sipped that villainous booze as if it were God knows what sort of sacred nectar. He glanced at the boxes set on the chests in the bedrooms and knew exactly what was in them.

He walked to the very end of the street, where there were clumps of people standing in front of the cinema. What's showing? Amongst the crowds he even saw a neighbour couple, and past their shoulders, a poster reading *The Anatomy of Love. A Polish Film.* That should be something, he humphed in contempt, but then he stepped back from that — Well, at least they'll have a beautiful girl to look at. We don't need that sort of thing, but it's no sin, after all. Marta must be home by now, for sure. No doubt about it. I don't want to see a dark window. I'd rather walk about the streets until morning.

He left the development and entered the old quarter of the town, with its villas and little family houses. The deep, dark gardens, the hazel shrubs, the lilacs and fruit trees, all evoked in him memories of his childhood in a little provincial town in the Sudetans. I always promised her that we wouldn't stay in this horrid city more than a year, two at most — and here it's already been twelve. The boys already speak with a local tang to their voices. Especially that Martin, he grew up here, he doesn't know anything about how we lived before. Maybe she's unhappy? What kind of a question is that! There are more important things in the world than being happy, for heaven's sake. If we're not going to believe that, we have no reason to be here at all.

Mr Vrána now found himself on the very periphery of the town, on the cable bridge stretching across the river. The wobbly bridge, they called it when they came this way on walks with the boys. He walked over the planks fixed in the iron construction, hung from the steel cables, and subconsciously took care at each even step. In a little while the bridge actually began to wobble under his feet. You see, boys, that's what you call harmonic waves — one man can set a steel colossus like this swaying at a proper rhythm. The colossus seen by the prophet Daniel.[11] Steel mixed with clay. Steel and clay in this town of foundries, in our own legs. Only a pebble is needed to send us tumbling into rubble. The boys become strangers, damaged, drunks, tail-chasers! Marta leaves and I won't ever get back on my feet. I was never able to understand how my colleagues could go on living after a divorce, how they can keep on doing anything in this shindy, this mess, this damn chaos, that they still go on treating patients and writing scholarly papers. I don't understand it and I never plan on understanding it!

The kitchen window was as black as a chimney flue as were all the others. Maybe she already went to sleep. He hurried through the flat to the bedroom. Nobody was there. He stood there at the door, in the darkness,

....

11   For the 'colossus' or 'great statue,' see Daniel 2:31 *ff.*

bracing his arms against the doorframe, and with a medical man's precision was able to circumscribe the uneasy feeling between thorax and abdomen. That old, long-forgotten duodenal ulcer began to make itself known — but that was of no significance in and of itself. Only far behind it did the real wound begin, deep and real, where there is no flesh. That experience of loneliness, in which you find yourself, Petr Vrána Senior, which you've been running away from all your life long. Like being dead before you die. Neither mother nor father, nor your work as a doctor, the sacred vocation of helping others, the drudgery, at which you forgot about all other things, nor any other power above in the heavens or down upon the earth or in the watery abyss can separate you from this fatal loneliness, which Marta has just set before you. A sinful thought became stuck in his brain. He that believeth in me, although he be dead, shall live,[12] but he'll have to die any-way. Now death, I'm familiar with death. I've seen more human lives burn out than most, and I can see no reason why this one, mine, should be any exception, if only Marta returned home. If only the key began to rattle in the lock right now and the angel of the Lord entered and said Yes, Marta's on her way home right now; everything's OK and shall be, forever and ever.

He wiped the saliva from the corner of his mouth and looked around. He saw nothing. He only heard Marta in the hallway as she took off her coat and shoes. Then she went into the bath. Then she went around him to the bedroom only to return, alarmed, until she found him in the chair in front of the television. Then she led him to bed and he didn't ask her about anything.

---

[12] John 11:25. Interestingly, this is the Lazarus episode, and Jesus is speaking to Martha.

THE TWENTY-FOURTH

You can't drown when there's kids around! Eva Topolská would frequently hear that saying, which is roughly the same thing as You can't squeeze blood from a stone, on the lips of her grandmother in Český Těšín. The good woman would send them her mother's way during those subdued kitchen conversations when her mother brought little Eva to Těšín for her grandmother to babysit. Eva's grandfather, who taught at the local lyceum, was a great lover of Leo Tolstoy and Charles Dickens, and he subtly infected her with his enthusiasm for them by translating their tales into fairy stories for her, during walks along the River Olza. The Christmas Carol, David Copperfield, but also — because here Granddad's heart was fully to be found, War and Peace and Resurrection. He traversed the long passages of those books in his soul, knowing them basically by heart, and creating from them short, pointed adventures to the rhythm of her little footsteps along the riverbank, such as, according to his paedagogical point of view, would be comprehensible to his little scholar. If she must understand that goddam Communism and the tug-of-war divorce her parents were going through, she ought to understand Pierre Bezuhov and Maslovova, too.

'And where's your Daddy?' he would ask his granddaughter, even though he knew that he was causing her pain by the question, but he just couldn't forgive all that… Because it still holds true, even now, that a proper sentence has subject, predicate, and object, right? And each proper family has father, mother, and child. Or not? Maybe that didn't apply anymore? The old man seethed, then, brimming with love, he looked down at the small curly head of his granddaughter.

'I don't know,' Evička replied truthfully, as if ashamed, as if she should feel ashamed about things she didn't understand. As if she was supposed to understand that her father was a great swine of a functionary, whose hand her granddad would never take in his own, even if the merry comrade would ever think of offering it.

You should be glad you don't, the old man said in his soul. But still and all. Every sentence needs a subject… If Olga only knew what she was doing. She chose him herself, and, more than that, tried to become like him, the troglodyte — and to a good measure she succeeded. Too little for him, though — and too much for me. And now she has no one. And that nothing that remains behind after him belongs to that little girl now, that suppressed subject. He and Evička gazed across the river at Poland, and the old man admitted to himself that he was glad that the world was meaning ever less and less to him.

'You're messing up that little girl's head with adult problems,' his wife would chide him when little Eva didn't know where to rest her eyes, at each mention of her parents.

'They've already messed up her head with adult problems,' the old man shot back. 'I'm setting forth examples, you understand, Olinka, examples that someday she'll be able to grasp. So that she'll know that in every sentence there has to be…'

'Sure, sure,' agreed the careworn wife of the teacher. I know, you don't have to tell me, she added in her soul, but what good is that, if the whole world has moved on somewhere else?

'You know, Oli, you can't drown when there's kids around,' she said then to her alienated daughter, when once again she needed her to watch Eva, for a whole week.

'And so you wrote her an excuse for a whole week?'

'What did you expect me to do? Otherwise I can say goodbye to the position, if I can't go to Prague.'

'You must know what you're doing. Her grandfather will make up for the schooling.'

Eva was sitting underneath the table at which Granddad and Mr Pěch were playing chess and smoking cigars. There, among those slippered feet and chiselled table legs, past the fringes of the tablecloth, she waited for her mother to leave.

Now nowhere and in nothing, in that vacant subject of her sentence, Eva Topolská, a big girl now, bit her lip until the blood spurted. She's pregnant, with a man she doesn't want. She's got nothing against him and never had — nothing against all those trysts and the whole style of life, in which they twisted themselves to the very borders of deformation. Do there exist any other borders besides the borders of deformation? When she was going out with the fellow, she was certain that, no, there aren't. Let's maltreat one another until we come to know who we are. And what did you come to know, then? Nothing! That's what Martin Vrána would say, who never yearned for any other borders himself, but he, that ludicrous boy, always believed that he'd overcome it all in the end, that he's undeformable, that he's a saint, of the same essence as God. She laughed.

Michael, the father of what she had inside her, had no truck with that sort of stuff. Eva's drive to allow herself to be demeaned, to allow the other to do with her whatever he wanted to, apparently suited him fine.

And now he'll never know what I have. I have — it warmed her heart that, and suddenly, she felt what a soft heroism it had been, that whole courageous game with life as its stakes, that game with the suppressed subject.

'I'm keeping the child,' she said, surprised at the simplicity of the sentence that she had just pronounced.

THE TWENTY-FIFTH

Moss and weeds are growing on the empty bottom of the swimming pool between the abandoned hospital pavilions. Through the cracks of the concrete walls push strong stalks of couch-grass and bindweed. They climbed down the rusty ladder to the flat level bottom, where no water of Archimedes was displaced. There was nothing there but a dry floor, set deeper than the surrounding park. People used to swim here.

Monika Tomská and Martin Vrána set foot on that moss and bindweed like astronauts on the surface of the moon. At the time of the Apollo programme, this area was completely off limits to people. The rehab swimming pool, which never functioned as such, was transformed into a reservoir for the fire brigade. But since the hospital never caught fire, the fire brigade reservoir became a fish-pond, which the director and his claque had stocked with carp. Then, sitting on the starting blocks, they would fish using poles outfitted in reels made by the Shakespeare firm, which they brought back from a conference in Great Britain. All around, wards: Internal Medicine, Infectious Diseases, Surgery, Burn Units, Pathology, Maternity — and in the midst of them all, the fat cats, jerking lines on which carp had been hooked.

Here in the empty greyness of the air, amidst the moss and bindweed, stand Monika and Martin before their first step, a small one for man, but a giant leap…

They first saw one another in that club where Martin was giving ear to the young mystics. He saw her a second time in these very park-grounds of the shuttered hospital, where his father had lived through most of his life. She studied social medicine here, the faculty of which was located in the former Neurology building. That was the same girl, wasn't it, who seemed so alone, and whose slanted eyes suggested an Asian heritage?

Even today he couldn't understand what it had been that had sparkled in their eyes when they met, the eyes of two people unknown to each other. What sort of spark flies from one stranger to another? What sudden, shared recollection between two who have nothing in common? Since the strawy fairy stories of fated encounters of people destined for each other have long ago been ground to dust. Dust that can give rise to nothing except allergies. People are not fated to one another, people are condemned to their fate.[13] They can't belong to one another, they can't belong to themselves, they belong nowhere. Has he not lived through enough already to understand that this not-belonging is the only home left to a person beneath these dangerous heavens? Unlike the unconscious creatures with their safe dens and cosy nests, man alone must stop deluding himself that he belongs somewhere, that someday he'll discover that other half from whom he was once separated, and that their souls will flow together and re-meld, like it's some kind of romantic movie. That some day, on the periphery of a poor, scrawny wood, he'll come across this Asian doe that will metamorphose into a girl.

They began talking. That it looked like rain was coming on. No topic led them anywhere in particular. Suddenly, they were together; before they knew it, without even trying.

He showed her his hands, dirty from the rusty ladder. Her palms were clean.

'I only held on a bit to steady myself. I never grip onto anything tightly,' she said. Indecisively, they looked around the overgrown depths.

'When I was little, I almost drowned in a pool like this. I was four years old or so. My mother told me that I walked up to the edge of the water and just kept on walking — I basically fell right in and began to sink to the bottom. She was still putting on her bathing cap when, suddenly, she became aware of the fact that I was nowhere to be seen. Nobody'd noticed anything. Then she dove into the water and pulled me out. I remember that, to this very day.'

....

[13]   The original Czech reads *Lidé nejsou souzení, lidé jsou odsouzení.* The close homophony of the related words has an immediacy, which suggests the quick progression of Martin's reflections. What is more, the Czech word for condemnation, sentencing, *odsuzení* is constructed from the participle *od*, indicating separation.

Suddenly, through the grey air hanging over the nettles Martin seemed to see a woman in a bathing suit and bathing cap fly. Sailing into the water, which is not. She becomes the diagonal of the vacuum. Her hands search for, and find, the head of the sinking child. She grabs her, pulls her close, beats the water with her legs and lifts the child up above her head.

THE TWENTY-SIXTH

They kissed at the door, which Monika was trying to close, and Martin to push open, although, of course, not forcibly. It was the urgent movement of two bodies pressed to a gap, the swinging periphery of which was constituted by the edge of the door wavering between Come and Go; meanwhile their lips and tongues touched each other with ineffable tenderness. The area of trust widened and narrowed like their breath. The more forcefully Monika's shoulder pressed the door against his breast, the more strongly her hand pulled his head in against her face, and the more strongly Martin pressed forward to cross the threshold in his desire to embrace her, press her down and make love to her, the more understandingly he gave ground under the pressure of the wood that was pushing him out into the dark hallway.

Their first date ended right there, on the threshold, where, following a modest and reasonable farewell, they still clove to one another. God only knows how long such things go on, while people grow convinced of the fact that they must, but can't, be together. When he extracted himself at last, Monika opened wide the door they'd been pulling and pushing against, and watched him, on the first step down, turn around one more time and then, without any urgency, bid her good night. It might well be a good one. She couldn't imagine that it could ever be otherwise with that man, whose life, as he put it, was almost over already. Then he would disappear into the dark depths of the stairwell, and she would close the door with great care, so gently as not to make the slightest sound.

And actually he never heard anything. The image of the girl, straddling a threshold between call and farewell, in the bright rectangle of the doorframe was never replaced in his mind with anything else. He carried it out the building with him into the intimately familiar streets of the city like a page torn out of time. Like a Japanese woodcut — an image that came to him surely on account of those slanted eyes of hers, of which they never spoke. Just like they never spoke about her father, who must be the effective cause of that feature, since there was nothing Asian about her mother's face — which he once had the opportunity of studying.

And now, as his steps fell into the well-worn grooves of chancy streets and far from cosy taverns to — at last — arrive at the unwelcoming flat that waited for him on Zborovská St., he sensed that he really didn't want Monika to be with him right now. It was enough for him to know that she existed, that there were other people out there just like Monika, as beautiful as an Asian deer. He was happy just to stand there, leaning against a pole and listening to how his heart beat, pressed up against the edge of trust. Or perhaps distrust? Who knows? With bated breath, he felt that he was about to lose his head.

With some disbelief he gazed at his hands, which, contrary to those of Monika, grip everything tightly and don't know how to let go. They get soiled with everything. That hurts, even when they're hidden in his pockets.

When he brought his kids over to his rented flat for the first time, he realised — with horror — that the only window in the place was absolutely filthy and that its peeling frame was mostly covered with greenish mould such as you often find in unused, unaired, enclosed spaces. Immediately, he determined to fix that. He dissolved some detergent and disinfectant in warm water and quickly washed over the window. His boy and girl were sitting on his bed, watching him with interest.

'What stinks?' asked his daughter.

'Chlorine. From the disinfectant. There's mould over here, you know?'

'Does it burn?'

'A little bit.'

'What if it burns up the window frame?'

'It's not really burning my hands, so…'

'But your hands aren't rotten frames.'

No, they're not, Martin said to himself in stupid joy, after which he softly pronounced his daughter's name.

THE TWENTY-SEVENTH

He went into the half-empty bar, where everything was slowly winding down, and he suddenly felt so good — as if reawakening to life after lying dead for a long time. As if awakening from that cacophony of people and things, which still, for some nonsensical reason, has to be kept going. That race of dead things, dead thoughts and feelings. How is it possible for us all to die like that, and yet keep moving about? If only we had died completely — back then at the twilight of the old régime. With one brave leap — like that dark-haired girl who tore herself out of the gendarmes' hands and flung herself down on the sharp rocks. At least then we'd be lying in a grave at the wall somewhere without a cross, a rare topic for social ballads. But this way…

He took note of the tall waitress with the topknot of straw-coloured hair pulled up above her head. He actually knew her, even the feel of her cold, hard fingertips, as once he placed some change into the palm of her hand. But he knew that she was no beastly *mondaine*, even if she was outfitted with all the proper shiny attributes thereof. She's a really strong, beautiful woman pulled this way and that, already past forty, to whom life somehow hasn't presented kittens and puppies. He sent a smile her way and ordered another vodka. How could we just die like that, just slowly die away?

Some people've already gone through with it entirely. Tonda Gona, he's already at the coal vein somewhere up in the big black mine in the sky. And Ivan Figura? The last time they met it was in this very same villainous bar, which back in the old Communist days was called Burgas, and now — Vegas. They happened to run across one another in the street. Martin wanted to give Figura the slip — didn't want to have anything to do with him. From the corner of his eye he noticed that he'd grown a little fat, or, rather, kind of heavy; that he'd lost quite all of his hair, or had it all shaved off — the skinhead look was coming in at the moment. Simply put, he wanted to slip by him and thought that Figura probably had the same intention in regard to him. He reckoned that, following their youthful tussle over Eva Topolská, they actually hated one another, or at least definitely didn't give a damn about each other, and here Ivan doesn't just call out to him, he literally takes him by the elbow.

'I've been looking for you.' A gambit befitting old Figura, as unconvincing as it sounded.

'How you doing, Martin?'

'You know. Could be worse.'

'It could,' Ivan agreed, with a tired nod. What happened to that liveliness of his? Martin asked himself, as Figura quite insistently invited him in for a dram, to this very tavern with its new neon sign.

'Burgas — Vegas, times change, the sun rises in the west,' Figura tossed out, and ordered the vodka. They drank, and looked one another in the eye. This was sometime in the early nineties, not long after the changes. Even back then Martin was aware of the fact that they were dead. The only thing missing at the table was Eva Topolská herself, with sunken cheeks and tiger wrinkles around her eyes. A couple bottles of vodka, and they could get shitfaced on that Russian invention for the destruction of Europe. With this sweet holy water[14] they might douse the last smouldering embers of life inside them. All three — get smashed and make a disgrace of themselves. Burn to ashes, a new Pompeii, all the while outside the agile students and managers with projects in their satchels hurry on by.

Figura drank like he meant it. Martin kept pace with him only every second shot — and even so his head was already aswim.

'It concerns me,' Figura declared mysteriously, following some preliminary words about these new days and opportunities and the company he has in Prague.

'What concerns you?'

Martin had been absent for a while. It seemed to him that Figura was sufficient unto himself, and so he wasn't really listening. But here, it seemed, he had need of someone other than himself.

'What? What we're talking about.'

---

14   In the Slavic languages, *vodka* is a diminutive of *voda* ('water'), hence the pun. Here, Balabán uses an even further degree of diminutive — *voděnka*.

                                                                JAN BALABÁN

'I don't know what you've been talking about. I don't give a shit.'

'O, you give more than a shit, I know. A shitload more. You have opportunities now. You can choose whatever uni you want. Go right ahead — Philosophy, Czech Philology… Go grab that Boháček or whatever the hell he's called, grab'm by the scruff of his neck and drag'm off his endowed fucking chair, kick the whole clique down the steps and they'll up and make you director and lick your arse clean. "Ah, professor!" they'll greet you with. Go ahead, tell'm you're a dissident and revolutionary justice, brother, is in your hands. Fuck yeah.'

'I'm not a dissident.'

'That makes no difference. You weren't in the Party, so you're as clean as that St Martin on his white steed. Rake'm all over the coals for Communists and collaborators and bring it on, start publishing scholarly works about whatever.'

'Go somewhere yourself, or go do it yourself, since it seems so simple to you.'

'Me? I can't.' And again Figura crawled right up in his face, nose to nose. His sweat, his breath, the gaps between his teeth.

'I can't because it concerns me. Didn't you read the lists?' Suddenly, Figura's face became completely expressionless. He looked like a wax figure. A slightly melted mannequin. Why must I be here with such a one as him, Martin asked himself. But he felt that, somehow, it was owed him.

'So, you read the political vetting lists, or not?'

'I didn't. Or maybe I did, or… I wasn't looking for your name there. I haven't given you much thought, you know.'

'Don't give me any thought. It's better you didn't. Don't give a fuck for me. You can all just shit on me, you know. Forget all about Figura.' And he burst into hysterical laughter. As if he'd sunk his teeth into something. And then a faraway look came into his eyes as he gazed at Martin.

'Tell me, Martin. Did I do you wrong? Did I do anyone any wrong, torture anyone, kill anybody?'

'I don't know. You've got to take that up with your own conscience.' What a stupid thing to say. I ought to have given him one in the kisser, Martin thought with regret, a moment afterward. That's vodka for you.

'With my conscience? You can just fuck your conscience, you know. Fuck your conscience!'

They stared at one another like two dogs. More frightened than enraged.

He was silent for a moment, gazing with fascination into his glass as if he saw God knows what inside it. And then he asked, 'And what's up with Eva? Do you ever see her?'

'Not much. I'm married, and…'

'But that's not a physical defect, after all,' Figura just couldn't let sleeping dogs lie.

'Pass along my greetings the next time you don't see her much,' he winked at him slyly.

'Greetings from the old structures.'

He got up, as if cramming himself into himself. He was gigantic in his long overcoat, as broad as a suit of armour. He tossed some banknotes down on the table in a gesture of *largesse*.

'So then, bye. Till next time.' And he strode away among the tables with his head held high and his cloak fluttering behind.

And me? Martin asked himself then, seeing his entire petty, plodding life as clear as a puddle of water cupped in his hand. Suddenly, he finished the shot in front of him and reflected on just how he might go and fuck that conscience of his, that heavy conscience, so damned heavy that he couldn't even squirm beneath its weight, to say nothing of going anywhere.

THE TWENTY-EIGHTH

'*Karcer*? A hole? What sort of hole? You ever been in a hole like that?'

'Nope. I only know the word from old German books about these boarding schools. Students there were subjected to arbitrary, disciplinary punishments, which were to transform young boys into good, proper Germans. One of these was the hole. I imagine it like a cold, dark *Zimmer* with condensation dripping from the ceiling, where a frightened boy in a thin nightshirt is lying on a bare cot, chattering his teeth, being punished for writing a letter without prior permission or jumping the fence for a date with a servant girl. "Fourteen days in the Hole! That'll give you some time to think over what you did..."'

'That's more or less how I imagine state homes to be. I was nearly sent off to one once, when my mother'd fallen on some hard times. The Home, the Hole. You know, we didn't have any relatives or close acquaintances who I could stay with while she was struggling. And so — off to the Home. Many a night I couldn't sleep a wink, terrified of that very thing. Just imagine — up until then, I'd never spent a single night away from home. Right, so — to the Home. I vowed that if such were to be the case, I'd rather drink the corrosives used to wash the floor and die.'

'You washed your floors with corrosives?'

'There was this little sticker on those plastic bottles of Kresol, or whatever it was called, showing a burnt hand and the words *Caution: corrosive!* A bottle of that stuff used to stand on a little shelf in the bathroom, and when I was a little girl, I was terrified of it. Of those hands, chiefly. And besides that, it said *Keep away from children!* But in the end I wasn't sent off to the Home. One of my mother's acquaintances, this peculiar person named Marie Sněhotová, who was maybe my mother's only friend, as far as I know, worked it so that I could stay in the hospital. Just think — in perfect health, I spent a month in the Paediatric Ward. But that was a hundred times better than that — hole… *karcer*, is it?' With a certain gusto Monika tried out the new word, rolling it over her tongue, surprised at the way it sounded, and looked over at Martin as if she were seeing him for the first time. It wasn't just a new word she was feeling out; rather, it was a new thing, which, that man there, it seems, understood. She'll find out about it all, but not by quizzing him.

Martin wasn't the quizzing type. He sat on the floor near the window and started to reminisce.

'When we were boys, we simply couldn't believe that one day, really, we'd be grown up. That we'd stop wearing long hair and scruffy trousers and carrying school satchels and somehow we'd take our place in this washed-and-pressed culture. That we'd become responsible people.'

'I for one still can't imagine it.'

'But back then it was a little different. We were somehow more aware of the fact that we were occupied.'

'Like, by the Russians?'

'That too, but mainly with the thought that our responsibility and our adult deeds had already, like, been determined, occupied, under the heel of that alien society, that lie.'

'All right, and so?'

'So, nothing really. We wanted to hold on to childhood, hooliganism, dickishness, as long as we could. Because everything else was repulsive. We even somehow, in this strange way, believed, or secretly hoped, that some sort of catastrophe, a nuclear war, which was always looming over our heads, would happen and release us of our opportunities, and consequently our obligation to make something of ourselves.'

'Maybe it was only you who hoped and believed that.'

'Maybe.'

'I remember being afraid, me and Mama, of anything bad happening. We were always afraid of being maltreated by someone.'

'Well, we were afraid of being made to maltreat others. But if the bombs began to fall, it'd all be different. At last, the pregnant world would give birth to what it had been carrying around in its belly.'

Monika was lying on Martin's bed. At the word *pregnant*, she shivered in distaste. You don't know what you're saying, she thought.

'But then the time came when it began to dawn on us that nothing will change, that even the war we'd been promised was not to come about. That everything's going to go on being exactly the same, and that we're going to have to crawl into our pigeonholes, like it or not.'

'I had to do the same thing.'

'You too were somewhere in that world, which we began to consider one big *karcer*, one big hole. We drank ourselves stupid in taverns in Prague, Olomouc and Ostrava; we blushed in shame in our schools on account of all that Marxist idiocy, we goofed off at night, and, half-joking, half-serious, we told one another stories of how somewhere in the cosmos there were happier places — maybe on Jupiter or in the Pleiades — and that people are transported to the planet Earth for punishment. Part of the punishment is their ignorance of the fact. We'd forgotten that we'd forgotten. We're all in a penal colony, though we don't know it. We'd say that somewhere our letters must be hidden, in among the pages of old books, under the tiles in church, in boxes in the pillars of old bridges. Somewhere, the message I wrote to myself before they wiped my memory clean is hidden. Before they brain-washed me. There is my real name; there I could find out what it was I did, and what I'm being punished for. How I got here, and how I might get out.'

Cold fingers touched Martin on the lips. Monika, suddenly, was stand-ing over him, pale and gaunt and shivering like a birch sapling. In those Hiroshima eyes of hers, as Martin secretly called them, a screen of tears sparkled. As if she were blind. She ran her hands over Martin's head and pulled it to her bosom. She felt a pulse inside her; she felt something dart about within her like a spasm. Like a word torn out of a deep darkness, a word that doesn't need to be spoken, because it proceeds from her very body into Martin's head. It's open. The lock, stiff with rust, begins to turn. And suddenly, everything falls into itself, and they, Martin and Monika, fall into one another. Everything around them is blue, only they are white, like two fingers, like two arms descending, on which you can rely, cling to, and nothing else need be, outside of them.

THE TWENTY-NINTH

Drops of rain began to fall on the window ledge. The drops were falling on Monika, too, who had left Martin's flat. It was now time for her to change into her white smock and trousers in the hospital dressing room, pull her hair into a bun, grab a notepad and rush off to the ward to practice social medicine.

Martin was sitting at the window with a coffee watching the turbid dawn slit through the clouds over the tarry roofs of the warehouses and old factories. There, at the railway line, the city ought to end. The brick hovels and the ramps, the approaches and the bridges and past all that there should be a pier, a strip of dirty harbour water and there, where the blinking red warning lights on the roofs of the prefab blocks emerge from the mist, there, the horizon, and on the horizon ships, and past the horizon, the measureless expanse of ocean.

But that's what it's really like; we're constantly on the edge of something gigantic, even if we only rarely become conscious of it, rarely giving ear to the crash of the waves with which infinity pushes into our empty stowages. Today, of course! Martin was calm and attentive. Today you can sense the sea in each plumbing fixture, as the water rushes through the pipes. When shaving at seven and you don't light the lamp, because the darkness and your whispering soul are vibrating at the same note, the same frequency. and thoughts of your children, whom you'll bring here this afternoon to be with them as if in a ship's cabin; you'll somehow set up three beds in this little, temporary, rented haven, and even this thought is free from anxiety, because the world is big, because Monika wears white hospital scrubs, because memories are a landscape I recognise.

Even before the old sceptic in him could whisper that this sudden joy would doubtlessly evaporate, he was enlightened by a sudden flash. A memory so strong broke in upon the present moment that, suddenly, he couldn't catch his breath. I've seen that before! A ray of light from the street had made Monika's bosom glow, her belly, her lap, when she hastily tore off her clothes in the blue darkness yesterday, suddenly coming on at once and making her flesh red and her hair like flame. I've seen that before. As a fourteen-year-old boy in the cosy little town of Hlinsko, washed in summer rain. Alongside the millrun of the old water spinning-mill and further on past the footbridge toward the building where the small-town cinema was located, jutting out amidst the provincial buildings. There was an exposition going on there, it was called Fine Arts Hlinecko, and they were presenting Rudolf Kremlička. His paintings hung on the walls like mysterious windows on to another world. Washer-women, women with toddlers, women bathing, heavy and rounded women, and then, in this corridor leading from the smaller room to the larger, on the green wallpaper was hung a small picture. And Monika came back to him in a heavy, rounded body, Monika, taking off her clothes, red, aflame against the green. And I am small and gasping with helpless desire standing before that blazing female world and others come suddenly, white again in the blue darkness and I'm large now and I enter the woman, who hurriedly took off her clothes and as a boy I'm running along the corridors of the dreary provincial cinema overcome with yearning, outside into the air, the rain, until I'm breathless, until the cry bursts out, and then at the next stroke I open the window and feel us both cool down, I stick my head outside, rain trickles over my body, I'm completely away and then as now I can't catch my breath, because I know that I've seen this before, before I even went along the millrun heading toward the bridge, before I saw her face the first time amongst those mugs in the club, before I could even think that I've already been here before.

THE THIRTIETH

'That was quite a peculiar situation, Nika,' Mrs Tomská began, sitting down on the armchair in the soft, homey garb, for which she had endured so much, with the excellent coffee she taught her daughter how to brew, the coffee you toss right into the cold water with a pinch of salt, cocoa and two teaspoons of sugar, and only then do you bring it to a boil until it begins to foam along the rim of the pot like the froth on a mad dog's lips, or a foaming horse. That's the moment you take it off the flame to let it settle. It always made Mrs Tomská feel good to know that Monika knew exactly when to take the coffee off the flame, and when to replace it there, for it to froth and calm a few more times, which is what makes a proper drink of the coffee at last, and not some empty infusion of the sort that they set before the office cattle. It's the reining in of the galloping horse and the calming of the frenzied dog that gives the coffee the strength we need.

'What kind of a situation?' Monika asked, leaning forward in her mother's direction. Just this — that leaning in her direction, signified docility; thus, in-bent and intent, will she really listen to what her mother has to say, and will be closer to her than if she were sitting on her lap. That angle, so well known from Pietàs and Annunciations is caused not by the cramped space of some shared den, but by the shared heart. That's the way Monika still knew how to lean near her mother.

'So this woman came to my office, a cleaning woman, most likely a brigade worker, she told me her name was Zlatevová Milica, that's how she said it. Milica Zlatevová, a Serb I guess, or some other South Slav. She was supposed to wash my office window, it seemed, if I would be so kind as to clear the parapet of the flowerpots and the other things, or better yet, if I'd go out for a coffee or something, in short, to let her alone there until she'd finished the window. And here, Monika, I realised that I actually knew her. This kind of lanky, but otherwise quite nicely built woman. Blonde — probably a bottle blonde — and though I may be wrong about this, I still seem to recall hair, dark hair, in her armpits. Broad-shouldered, like a man; a handsome woman.

'So I'm getting up as if I were to go off to get something done somewhere while she was washing the windows when she turns to me with: Mrs Tomská, Madam Magister, and now she's already standing on the parapet, huge in these like gardening coveralls she's got on, with a rag in her hand, and her hand cocked like this, and she asks me: You're a translator?' Mrs Tomská took a sip of her coffee and glanced at Monika, who was bending in towards her, still at that same angle. For how much longer? she asked herself longingly.

'Yes, I'm a translator, I said.

'Do you think you could loan me a dictionary? Any sort of one you don't need — you probably know all of those words through and through already, I bet.

'But what sort of dictionary?

'I need to borrow an English dictionary, so English-Czech and Czech-English too, otherwise I'll go nuts at these windows already.

'And that's when, you know, Nika, I saw it was bad, I remembered her, I knew her, this was that tall bruiser of a woman, the kind that wears that — what you call — those elastic jeans and a leather jacket to the waist, the kind with the zipper running obliquely?'

'A switchblade,' Monika completed the thought.

'That's the word I was looking for,' Mrs Tomská frowned before continuing, 'And that sometimes I've chanced to come across her in the evenings, aggressively made-up.'

'But Mama —' Monika tried to snap back, because what did her mother know about aggressive makeup?

'No, Nika, I saw her once, she was going down the street there from those prefab stages, as if in the direction of our bus-stop, and she had these sort of lines on her eyelids and eyebrows, painted, like tiger stripes. She looked dangerous. And then on top of it all, her name is Milica.

'But Mama! Milica doesn't mean militia, it means *milující, milostná, milovaná* — Affectionate, Loving, Beloved.' Monika was happy that she herself was also loved, that so far she'd kept it secret from her mother, that her mother senses it nonetheless, and notwithstanding that, she remains inclined in her mother's direction, or maybe for that very reason.

'And now this beloved and loving Milica of yours says: Let me borrow that dictionary, Madame Magister, otherwise I'll go nuts at these windows. So I go and find in the back of the shelf old Poldauf, which I knew by memory, for sure, already back when you were small, otherwise I could never have become a translator, it stands to reason.'

Her mother suddenly appeared so lovely. Monika gazed at her bright eyes, her long fingers and neck, which still lifted high that clever head of hers. Clever… those were her words. This clever head puts food on the table for both of us. That sentence I've known as if I drank it in with the milk from her breast, the happily loved Monika said to herself. If she could, she'd curl up in her embrace and bury her slant-eyed face in her bosom, but she can't — that would break the angle of inclination and the land of the heart, the heartland, would be lost at once.

'And then she asked me, Madame Magister, how long does it take a person to learn that dictionary — a month? Two?

'You want to learn the dictionary by heart? Memorise it? I asked, surprised.

'Yes, *pamyat* — I've got a good memory, she said and then, methodically, I mean that in the literal sense, methodically, she wiped the dirty water from the window. I remember everything, and I'll memorise that dictionary too.'

Monika was waiting for her mother to laugh, or to wink or something, but she remained serious, ladylike, with a peculiar tenderness stifling any hint of irony that she might have expressed.

'Yep, I'll learn the dictionary, she said, and her work seemed to go from then on like play. She'd squat down like this and then wipe the clean strip up the wet window, as if she were using her whole body, saying all the while: I'll learn me all those words, I will, in order, and I'll become a translator like you, or I'll go off to America or England and I'll find a job there — why here?

'And so I loaned her that dictionary, or really gave it to that Milica, old Poldauf, devil take him. And at that Milica says You've got a heart of gold, Ma'am. And she sticks the dictionary under her arm, grabs her bucket and leaves my office.

'God will repay you, Ma'am, she added at the door.'

'And she was off to America,' Monika concluded.

THE THIRTY-FIRST

Even from far away it was obvious that those two were just wandering about the streets, rather than being on their way somewhere. Happier outside, say people who can't endure being at home because of the unbearable presence of some family member. At least outside, say those who don't have a home to be in together, and so they walk about among the cold gardens of early spring as if they were interested in whether something was budding there or not. How cheery a vibrant crocus would be right now, on this gloomy afternoon! But the unbelievably yellow and violet colours of the crocuses are still hidden in their seemingly dead bulbs in the soil; or, rather, those colours don't yet exist — there's nothing there but the white blindness of anticipation beneath the dry clay upon which the twilight falls.

If one came closer, one would recognise in these two figures there between the fences Martin Vrána and his son. That's how they would meet and walk about in the first years after the divorce; that's the way it was when Martin borrowed him or his sister or both from their mother, who couldn't bear to look at him. They'd go on long walks, or to a buffet or a pizzeria or a restaurant, where he could pick the kids up, but it was usually long walks. The words flow easily when one is walking, flowing on just like the day flows toward evening.

'What if we're not alone in the universe after all,' the boy pondered. 'You know what, Dad? I reckon that I'll live to see the day when some sort of other intelligent being appears to us,' he said, his face becoming very serious at those words. 'For sure.'

'Yeah. In ships as big as stadiums,' Martin mused in turn, ironically.

'But I don't think it'll be like in that stupid film Independence Day, not at all. I'm thinking about some sort of signals, some sort of message.'

'And what do you think that that other intelligence, or so to speak, other intelligences, are going to look like?'

'I try to imagine them as, as…'

'As some sort of squid or green jelly or light waves?'

'That's stupid — jelly! I saw that in a movie once too, how this living jelly spreads through the city and eats away at people. It was completely gross.'

'They had that running in the cinema?'

'No, we borrowed a cassette.'

'O yeah, you do have a VCR.'

They were quiet for a moment, as they always were after each mention of what's changed at home since Martin left. Especially that VCR which Martin, while still a valid member, if not head of the family, always declared that he would never buy — why? So that the shit on TV should eat away at the kids' brains even more?

'Yeah, we do, yeah.'

'Whatever. Mama knows what she's doing.'

Their eyes fell upon a half-dilapidated gazebo crumbling into dust in the corner of a garden belonging to a noble-looking villa with dark windows. Gazebo, bower.

'When I think about it,' the boy resumed after a few moments, 'they'd just look like people, wouldn't they.'

'And what if there were people there, somewhere, far away,' said Martin, giving his head a toss in the direction of the sky, from which the light was slowly ebbing.

'What — you think that they are human?'

'I'm simply imagining that the universe is populated by people. That on planets in far off solar systems there live people, as if on islands in the sea of this gigantic galaxy.'

'I've also thought of that,' his son said in answer, 'but rather as when someday people will start travelling at speeds greater than light and they begin to colonise other systems, but — other humans? Out there now, like you say? I can't understand that. How could they be there, and we know nothing about them?'

'Well, just so. They're people that we don't know exist. For instance, they spread about the cosmos a long, long time before our culture arose — maybe the earth isn't the home planet of the human race. Maybe we're the descendants of some expedition or other, which arrived here a hundred thousand years ago. Like they got trapped here — They'd flown so very far, lost contact — shipwrecks…'

'OK, I get that. But they'd've been people with an advanced level of technology, not some primitive cavemen. And what about those primitive early humans, those skeletons, those stone wedges that they dig up?'

'Eh — who cares about them bones? God only knows what sort of monkey they belonged to. And those primitive cavemen, well, they're the descendants of those shipwrecks, even if, somehow, they mixed in with the apes.'

'But Dad — that won't work. People who travel around in spaceships, conquering such distances as we can't even imagine, aren't going to transform themselves into some sort of primitive hunters who worship totems.'

'O, people change, boy. And people have real short memories. As soon as their computers shut down, they were suddenly naked in the wilds. You yourself — do you know how to build a refrigerator?'

'No, but…'

'Or a power plant?'

'A wind driven one, maybe.'

'Who knows? I think that people, depressed people torn away from home, are even going to start fighting amongst themselves, harming themselves, destroying the majority of things they've brought with them, and then, after five or ten generations, they'll even forget where they came from. They'll have nothing left but those totems and rituals and the secret teachings of some sect or other, the builders of the pyramids and so forth. And then quite simply the planet of their exile becomes their home. They have to forget about their original home, otherwise they wouldn't be able to go on living. You understand me? You can wait ten years, a hundred years, but ten thousand years? You can't wait on a rescue mission that long. You can only believe in something like that, you can already only suspect that your real home is somewhere other than this earth. Like the Polynesians who believe that after death they'll paddle off in their canoes to where the ocean meets the sky, and then up through the heavens to where their ancestors are. You can build pyramids as some sort of cosmic symbols, but your grandchildren already aren't going to know what those symbols mean…'

'Dad, it's getting pretty late,' said the boy, touching Martin's elbow. His face took on a worried look.

'You're right. Let's head back home.'

They picked up the pace, no longer just wandering aimlessly. In the depths of the villas lights came on and Martin became unpleasantly aware of how cosy it must be, there.

'I don't think that's the way it is, but it might be,' the boy reasoned.

'Who knows? But it is really late, and you've got to hit those history books, the rise of Fascism, what we were talking about.'

'Of course. I'll read it.'

They came out of the neighbourhood of the villas and into the lit streets and headed inexorably in the direction of the boy's home.

'You know, boy, even though we don't live together, that doesn't mean that…'

'I know.' The boy was suddenly older than Martin was. Martin was ashamed of the tears that he somehow fought back. He thrust fifty crowns into the boy's hand. 'Buy yourself that computer magazine.'

They embraced one another clumsily and then the boy disappeared past the door, through which they had passed together so many times, before.

THE THIRTY-SECOND

'Good evening,' Martin greeted the empty space, and immediately switched on the television, so that he wouldn't have to think. And yet he was thinking, scanning all four channels with the remote. A show at all costs. He settled on Eurosport. He never watched sport alone, really; never watched it at all unless he was with his boy — hockey, or ski-jumping. Today they were showing track and field. He let it run. The running track suddenly seemed more interesting than all the other programmes.

The hundred metres. That takes soul. To prove something over such a short distance. To prove everything over such a short distance. Five women in blue kits with the logo of the sponsor of the championships were milling around the starting blocks. Martin suddenly perceived their rather boyish figures, their intent faces and the precise movements they made, which were intended to loosen their muscles. The warmed-up, black American girl was transferring her weight from heel to toe, as if to say, Let's get a move on! The strong Russian won't budge an inch. Single-mindedly and somewhat grimly, her eyes were locked on the hundred metres before her. The determined Polish girl was bouncing on her toes, resolved to give no ground. The Kenyan was prowling around the starting blocks softly, like a leopard, and the German was shaking her forearms and working on controlling her breath. Suddenly, all of the women began to undress. The blue nylon kits fell into plastic bins taken away by the hands of young girls, and now the athletes stand there in their lanes, dressed in elastic shorts and bodices which only cover their breasts. Their thoraxes rise and fall rhythmically in an attempt to shore up a bit against the oxygen debt they're about to incur.

Suddenly, Martin sees these athletes metamorphose into quite different beings, even though the Pole signs herself with the cross, the Russian clenches her fists, the German lifts her arms above her head as she takes in a deep breath — suddenly, they become more denuded than if they had been naked. The hundred metres lie before them like a solid block about to be pierced by the starter's gun.

As they kneel with their feet at their blocks, they are now dispossessed of everything. The world around them disappears, along with the stadium, and their names, and nations, and families. They are pure beings, merely touching the lonely edge of the material world with the tips of their fingers and toes. Then comes a false start. They burst out and up, and then fall back like birds that have been shot. O, don't do that to them, damn it, says Martin in a disburdening of his own energy, his lungs pumping as if he were about to run the course himself. Then comes the second shot, and the runners abandon the material world, each in her own style and all in a single burst. Now, nothing can be seen but running itself. Bodies at work, which entrust themselves to the abyss before them with absolute confidence and absolutely everything they have. Cameras take them in from every angle, but can't capture a single detail, because no such thing exists here. All of a sudden, Martin sees that these women have completely left the space we inhabit; that they are there, at a place into which a person can glance, glimpse, only a few times in one's life, if even then, after which the one so privileged lives on this, feeding on it, singed, perhaps even contorted and with bruised organs, without awareness, in awareness!

The German crosses the finish line first, with the Kenyan just a few millimetres behind her and all the rest pass through to the other side in a wink of time, faster than you can say boo. Once again they're here, in that stupid stadium, their short road ending in cheers and uproar at which they once more put on their names, nationalities, and kits. Martin follows with his eyes the violently labouring body of the heated American, who finished third, how she opens her eyes and makes sure of where she is and which one she is and all… I run hard until I'm caught up, ravished, Martin says to himself, and that's everything. Only in that way, boy, can we return for a moment there, where we have never been before.

THE THIRTY-THIRD

Again he was at a train station three quarters of an hour earlier than he needed to be. He got that from his father. Better an hour early than a second late, old Vrána used to say to his sons. But still they were always and everywhere late, that's how Martin saw it right now. In time for them to understand what it's all about; too late for them to care. There remained them the irony of latecomers, who would say to themselves, Just don't shit yourself!, and then watch as the well-fed buttocks of other men stuffed themselves into trains that they, the Vránas, wouldn't be taking now.

And thus Martin gazed around the long, so long platform of the tube station in London. The boarding platform of sandy yellow concrete was fitted at the very level of the train doors, which passed through here like arrows out from the City to the suburbs, and back again. Here, one enters the carriage slowly; nobody clambers up the steps as in Svinov, Prague or Paris. Here the platforms and the carriages are at the same level, even if there's not much else here that's on the same level. This station, parallel to the bend in the Thames, is called Lambeth. It's written there in black letters on the low, sandy-yellow building as an incontrovertible truth.

The unknown, and yet not alien city of London surrounded Martin with its small crouched neighbourhoods of unexpected extent. Never before had he been able to imagine that there might be so many ordinary and yet all the same interesting buildings in one city. Buildings of dark brick with black, cast-iron pipes climbing up over exterior walls. He never knew what the city looked like, in which he had lived in imagination for so long, that London. The City won't surprise you; you know the City from school and books and all, but here, past Vauxhall Bridge there's this little train station and houses around it like forests, forests of gables, roofs and chimneys, full of such usual lives as didn't reach into our prefab flats…

And so three quarters of an hour, as always. He sits there on a bench, while a blue and silver train speeds through the station, not stopping, but whizzing on to the wealthier suburbs. Sit here and look — past those trees there, the four smokestacks of the old Battersea power station rise, which you know from the Pink Floyd album cover, from the greasy, threadbare vinyls smuggled into Czechoslovakia… there was also that inflated plastic pig hovering against the yellow sky. Now, there's nothing hovering there — on the contrary, the dusk flows on quietly.

Just that morning he spoke with Eva Topolská on her mobile. She's been here for over a week at some sort of conference; she's trying I think to arrange something here for a Czech institute of European reach. And so she rang him up and they found one another in London, where Martin was attending the meeting of a certain Czech foundation that had its hand out for European funds. And so they called one another and thanks to some little flashing lights screwed here and there on towers and chimneys, they set up a meeting place.

Beneath the satellites, old London. Beneath the satellites an old English love and a thousand words a year. The memory of an old teacher with a wig and thick glasses and the unique talent to teach people English. Childless, always with her students, for a whole fifteen years under the régime of Dr Husák she preserved her old tickets from the London Underground so that she could show them to her pupils. And now we can freely exchange Czech crowns for British pounds, the teacher is dead and so, fortunately, is Dr Husák. We can work here in London without a problem, Ma'am, your pupils, Martin and Eva, though we don't know English even half as well as you did, Ma'am. Dear is now cheap and cheap's gotten dearer. When I think about your breath, when you danced with me at the ball after the maturity exams, and you told me, suddenly and privately, switching to the familiar form, You're my good student! I know that you had more in mind than just my progress with that language, which any old ox can rinse his mouth with these days.

That love is conveyed only by a movement of the heart and that heart is, for us, even for us bloody foreigners, only London, only the tranquil speech of Dr Johnson, not the babble of Dr Husák. Another world, Europe beyond the borders of Europe. Britain, who sneezes at us and lauds in its cathedral Lord Chamberlain, whom we must hate a priori because of his

Machiavellian swinishness; who knows where it arose, this love of ours for a city that knows nothing of our very existence, this love for London bent around the River Thames that runs through it, Ma'am?

And so they met in Lambeth. Eva wasn't thrilled at that. To travel to some out of the way neighbourhood and meet up with an old friend at a railway station… but since that was the only option… She took a taxi to the last train stop before Vauxhall Bridge and then got into the carriage — maybe 2000 metres from the place agreed-upon. She asked herself why she couldn't take the taxi all the way to Lambeth, but she went along and played her role in his comedy, that she arrive by train, she couldn't refuse him that, and suddenly she became as sentimental as he, emotional as she never in her life permitted herself to be. She stood in the carriage for some two minutes. You'd like to say that that awesome magnetism that they shared was what drew the train over the steel rails, that one was drawn to the other like the only two living beings in an otherwise dead world, but who would want to say such a thing, to enunciate it aloud, to embarrass oneself in front of one's own self…

She exited the carriage and saw him sitting there on a bench on the long platform. Propped on his elbows, tired, like any little crow anywhere in Svinov, Havířov, Paris, or anywhere in the world.

'I really didn't want this,' she said, sitting down next to him. 'Really, I didn't, Martin.'

'Neither did I,' he replied and they clasped hands and held on for a while in an indifferent, and yet again emotional contact, the same as when they were going out together, when they were the old teacher's best English students. Like back then at the train station in Havířov-Suchá.

'Which never was.'

'No, it wasn't.'[15]

And then came the questions and answers. The phrases were borne away like empty wrappers on the surface of a deep river. They told each other why they were here. What they do. And what they don't do anymore. All in vain, all beautifully golden vanity. Both were nicely dressed and combed, too nicely for a train stop, unless in Lambeth. There are places on earth where even a socially groomed woman can sit just so. He wasn't dogeared

....

[15]   … 'dry.' *Suchá* means 'dry' in Czech; Martin and Eva are punning, sharing an inside joke.

either — he was wearing a suit and a greatcoat and nice shoes and a clean shirt. Such people as might appear even in noteworthy films.

'Why did you call me?' he asked.

'Just so. A while ago I got the number of your mobile. I was feeling sad in the hotel, so I started ringing up friends. I didn't know that you were in London.'

'I don't believe you.'

'You don't have to.'

'What sort of phone do you have? Mother of pearl?'

'Maybe.'

'Like pond mussels.'

'Maybe. Doesn't matter. It's like a pond mussel.'

'Eva.'

'Martin.'

'Martin.'

'Eva.'

They talked a long while and across the river the four smokestacks of the old power station rose in the air and, behind them, bluish-grey clouds slid over the golden late afternoon sky.

'You know I'm afraid even to touch it.'

'Touch what?'

'Our life.'

'We had a life?'

'Exactly. The one that we didn't have, the one that didn't come to be.'

'At least it couldn't go bad,' said Martin, with sudden harshness.

'You've had a life go bad on you, maybe?'

'More than one. Some I've made bad, others I haven't allowed, and it seems to me that one's still constantly not coming to be.'

'I don't believe that of you. About me I'd believe it, about you — no.'

'I'm trying to speak like you.'

'Why did you want me to come here, exactly?'

'I'm staying nearby. But chiefly, because the place is called Lambeth.'

'It sounds like a little lamb.'

'It sounds like…' Martin took a deep breath.

'There is a Grain of Sand in Lambeth that Satan cannot find
Nor can his Watch Fiends find it, 'tis translucent & has many Angles

　　　　　　　　　　　　　　　　　　　

And thus he reaches out for it in vain

For as he gazes at it, he sees what is not there.[16]

'That's what you were thinking of? William Blake?'

'You know, there exists this unprovable and yet irrefutable legend, that somewhere in the garden of one of these old houses the Lake poet Wordsworth surprised William Blake and his wife, seated on a garden bench beneath the woodbine, as naked as Adam and Eve. The Lake poet supposedly turned aside his chaste eyes, but then he kept flapping his gums about it so, that it entered into every literary history.'

'I've read that too, but I didn't know that it happened in Lambeth.'

He accompanied her back to the bridge over the Thames. No supper, no hotel. Just a fleeting brush of soft lips and then each returned their own way.

....

[16]   The first two lines are from Blake's *Jerusalem*. The last two are Martin's, or the Czech translator's.

THE THIRTY-FOURTH

'I still forgot to tell you…'

That sentence sounded to Eva Topolská like the refrain of some heavy song. Like this great, sad woman singing this long, reproachful song, or prayer, in which the weight of life is submitted to God alone — who else? What of all else have I forgotten to tell you? She walked along the embankment of this beautiful, foreign river and there, inside her, in the place she strove to avoid as much as possible, something black arose. She only wanted to watch it. To call it to life for a moment only, to make sure it wasn't dead. That's why she wanted to meet up with Martin in London, and satisfy herself that she had been alive back then, that she had been through all that, that that was her back there.

That's what these mobile phones do. You can be anywhere. That's no advertising slogan, that's the truth. You ring somebody up just because a friend in common gave you his number. Because you have this feeling, or maybe somebody told you, that he'd be in England, or, rather, no, you didn't suppose that; he has to be at home after all. Somewhere in northern Moravia, among the collieries, somewhere in northern Czechia, amidst the exhausted quarries, somewhere in some unreal land, where everything is disappearing. Buried in ash like the shadow of years one recalls with sweetness, because they no longer exist. Because you are no longer a young freckled girl in his embrace, but a damnably independent woman, who does little more these days than ride around in taxis and ring people up. So you pick a number, you can be anywhere. And he's not sitting there amidst the exhausted quarries, he's here, on the other side of the river, and makes a date with you at a train station.

She felt that black and bitter thing in her begin to swell. That scream! You can't manage it any more. There's nowhere to step aside. She leant forward, bent; it's like a shaft piercing her midriff, right where she lives. I didn't want that, she says to herself, and takes a seat in a café on the embankment. I didn't want that, but it just goes on. Obsessively it returns to her, however often she's used that sentence, however many times she's given way to that silent scream inside her. How many benches has she sat down upon, how many cold sheets has she slipped into, how many pills has she taken until they carried her off to a safe place, how many times has she heard, constantly, those same words?

It went dark before her eyes. Between the lashes of her semi-closed eyelids, the Thames looked like a rolling belt of coal, while on the other bank, the grey buildings and towers began to quiver. A glass of water, please. She plunged her hand into her bag and rummaged around for her pills, but it was the phone that her hand came into contact with, her little silver Ericsson, which knows what you're thinking.

Martin was staring into his pint at The Ploughman, and it didn't occur to him at all that the annoying beeps he was hearing were coming from his own pocket. The thought wouldn't even have crossed his mind had the waitress not come over and said I believe that's yours, sir, at which he replied Thanks, pulled the gizmo out of his pocket and stepped outside onto the pavement. It was Eva's voice he heard on the other end:

'I still forgot to tell you…' then, sounds interfered, of the sort you hear when somebody's calling from a café or the street; quite a while they lasted, then a couple intaken breaths and a pause, like the closure of the first line of a letter… '…that Ivan Figura, you know, we mentioned him when we were talking, he's dead.'

'That's horrible. What happened to him?'

'Did himself in.'

'He killed himself?'

'Yeah. Suicide.'

'But — you don't know why? I know that it sounds stupid, but…'

'I know.'

'Would you maybe like to get together again? I can get a taxi and come over. Where are you?'

'You can be anywhere,' Eva laughed. 'No, don't come. It's better this way. I'm nowhere…'

'All right, then. But why did he do it, really?'

'They were really tormenting him.'

'StB goons?'

'They never tormented you?'

'Sure. I was afraid of them, too. But that's over and done with.'

'You stopped being afraid of them?'

'Sure.'

'Tell me.'

'Tell you what?'

'How you stopped being afraid of them.'

'Listen, Eva — this is going to cost you a fortune. Wouldn't it be better to talk face to face?'

'No. I've got limitless credit, so no, no worries. When did you stop being afraid? I'm curious.'

'Just like that, here on the street?'

'Yeah. We were always closest when we were out in the street. So — how did you stop being afraid?'

'Quite simply. One morning, I think it was 1990, I woke up in bed and I realised that I was missing something. That something's not here. It was a nice bright morning, the swifts were screaming outside the window, the children, my wife at the time…'

'Dana?'

'Yeah, Dana. Thanks, keep the change.' During the conversation, Martin had returned inside to pay and fetch his coat.

'OK, I'm back. So, they were all still asleep and I suddenly felt that I'm not afraid of the StB. They never did much to me anyway, but that fear — that fear was functional.'

'What did they do to you?'

'Two interviews and a sort of pressure, because I had been abroad when I was a student, and had some friends among the emgirés and the Chartists — they could have been interested in me for that.'

'They were. For sure.'

'How do you know?'

'They'd ask me about you, and Ivan as well. Always.'

'You were seeing Ivan?'

'Sometimes. In Prague.'

'And they interviewed you, too?'

'Just like you, it seems. Not much. But how was it again with that fear?'

'Quite simple. I suddenly felt that that fear, that feeling that you've been handed over into the power of beasts who could show up and ring your doorbell any time of day or night — was gone.'

'Beasts can still show up at your door, even now.'

'Maybe. But that's when the fear left me. There only remained this pure void, a void like a place for hope… But what about that Ivan — how'd he get mixed up with them?'

'They recruited him when he was in the army, and then they wouldn't let him alone.'

'And he? Who wouldn't he let alone?'

'I don't know!'

'So, after the changes, he could've just sneezed at it all, right? I spoke to him about a year ago and he told me that he'd never hurt anybody. Your ear's not getting red from holding your phone to it, is it?'

'I don't know, Martin. I can't see my ears. You know, he never stopped being afraid, I guess, and that's why he could never feel that space for hope, as you put it. You never signed anything for them, did you?'

'And you did?'

'I won't answer that question even to myself.'

'So where are you, Eva? Down here by the river it's as dark as an old British whodunit. Come on, let's meet somewhere for supper.'

'I'm nowhere. Yesterday I was at the Tate. Have you seen Munch's Sick Child?'

'Sure. Many times.'

'The original's quite different from the reproduction you showed me back when we were in school.'

'Everything's different. So damned different.'

'For sure. And I still forgot to tell you…' Then there was a noise, like when somebody shouts out in the street, and then a silence, like when somebody hangs up.

THE THIRTY-FIFTH

'I didn't know you had a sister,' Martin said to Monika.

'I didn't either, for the longest time. She's my half-sister, from my mother's first marriage. She's a lot older than I am. I saw her a few times and knew her back then as this young lady who came to visit my mother from time to time. Mostly I remember her as being very tall. Estera.'

'So her name is Ester.'

'I've always heard her spoken of as Estera. I don't know why.'

'I know so terribly little about you,' Martin complained. 'Nearly nothing.'

'On the other hand, I know more about you perhaps than everybody else taken together,' Monika laughed. 'So many adventures. You know that you're constantly telling adventure stories?'

They kissed in the frosty mountain air. They kissed as if each were searching for his place in the other. They searched for each other in the tatters of the mist which the wind was pushing across the mountain ridge. With that hood on her head, bound even more tightly round her face with a scarf, Monika looked like an Eskimo — her slanted eyes, her small bosom, her small hands in Martin's sleeves. A wind as cold as water from a cataract struck them in the face so, it was a wonder that it didn't topple them down into the gorge of fallen trees, which opened at their feet. Some of them were still hanging by their roots, crowns downward; others were caught on rocks, broken apart like suicides. Holding on by their fingers, caught by their hair, and yet sure to fall down into the valley spreading wide its tranquil landscape far below.

'Does she look like you?' asked Martin, gazing inquiringly into her face.

'Estera? I don't know. I never saw myself standing alongside her. She's certainly a lot taller than I am, and… Stop looking at me like that!' Swiftly, she untangled herself from his embrace, stepped back, and covered her face in her hands.

'How am I supposed to not look at you?'

'That... searchingly...'

'But, Nika...'

'No, don't call me that — that's what Mama calls me!' She stepped back another pace — and that was already a little bit dangerous to do up there.

'Ever since I was a child everyone's always looked at me, searchingly like that. Everybody except Mama. I know why you asked me if Estera looks like me. What you wanted to know was does she have eyes like mine.'

'You mean, dark eyes?'

'No! Slanted eyes!' Monika cried. 'Not dark, slanted! That's what all of you want to know, because you all say: Well, she had her with some Vietnamese, Chinese or Mongol...' She pressed her hands to her eyes and the trembling of her chin alone showed that she was crying. It wasn't fun, having to look at that chin and those hands, vainly trying to hold back her tears.

'Monika.'

'Don't come near me. Let me be!'

'Don't worry about it; it's not important after all. Who makes distinctions among people here?'

'Who doesn't?'

'I don't.'

'O, what a broadminded fellow you are! Who can go around with a mixed-breed now that his latest marriage has fallen apart!'

She tore her hands away from her face and looked straight into Martin's eyes, narrowing her own to slits.

'Come on, you know you're beautiful.'

'No, Martin, I don't, and I don't know who my father is. I don't know a thing about him.'

'Your mother never spoke about him?'

'No, never. When I was little, we never talked about him. And when I was older, I was already too afraid to ask, because we'd never spoken about him. But when I finally did, my mother said — Don't ask. She knows how to be real tough on that point. She's a great person, but she's as hard as stone. I've never seen another woman like her. She'd let herself be put to death rather than break her silence on that subject.'

Monika spoke so straightforwardly, without the slightest hesitation, it was as if she'd already prepared that speech. Like a scene learned, one that would someday have to be played out. Martin almost felt as if his presence there were unnecessary. She could just stand there on that mountain ridge, disappear, and appear again as the mists flowed over her, and with eyes closed, soliloquise to the empty spaces. But it wasn't like that; he wasn't empty air; on the contrary, he was full of something heavy. The landscape below suddenly became dreadfully empty and pointless.

'So when you asked why you have… why you don't have eyes like hers?'

'You have a beautiful way with words, you do. She said I should thank God that I'm a healthy and clever girl.'

'And she was right.'

'But you see, it never bothered me, my appearance. I like myself, and even though you're not supposed to say such things, I'm not afraid of any mirror. It does bother me, that I don't know who I am. But let's get out of here,' she said, hoisting her knapsack on her shoulder and setting off down the path without a backward glance. And who do you think knows, Martin said to himself, setting off behind her. In the distance, the tip of a television tower poked up through the clouds, where, to all indications, Monika's sister worked.

The evening was coming on. The sun was setting beyond the horizon, and the first stars were appearing in the sky. The valley below them was full of mist. It might even be raining down there. The path leading to the tower stretched out like a white line through the dark mountain meadows. All around them rose the flat, stony mountain summits — Šerák, Keprník, Vozka, Petrovy kameny. Black rocks on the roof of the world, and above them, nothing. A gigantic abyss of air that thins out in the direction of the stars and blackens to night.

'We're sitting on a rock hurtling through space. Can you feel it?' Martin asked Monika, as they sheltered from the wind behind a block of stone.

'And there, where those red lights are, lives the sister I don't know, and who wouldn't recognise me if she saw me,' Monika said to him in reply. 'We were crazy to come here. She might just as well be living there,' she said, pointing, 'on whatever that big star's called.'

'That's Jupiter,' explained Martin.

'She might just as well be living there. It looks just as far away from here as where she is.'

'Come on. We're almost there.'

THE THIRTY-SIXTH

'So, you can get a good night's sleep here, and tomorrow, as I said, leave the key in this pipe.'

'Sure, boss,' answered Martin. 'You've already told me that.'

'Most important thing is that nobody see you here. They'd say things like "we have our stuff here," and so on.' The guy with the bald skull and thick whiskers pointed to a row of doors leading to workers' quarters.

'This here room's in case of need. What more is there to say.'

'I know. I stayed here once before, back before that tower was built.'

'All right then,' and the door closed behind them.

'That's what these bosses up here in the mountains are like in their flannel shirts and whiskers. They act as tough as the Mountain Service, but the majority of them have weak livers,' Martin declared.

'But we can be glad that he let us sleep here, Martin, and he even gave us Estera's address.'

'It wasn't out of the kindness of his heart.'

He opened the window and lit a cigarette.

'Can you smell that odour? Like glue or some sort of adhesive? I remember that from back then, when they put us up here in our work brigades. We stayed downstairs somewhere on the ground floor. Back then I didn't know anything about this room. I guess it served some sort of nefarious purpose.'

'As it still does,' said Monika gaily, peeking out from behind some drapes, which hid a double bed in a dark, studio recess. 'At least we know where Estera went off to, since she left a forwarding address for mail. So we'll forward her some. I'll write her a letter: Dear Estera.'

'What's her full name? You don't even know what your sister's last name is.'

'Now I do. Ms Ester Kocíchová. But you know yourself that Estera suffices. Everybody calls her that.'

Suddenly, Monika's good humour began to irk Martin a little bit. But more to the point, he was a little jealous. He felt a little alone now, because of this newly rediscovered sister of hers.

'Well, I'm going down to that *wawrshroom*[17] as this here lighthouse keeper puts it.' And Monika slipped her hiking boots onto her bare legs. Martin peeked out the window of the tiny worker's lodging that crouched not too far from the television tower, listening to Monika's steps as she thumped over the wooden stairs. Ms Kocíchová, technician and systems analyst, departed here a month ago for the GSM in Pardubice. Mobile networks pay. And that great woman couldn't even send her little sister a letter. Perhaps she never had. Martin thought about his own brothers. They also never wrote him, but his parents always knew where they were. Petr, in Germany, an important man in that unimaginable Hannover of his, has a beautiful family. His older boy — also named Petr — is already in high school. Tomaš is still in Prague, still one foot in Prague, rather. Mama speaks of him with anxiety. Maybe she speaks of all her sons with anxiety. We Vránas are anxiety-laced folk. And just look at Monika — she won't find her sister and is going to sleep in a cubby hole, and off she goes in hiking boots to wash and brush her teeth in a *wawrshroom* on a summit of Hrubý Jeseník and is almost singing all the while.

They shut off the light. Immediately, it was as dark as the inside of a sack. They sought each other out under the covers.

'I can't see you.'

'That doesn't matter.'

'Martin.'

'Yes?'

'Martin, lay down on me.'

He obeyed, completely covering her body with his own, carefully. He felt her breasts pushing up against him, the arc of her ribcage, her mound, her gentle thighs — and he hardly dared breathe.

'I feel so good right now.'

'I must be real heavy.'

'No, lay like that, exactly like that. At least now I won't fly off into the cosmos, which you're constantly going on about, and which just makes me scared.'

....

[17] He calls it an *umývárka* rather than the generally accepted *umývárna*.

He thought she wanted to make love. She did, but not just yet.

'In a bit. Now, I've got to tell you something, and you've got to remain on me like this. You've told me so much about your childhood, your mother, father, your wife.'

'My ex-wife.'

'…your wife, your children, about the little boats that your[18] boy always had to have in bed with him, so that he wouldn't drown, of the night fears of your daughter, and about your mysterious Eva, whom you never stopped loving despite your marriage, about your brothers in Germany and Prague, about how you'd go into the forest with your children when they were little and tell them about the mushrooms that grow mysteriously underground…'

'Monika!'

'No — just bear with me; at least you'll see that your words didn't just disappear into thin air when you told me how your daughter crawled beneath the table in fear when you were quarrelling. About your son, who ran out into the corridor after you when your wife was screaming that she hated you. How that helpless little fellow wanted to soothe you. I remember it all. You poured it into me like iron, and it's not yet cooled.'

They turned on that bed, gone squeaky with so much tussling over the years so that now Monika was on top of Martin. Her elbows were pressing down on his shoulders, and suddenly, there was no stopping her mouth.

'My life, growing up, was completely different. I experienced no adventures, only things which later I tried to forget. That's what Mama taught me. But it's impossible to forget everything; you can only not think about it. I'm not too heavy?'

'No. Stay like that.'

'I always was aware of the fact that I was my mother's sin. Now, she loved me, she gave me everything. She helped me with my lessons, so I never had any problems with learning — she'd explain everything to me. She always had more than enough time for me. Our house was as cosy as a boat. A little boat. But all the same I remained her sin. She never went anywhere with me. She always just waited on me somewhere, and then we went home. I don't

....

[18]   Monika uses the plural possessive here, *váš*, which emphasises the boy as both Martin's and his wife's; a little later in the sentence when she speaks of 'your daughter' she uses the singular, *tvé* — i.e. 'Martin's daughter.'

think they knew she had a daughter, even at work. I mean, somebody had to know — salary additions for a child, tax relief and so on, but she knows how not to draw attention to herself. She's clever — when she doesn't want you to see her, you won't. She hid me, and she hid herself, as far as I know. But that's not what I want to tell you.'

She lay there on Martin like a cat, like a little lioness. It felt so good, she could have stayed like that forever, as far as he was concerned.

'I want to tell you that I also had a child,' Monika said, going as stiff as an iron rod.

'Had? You don't have any more?'

'It died in me, six years ago. I was in my fourth month, and I wasn't all right.'

'What do you mean?'

'Don't ask. I'll tell you everything myself. It was my own fault. I was rebelling against my mother — toward the end of high school.[19] You know what that's like, when someone flies toward their own misfortune?'

'I do, even if you weren't flying at the same misfortune as I.'

'No, much worse. I was eighteen and absolutely crazy mad at the fact that I look Chinese. So I'd dress up and do my hair that way, even though I don't have the foggiest idea of who I am. I was going out with this boy who was more interested in the Chinese girl than in me, and at the time I wasn't completely in my right mind, I'd say. I was a little unbalanced, having run away from my mother before my maturity exam and all. You know those gloomy clubs, where people sit around not talking much, listening to music, toking and then going off with somebody to thrash around a bit with them, then music and it's bad and it's good and life is such that you have no idea whatsoever and that's just the point. Staring off into space and not giving a damn. You know what that's like?'

'Yeah.'

'You've experienced it?'

'Yeah. In another way, maybe, but yeah.'

'Well, I didn't. I was never fully in it. Just like I never was a Chinese girl. I was only always alongside it. Even if he did with me like…'

'Moni!'

....

[19]   In Czech, *zdravotní škola*. Monika attended a high school with a medical profile.

'You have to hear me out… Even if he did with me like we were on a trip, but I was on no trip at all. I never trusted him, but then again I never trusted anybody. Only my mother, and even with her I held back a bit. And then I held back from that boy. He wasn't much of a boy anyway. A kind of a person that comes your way, and then when you leave him, you don't know how you came upon him in the first place. That's when I returned to Mama. Stressed out, skinny as a rail. Outside my own self, and, best of all, pregnant. We wanted to keep it. Both of us, Mama and me. We wanted that child. I was over the moon with how wonderful she was. She arranged it so that I could repeat my last year; set up my doctors, everything. Because of me, she didn't go to work for a month, I reckon. I don't know how she did it, and all the while she's calling me her girlie.'

'You didn't go through any hell for all that junk?'

'No. Cold turkey wasn't so bad on me. I'd just lived really stupidly, you know. But consequences, O, I have my consequences, and they'll be with me as long as I live. I lost my child, the child I wanted, and I constantly feel that whether it was the junk, or the terror, I'm the one who killed it. There had to be a delivery, Martin. I was in the maternity ward like any young mother, and I had to push a dead child out into the world.'

'Moni, that can happen to any woman.'

'I know, because it happened to me.'

Then she laid her head down alongside his and breathed into his ear just like after lovemaking.

THE THIRTY-SEVENTH

Everything will suddenly fall into order, everything will settle and become real. Even the Stage 4 estate grew as familiar as a washtub to become simply another place to live. People grew old, kids stopped scruffing up the lawns, breaking the saplings and the bushes, and bellowing over the staircases. Nothing but peace. Even steel gets tired, even steel set in concrete. The prefab towers sagged a bit, cracked a bit, just like the people who live in them. Nobody remembers any more the days when all of this was new, shapely squared buildings arising from the marsh, and everybody young, with small children, as if in those days no other families but young ones even existed.

So many preschools, so many nurseries, so many elementary schools — transformed today into secondhand shops, pawnshops, taverns, distributors of barrelled wine and arcades. The old woman fixes the curtains on her window and turns back to the safety of the things she knows. Only memories torment her. Those nurseries, to which I dragged the boy each morning by the hand. And when I was changing him, he always fought back, grabbing me by the coat and wailing 'Not among the children!!!' These days those same boys go there to drink beer. They're all big fellows already, and ought to have wives and kids of their own at home, but maybe they don't, or they disappeared somewhere, 'cos how otherwise could they have closed so many schools and preschools? Where will it all lead?

The Communists built Nová huť', and we all went to work there, thinking that it'll all turn out well, that there'll be prosperity. But there was no prosperity. Back home as a girl in Kysuce I sweated my share, and here in the foundry as well — a person hasn't much of a choice. Now the foundry's deep in debt, the mines are closing down, the men are out on welfare and the boys head straight to the dole after school, and it's surprising that nobody misses the work. They just keep on driving their cars, even the unemployed, to go fishing, to go on vacation. We were in Bulgaria twice, always and only on ROH vouchers, and only because my husband was foreman and president of the plant committee, otherwise we wouldn't have been able to save up enough. And now, people are going and going wherever they please. Always flying to their Eurotels and Paegases, and that Ilonka of Ivan's, Ilonka, after me, but he wouldn't permit her to be christened and now, how does it all turn out. It's good she has a telephone, I'm just waiting for her to drive up in her car. She's a clever one, that girl; at her age, eh! I went about in hand-me-downs. But let her enjoy it, my golden girl, she's got it hard, too — seeing her dad once a fortnight, and her Mama constantly in the air somewhere, divorced, everybody's divorced. And I say to him, Ivan, don't be stupid, and he, Look Mama, it just didn't work out. Well if it didn't, it didn't. You must know if anyone does, searching for happiness in that Prague of yours — Who can stick it out with a girl from Prague? They're entitled ones, they are. They've gotta have two crates full of clothes, three maybe, and if all that makeup won't fit in one bathroom, why, then she'll have two bathrooms. My old man meant something too, after all, but we had no need of so much stupid rubbish, and moreover that Ilonka in Prague, always alone, what's up with that! Here at least there's peace and quiet. Clean in the old digs. It's not as messy with vomit on the stairs as it used to be. They sold it to us, and when we pay it off, it'll be all ours. It's not a bad place to live, and when Ivan gets sick and tired of that Prague, at least he'll have somewhere to come back to.

What's on the agenda for today, then? To the post office, to pick up the pension. They don't deliver it any more. There've been so many muggings. It don't take much effort to smack around a postman, and to mug an old lady, it's even easier. What can you do? Visit the graveyard, hoe around the old man's plot, and in the afternoon, in the afternoon, see what's up with Esmeralda, if she's gonna end up at last with that Alvar, that young José, he ain't got an ounce of sense in his whole head either, he don't, they're like little children, they are…

She grabbed her bag and her coat. Carefully, she locked both deadbolts and took the lift to the ground floor. To see if any mail came. Yeah, something's there. She opened the mailbox with her key. A letter. Whose writing is that? Return address? It's from Jana… Can it be? What could she still be writing to me for? She hasn't written in, what, three years? Since they got divorced… She wanted to open that letter then and there, it shook in her hand so. But she never did such a thing, read a letter out there in the corridor like some… She thrust it into her bag and set off for the post office. What on earth could she be writing to me about? What could that woman want to write to me about, after three years? old Mrs Berezová said to herself, shaking her head in disbelief.

THE THIRTY-EIGHTH

A little roller on the wall, a smoke-stained ceiling, a faded Mánes in a dusty frame. That's Romanticism for you, said Kosinský to himself, that same Kosinský who'd weighed on the conscience of Ivan Figura for more than twenty years now. He looked past the heads of all the other patrons in the At the Grinder pub in the Holešovice section of Prague. What are we waiting for here, really? Suddenly, he was upset — this happened sometimes, when life went stagnant like that flat beer, a third full, and you either order yourself a shot of something stiff, or you bugger off, and quick. Then, an unbelievably thin little fellow with a recessive chin and a pointy forehead entered the local. This was Prop, an old pal from the underground. He could hide behind a whip, he could, like in that nasty concentration camp joke. Kosinský glanced down at his irrepressibly expanding gut, and resignedly poured the rest of the beer into himself.

'So then that snitch who ratted you out back then has bought the farm,' said Prop to Kosinský, tossing down a magazine on the table in front of him. There was a headline with the word suicide, and a little further on, a question mark.

Out of habit, Kosinský brushed some non-existent hair from his face.

'Since when have you been reading shit like this?' he said, picking up the copy of *Super* that Prop had pushed in front of his eyes.

'Since they started writing about the voluntary exit from existence of the police confidant Ivan Bereza alias Figura.'

'Holy crap!' exclaimed Kosinský, rising so suddenly that he almost upset the table and the beer resting upon it. Standing, he read the lines that followed: *found by his own daughter on the kitchen floor overcome by gas fumes… all evidence points to suicide, even if the coroner is not eliminating the possibility of… a settling of scores amongst entrepreneurs…*

'That's him,' said Prop, noting significantly, 'the mills of God grind slowly…'

'Shut your gob. It's no certain thing, after all, that it was him who sang about the letter back then in the army. Somebody snitched on us, and then his name was on those lists, and that's all there is.'

'No, that's not all there is. He became a confidential agent in that very same year, and you were tossed into prison for a year for dishonouring the army, and if it hadn't been for that amnesty…'

'Fuck your eyes, you talk as if it was you that was locked up,' Kosinský tossed at Prop. He still wore his hair long, at least there, where it was still growing, and his eyes, bad to begin with, had been ruined all the more by a lot of basically unsuccessful editorial work. Back then, after the changes, they raced to publish everything they'd collected over the years. But what a hellish grind it had been to transcribe all those typewritten pages into digital form! Thanks to his imprisonment, for a certain time after the revolution, all doors stood open to Kosinský, everywhere. He obtained some computers, set himself up in publishing, and sat on committees of all sorts, but after bringing out a few books, they got bogged down. The business collapsed. Doors and hands that had been too swiftly spread open were just as swiftly closed, and they were happy in the end to pack up and get out of it all with nothing more than a few small debts. A few years passed, and Kosinský was thought of again more as an ex-con than a hero. Once, a little liquored up, he told Prop and a few of his mates that *If the Communists had beaten anybody, they sure beat me.*

He thought back to that letter from his army days: a man killed because of sloppiness, a murder covered up, human rights. He still felt the same way today. He didn't much like to talk about it with his wife Alice, without whom he'd've long ago been in the nuthouse or somewhere on the skids. He'd bellowed through so many nights, and she'd agreed with him so many times, that they were both sick and tired of it already. Of that wrong, which stirs no one anymore. Ridiculous and exhausted and with that prison baggage, shunted to the siding, with no money and health gone.

But exhaustion was not to have the last word with the Kosinskýs. They had a plan, which they kept entirely to themselves. They'd go off to a cottage in Lomnice, taking Kosinský's archive with them, and there they would slowly record in writing all the events that they could remember. Kosinský would supply the material and Alice would write; she has a perfect style, she's a trained Bohemist. They'll write a book together, which will be the greatest accusation of the whole age. Not an accusation, but a testimony, Alice always corrected him, that grand woman in her big hair and flamboyant clothes, whom no one would reckon for a PhD. So, to Lomnice. And so, Figura would also find his place in that book.

'So what was it with him, really?' Kosinský drew his gaze back to Prop. 'You know everything, after all, don't you?'

'Well,' Prop lit himself a cigarette and took a sip of beer, 'according to the official version, his daughter was to stay with him that weekend. He was divorced, and so got to be with her only from time to time. And this daughter, Ilona I think her name is, had her dog with her, and he starts to whine strangely when they get near the door. And the girl, fourteen years old maybe, when she opens the door and gets inside, there's this horrid smell, and she finds Daddy in the kitchen lying on the floor with his head in the oven. He was already dead.'

'Dear Lord Jesus a fourteen year old girl, at her Dad's. That's a blow, that is. Something like that'll have a lasting effect… Well, all right. But what's the word you hear round about?' Kosinský continued, a moment later.

'What do you mean "round about"?' Prop put on an expression of seeming incomprehension.

'Your own confidential sources.'

'My confidential sources tell me that Mr Figura was a capable businessman. A couple firms, you know, and ups and downs, switches, like on a mountain bike — cars, homes, anything you can name. He had a solid business and legal education and contacts. And he always said that he was as pure as the driven snow.'

'And what do you think?'

'Well, yeah. Everything pure, pure white.'

'Like a white horse?' said somebody at a nearby table.

'Well, there is that question mark over the suicide. In the papers they're writing that he had these bruises on his head — whether he banged it himself, or somebody helped him.'

He was unable to form a picture of him. Neither lying dead on the kitchen floor, nor back then in the army, when Figura probably betrayed him. Just a kind of a shadow, like a blurred photo from an old newspaper. Could be anybody. Suddenly, Kosinský got up to leave; he was feeling a little unwell, quite unwell actually, and everybody around him seemed faded and expressionless.

'It seems to me,' he said to Alice later that evening, 'that that Figura was from Ostrava, or somewhere thereabouts.'

'He was. I mean, we knew that.'

'I was there only once. But I believe that they have a little white horse on the city crest. I saw it on a trolleybus at the railway station.'

'Yes,' Alice confirmed. On its crest, Ostrava has a little white horse and a green four-leaved clover against a pale blue field.'

THE THIRTY-NINTH

'Little white horse / They haven't killed you, of course.' Those two lines formed the refrain of a long-forgotten poem written by Martin Vrána sometime in those dark seventies, when Ostrava was indeed a dirty city, both inside and out, so to speak. Back then, on account of the dirt, those little white horses on the logo of the transportation authority couldn't be made out at all on the sides of those legions of buses, buses and buses that one took from the housing estates to work and to school. Back then, it was cloudy even when the sun was shining. Today, when the decrementally wide-spread and dusted-off factories are barely breathing and fish have returned to the rivers, what's chiefly left behind is grime on the undersides and undercuts of thoughts and deeds, just like in any other city. But back in those days, when they heroically laid down suffocatingly thick eiderdowns of smog upon the city quarters, Martin would find, in secret, hidden and crouched places and moments, something white, shining in the gloom like a miracle. Maybe it wasn't a whiteness at all, but merely the desire for such, unattainable, on the borders of lassitude and the unconscious, a sort of faith which cannot be stained by that filth seeping from the Communist machines, something to which that scum will not stick as it does to the sides of the buses and to windows and generally to everything, which you have to keep washing, and which goes filthy again immediately it's been washed.

Back then, each week the Vrána brothers would go clean up the Protestant chapel on Ocelářská St. The careful, weekly scrubbing and ordering of the former pub hall, which the working-class founders of the local Protestant parish once rented for pious use was in and of itself a pious work. How many times must a taproom be cleaned before it can become the house of the Lord? How many buckets capped with foaming detergent, how many rags, dusters, scouring brushes and brooms does a black barrelhouse demand, before she becomes whiter than snow? The unending process of cleansing, bucket brigades of the parish elders and their families, just like the Sunday road to church through the streets of the gypsy ghetto, just like the Thursday Bible hours in that quarter where the proper citizens of the prefabs wouldn't dare set foot. For which reason, after Bible study, they went off to the bus stop in groups, and even so, the old stoolie across the street could see the whole thing as if on the palm of his hand, as he continued to monitor this activity, which was tolerated anyway — all of these exercises, which conceivably had their own inner theological and liturgical significance, Martin came to perceive as one great stubborn process of cleansing. And in his adolescent, romantic ardour, he might even be able to mumble something about ten righteous men in Sodom, who always, again and again, make something clean by their Sabbath attire, by familial will, by backsides in polyester trousers, by shutting off the morning television, by detergents and rags, hymns and prayers, and their searching for ways to bring the gospel to life, to cleanse the hand of the dirt that's eaten into it deeply and, in this way, to make the world a little whiter somehow. Such was Martin's most beautiful, and actually his only experience of the meaningfulness of the Christian community. Everything else he dared do, and eventually handle, by himself. For this reason alone was the cleansing of the whole community necessary, because in general, a person doesn't wash himself all that often.

And so in good faith Martin was scrubbing with a damp rag the red coconut-fibre carpet that ran the length of the chapel between the rows of folding chairs all the way to the Lord's table, when a knock came on the door. Martin unlocked it, and there, on the other side, stood a boy of about eighteen in a denim jacket with a cigarette dangling from his lips.

'You cleaning in there?'

'Yeah.'

'I live upstairs. Every Sunday morning I hear you all, those organs or what have you… You wake me up, actually. On Sunday morning I'm usually sleeping off a spree, and when I hear those organs, I say to myself O Fuck it's those Evangelists again.'

'We're called Evangelicals,' Martin corrected him.

'All right. Whatever. That's not the point,' the boy said. He seemed quite friendly.

'Can I come in?' he said, with one foot inside the chapel already. What now? Martin was filled to the neck with a sense of the inappropriateness of it all. But you can't refuse anyone entry to the house of the Lord, and anyway, who knows what he's looking for here — would I even dare get rough with him? He doesn't seem like a thug, but what if…

'You can, but there's no smoking in here.'

'What, you don't smoke?' asked the visitor with surprise.

'I do, but not in here.' The boy tossed his smoke away and came in.

'You've got a nice place here. Right enough, you do,' he whistled, nodding toward the Lord's table, with its relief of an open book and an alpha and omega.

'That's a good picture,' he said, in reference to a plaque on which the Lamb of God was carved. 'I figured you'd have a cross there.'

'Catholics have crosses.'

'Is that right? I only hear those organs all the time, you know? That them?'

'It's a harmonium.'

'Organs, harmonium, same thing,' he said, pulling out another cigarette and setting it between his lips.

'Hey man, you really can't smoke in here.'

'All right. I'll light it up outside. But you do have it nice here, and when you're singing, I can hear it all. Here's where I live, exactly here,' he said, pointing at the ceiling with his finger. 'My bed is right here above your altar.'

'So, come by some Sunday. You'll see what it's all like.'

'No man, I don't think that'd work. You know, I'm usually off with the gang to Permon on Saturdays and it's a long road — we're usually not back until well after midnight, so there's no chance of me getting up so early. I sleep till dinner time. Yeah, but you've got it nice here. But now I really do need a smoke. C'mon outside. My treat.'

They went out in front of the chapel and lit up. Both were in jeans and denim jackets; both had long hair. They looked just like two lads from the neighbourhood having a smoke together on the corner outside a tavern.

Martin had a look up Ocelářská Street and saw there sister Marie Rosenzweigová, an old white-haired lady who dedicated her life to Christian service. With her cane and her threadbare green coat she was drawing near with an alacrity peculiar to herself. She often came round to help out with the cleaning. When that visitor of his knocked on the door, Martin had thought it was her.

'I gotta get back to work,' Martin said quickly, crushing out his cigarette beneath his shoe.

He'd barely taken his broom in hand again when Marie was already bustling through the door.

'It's lovely, Martinku, that you're cleaning up here. I came by to dust, and we also need to take down the curtains. Sister Chrobáková will wash them if I take them over to her.'

Sister Marie set her cane aside and began to buzz about the chapel briskly. Feeble, emaciated, nothing but wrinkles, but with a smile and eyes that had a girlish shine to them. But she was a girl, after all, an old maid. A butcher's daughter, she stopped eating meat at fifteen — never even a slice of salami or a frankfurter, even though she delivered them in her basket to her father's wealthy customers. When she was twenty, she went off to Prague on foot, and when she got there after maybe a week's march, she succeeded in being received by His Excellency, Prof. Masaryk, President of the Republic. He devoted a few minutes to her, during which time she revealed to him what lay on her heart, and he helped her to a place in a mission school. In such a way, Marie became a missionary in the dark primeval forests of Vítkovice in those times of unemployment and universal drunkenness, during the war and after it as well. She nursed and tended to the incapacitated elderly, led the children of alcoholic families off to school, and the most various castaways and shipwrecks to Christ, until the Communists shut her mission down. When that happened she continued her work on her own. Old now, already a little senile too, but always out in the streets. Somebody always needed something, something that she could still handle.

During the evangelical services, always after the sermon, she'd request permission of the vicar to pray. She prayed aloud: first on behalf of the president, that the Lord would keep him in good health, and then for all the rest. It was always one and the same prayer, which most evidently played testingly on the nerves of the more dignified members of the assembly. When she prayed the Lord's care upon the health of His Excellency President Gustáv Husák, some of them in spirit (and not only) smacked themselves on the forehead. But Marie had shared one good experience with one president, and therefore believed that all presidents were alike.

It was this Marie whose thin little arms were steadying the ladder for Martin as he took down the curtains.

'You know, Martinku,' she said, 'my biggest concern is the youth of today. We oldsters are on the quick march to the Lord already, all of us, but the youth, the youth is the hope of the Church. So be careful up there now, and don't lean out so; come down rather and we'll shift the ladder so you don't fall.' Let's not shatter the hopes of the Church, thought Martin.

And so they took down all the curtains and packed them up nicely. Martin finished scrubbing the carpet. Marie wiped down all the chairs with her dust rag, and all was soon in order.

'And now, Martinku,' said sister Marie, taking him by the elbow, 'let's lift up a petition to the Lord together.' She knelt down and her gaunt hand, suddenly full of strength, pulled Martin down to his knees as well. They folded their hands and Marie prayed. And that prayer was to remain with Martin for the rest of his life. Amen.

THE FORTIETH

Seventieth birthdays tend to be grand affairs. At least in those families where birthdays are still affairs at all. Such was certainly the case in the family of Petr Vrána senior, Christian doctor, father of three sons.

'That cursed, lucky seventy…' Martin said to himself, searching among his clothes for a clean shirt. '…Seventy years lasted the Babylonian Captivity. Seventy years between each passing of Halley's Comet — few they are who see it twice. Seventy times you're supposed to forgive your brother,[20] so me and Dad still have a nice stockpile left over. The Soviet Union lasted seventy years? Or no? More or less — and that union was supposed to be eternal. I'd be interested to learn how old Oedipus was; if he killed young, he might've lived to seventy. It's doubtless old age at any rate.'

He knotted his tie and put on his suit, which otherwise he wore only for official purposes and court appearances, for which reason he kept it in a plastic bag in his armoire, protected from his other clothes. And now he hesitated, wondering whether he shouldn't zip himself up again in that plastic bag so as to protect himself from the celebration. Monika didn't want to go with him at any, I mean any, price. Finally, she consented to buy a little bouquet and show up for a moment to pay her respects to the old gentleman and then leave, leave at once, because she's got to study, really. Really she didn't, but otherwise, maybe she's right.

Then he went over to his ex-wife's to pick up the children, whom he was to take to the party chiefly because grandchildren are the light of their grandparents' lives, mainly because they're still little and unspoiled, and so you can see how your seed multiplies like the grains of sand upon the sea-

---

[20] See Matthew 18:22.

shore, as Jacob saw with his head resting on the stone.[21] His ex-wife would not be coming to the party, but she did send a present through Martin. The children were happy, because they liked parties; probably because they knew that they were the light of their grandparents' lives.

At his parents' flat, Martin's children went off to join the scrum of their cousins, and he went over to greet his father. And again that peculiar, anxiously irate smile — his manner of coping with such patriarchal situations, an elfin thorn of anger.

'And so you've come after all.' As if the matter of his coming were ever in doubt.

'Yep.'

'That's good. Have you brought the children?'

'They're with the others. Dana sends her apologies, you know, after all; and Monika, Monika's up to her neck with study, but she said she'd drop in sometime during the afternoon.'

'She ought to come to dinner.'

Martin shrugged his shoulders. In his father's eyes he could clearly read what his Dad thought of him and all of those things, but just at that moment — thank God — his oldest brother Petr from Germany came bursting through the door along with his entire family.

'How happy I'd be to have a talk with him sometime,' Martin confessed to his brother Tomáš in his parents' bedroom, into which both of them had ducked out of the universal uproar.

'You mean Dad?' Tomáš asked, who still wore his hair long, still balled all the girls, still treated his wife shabbily, still was pushy in an unhandsome way and generally still caused his parents the same sort of grief and worry as when he was young.

'I was thinking of Petr. Such a sound chap, and hardly a word escapes his mouth. I haven't had a real conversation with him, seriously, since he emigrated.'

<hr>

21   A conflation of two Old Testament references. During Jacob's dream in Genesis 28, he is promised that his seed 'shall be as the dust of the earth: thou shalt spread abroad to the west, and to the east, and to the north, and to the south' (28:14); whereas it is to Abraham that the Lord promises: 'I will bless thee, and I will multiply thy seed as the stars of heaven, and as the sand that is by the sea shore' (Genesis 22:17).

'Maybe he's forgotten, seriously, how to speak Czech,' Tomáš re-marked acidly, rummaging about his mother's chest of drawers for something.

'And here we go!' he cried. 'Remember this well, Martin — in the bed-room of every proper Protestant you'll find a bottle.' From beneath the linen he extracted a barely broached bottle of cognac. And they helped themselves.

Later, Martin went off to his mother in the kitchen. She was in over her head with it all, the fancy tableware, the soup, gateaux, salads, pota-to purée and, still at this zero hour, she had to fry up fifteen schnitzels, all the while mastering her emotions at having them all together here at once, under her roof. And to top it all off, the invasions of all the overheated grandchildren. Martin, perfectly set at ease by the cognac, expelled from the kitchen the grandkids clambering up after the cakes with the reminder that he was the Nasty Uncle. He took off his jacket, put on an apron and was already at work turning fifteen schnitzels in the pans, happy to be with his mother for a bit. He sensed that this would perhaps be the only real time they'd have alone the whole party long, and it meant so much to him.

'Don't be stingy with the oil, Martin, let them float rather than having them stick.'

The schnitzels were crackling; his mother's hands tossed the salad greens into bowls, preparing all the transient beauty of the food that one proper way, so that it might reflect the splendour of the grandest of feasts. To which we all shall suddenly be summoned, when that exquisite board, made up of course from two smaller tables pushed together beneath a tablecloth snow-white and starched like the robe of a high priest, will founder beneath piles of dirty tableware and stains. When our beloved and loving bodies will be reduced to a little bundle of bones, which the half-drunken gravedigger, according to ancient custom, will set at the head of the next arrival in the pit. Only this brief flicker, at which Martin and his mother were presently labouring, and which, God grant, shall descend upon the table like the fire upon Elijah,[22] only this has meaning,

....

22   An obscure reference. In 2 Kings 2:11 (4 Kings 2:11), we find the familiar passage of the chariot and horses of fire that descended to Elijah to bear him into heaven 'by a whirlwind,'

                                        JAN BALABÁN

and for this reason fifteen schnitzels must be turned on the pan, pyramids of potato purée must be heaped up, plates must be polished to a sparkle, the soup tureen warmed and the cloves finely diced indeed.

....
while in 2 Kings 1:12 (4 Kings 1:12) as 'a man of God' Elijah calls down the fire of heaven to consume some people he's not pleased with.

THE FORTY-FIRST

After the party, Martin took the children back to Dana and made his way back to his little flat more or less by muscle memory. He fell on his bed, lit up a cigarette, only to crush it out immediately and toss it out the window. What now? He hated such compulsory questions as much as he did his aimless wandering from window to door, and his useless crashing on the bed and getting back up again neurotically and sitting down at his table, the pointless picking up and setting back down of the work in front of him. He suddenly had the sense of it all being wrong and that it always had been wrong, that we're just playing at it, that we're merely sort of celebrating, that we just kind of muddle along gaily, doing well at the very edge of the abyss.

He glanced at the mirror on the wall angrily, his face heavy, as if worked up out of ash, cinders. In the gloom he could only make out his father's traits — he couldn't see himself there at all. Suddenly, he understood what nonsense it was to wish to see oneself through one's own eyes. When he's alone, a person probably ceases to exist. What a dreadful mistake it is to think that when I'm alone — and I'm almost constantly alone — I am myself. That's exactly what I'm not. The old pious women believe that the time they spend in church will be added to the length of their lives. And as for me, I know that every second spent in this wretched loneliness will be cruelly cut off from the remaining balance of my life. But what then, Monika? — I'm supposed to let someone in here? I'd rather go off after a whore and screw her for money, just so I could remain alone all the same.

The reflection in the mirror had now lost any sort of sensible form. It was just a glossy smudge on the dusty pane of the glass, that's all. He sensed a queasiness; he felt something move about inside him, something foreign still, but which was sure to take up residence within him sometime soon.

He felt his physical disgust transform itself into some sort of complacency in the face of everything being wrong. Wrong, wrong, wrong!

He unscrewed the cap of a bottle of vodka and took a deep pull.

'Who drinks alone drinks with the devil,' he said aloud, and took another drink.

With each successive swallow of the booze he felt a greater… not a greater thirst, but a greater hunger. The warmth in his stomach, the astringent, persistent sense of the exhaustion of all his reserves.

I've got to walk it off. He grabbed his jacket and his shoes and headed out. But the early spring is the very worst time for something like that. The bare earth and the bushes along the railway line were covered with litter. So many crumpled plastic wrappers, bottles, cinders, fag-ends and piles of dog shit. What's going on here? Here in this subway beneath the rumbling corpus of the railway — what is this greasy filth, with which the water is clogged, ankle-deep?

Who makes us live here? Here amidst these bushes, from the bare branches of which tatters of plastic flutter? Here, where iron plates crumble to rust, where even iron is exhausted, handrails sag, tracks are empty, buildings shuttered, windows grim and grimy with poisoned perspectives and retrospectives on the low sky from which this dreadful April drizzle is seeping. Who was it fixed these sights before our eyes? How am I to walk off my despair, how do I get rid of this dreadful hunger?

I beseech you, merciful nettles, strike up from the soil; burdock, by your grace, spread your leaves over this filth. Crowns of the trees, of the Judas-aspens, cover it all, with your green and grey anxiety, block from our view these emaciated structures, which are unable to bear even their own weight.

He stopped on the railway bridge that crosses the brown waters of the Odra. The muddy spring current seemed to push the bridge backwards, upstream somewhere. Martin's head was spinning. He didn't know where to direct his steps now, at all. It would be best just to remain here, without having to decide which bank to head for. He stood amidst the webbing of the trusses as a train clattered past behind him.

One can always find a taproom where they'll be glad to pour one for a man who drinks with the devil. And soon there were those three rusty rums at the station buffet. When Martin had swallowed down the third, he felt that anything might happen now. He glanced out into the street above, which the disk of the sun at evening was slanting like some kind of clumsy, grinning face. Its light flowed over the contours of all things like mercury, and it seemed as if mercury was flowing through his veins as well. He sensed an acrid, sharp taste on his tongue, felt a flame in his belly, in that painful cavern of his body, for which he suddenly felt sorry. He felt sorry for the whole world, writhing in the throes of the all-encompassing, all-penetrating void.

'I've never yet felt such a hunger,' he whispered in a tremulous voice, as if he wished to share that thought with some dear being.

Then he took three steps outside and at the fourth he was slammed off his feet by a dreadful impact. He rolled over the hood and his head struck against the windscreen, a few centimetres away from the terrified face of the woman who had been driving. The centripetal force of her violent braking had lifted her out of her seat and propelled her so close to him that, in that fraction of a second, it seemed as if they were about to kiss through the glass. The car came to a stop and sloughed him off the hood, and he, his hand flapping helplessly as a rag, fell, striking his head against the travertine kerb. The woman kept her calm, stepped on the gas and drove off before anyone could note down the registration numbers on her license plates. And Martin, in some recess of unconsciousness, experienced a moment of rest.

THE FORTY-SECOND

When it became clear that evening that Martin wasn't coming over, Monika actually breathed easier. This had been her first peek inside the Vrána family and even now, after her bath, after a little wine (which she'd actually bought for Martin), even with a little wine in her head and her gaze fixed on the lit windows of the buildings far across the way, she was still agitated. This was a feeling not entirely unlike that which once took hold of her after some scumbag had tried to rape her in the park. He threw himself on her from the rear, and with his horrid arms and his horrid words overcame her at first. Up until then, Monika had never known that she could scream so loudly. That scream, which must have been heard all the way on the other side of town, saved her. And when he tried to stifle her with his hand she bit him so hard that her mouth filled with blood. Later, she wasn't sure if that blood was from his hand, or from her own battered lips. She screamed and kicked, kicked, kept on kicking until, suddenly, she found herself alone; ruffled, sure, but unviolated, unpenetrated, the victor who had successfully defended herself. Only it took a long, long while for her to get over that feeling left by the ferocious grappling, the agitation, the feeling that she was about to die at the very apex of her throbbing life.

No one laid a finger on her today. She only gave some flowers to an old white-haired man, whose gaze pierced her, deeply, very deeply, after which she somehow allowed herself to be wedged in amongst all those relatives, set at the mercy of a benign interest and the attention of people who somehow dreadfully belonged together, to one another. She kept quiet and breathed in shallow breaths, as if in a submarine, where oxygen must be conserved. And then a family picture and Martin's hand absurdly on her shoulder. She shut her eyes at the exact moment that the Nikon in his brother Tomáš's hand flashed. It was almost a swoon. It seemed to her that everyone was speaking dreadfully loudly in a language that she understood only very imperfectly. She excused herself as quickly as she could. Even at parting out in the corridor she couldn't say anything personal to Martin. For all the love she bore him, she couldn't forgive him that. When he kissed her on the lips, it was the kiss of a stranger, a member of some clan, and she's an alien, she has no clan. Thank God. All those men and women and children pushing forward. Away, away!

In the darkening room, clenched by a vague fear and anger at Martin for doing that to her, she rolled back her thoughts. She thought back on that surprising, staggering feeling of reality when she ran away from her mother. The whole world had suddenly bristled against her like a deep, deep forest surrounding a little child. That doesn't just happen in fairy tales; fairy tales are about that. How quickly did she take back her plan, the plan of a young woman, to find her own lodgings, somehow, to find a job and live on her own, going wherever she wanted to go, sleeping with whomever she chose to sleep with. Liberated at last from the clan, from that most tightly-knit clan of all, the clan of two. But what was she actually doing? Merely putting off the moment when she would have to admit that she couldn't handle this a single day, a single night. She sat around in empty clubs with empty people. She slept with a boy she didn't trust, with that beautiful, long-haired Igor before whom she felt ashamed, really, especially when the light of day overtook her. She felt ashamed before him, and for him. They crawled into one another's arms just to beat away that shame. To let yourself be fucked, to let yourself even be punctured a bit and feel that force spilling through your veins, that alien force. To lay on the floor of some room like wrung-out rags, a room being paid for anyway by Igor's mother. To feel the edges of reality and do nothing with it all. To not allow anyone to chatter you into life. If only it were possible to be alone!

THE FORTY-THIRD

Ester Tomská, that important, tall woman, who, following an unsuccessful but fortunately — as she said with a bit of nostalgia, into the depths of which she allowed very few people to gaze — fortunately childless marriage, returned to her maiden name, had reckoned that nothing in life would be able to knock her off balance again, so soon. She cared for her peace and privacy, to which access was forbidden to all save one good friend, with the same sort of quiet toughness as her mother. Like that mother, who had once hurt her, and whom, as the years advanced, she began to feel respect, again. However, that was taking place only on the inside, in the development of her thoughts and attitudes, whereas on the outside she was unable, or unwilling, to break the frosty silence that reigned between them for more than twenty years now. Just here or there she'd catch herself thinking of her mother, or perhaps speaking to her in thought. She thought of her rather as if she were dead, as someone whose legacy we come to terms with as the years pass, and our bitter memories become sweet with the passage of time.

Her work in systems analysis afforded her a lot of time to wander about in thought and in the vicious circles of memory. For she was a good, even an excellent, analyst, and her grip of communication systems and languages superseded by far the requirements of those few primitive tasks, which the well-paying mobile phone network demanded of her. Only during the occasional periods of troubleshooting, or in the crises which could occur in the network, could her job completely consume her for a few hours or days, filling her with the happiness of problem-solving. Otherwise she remained at the mercy of simple tasks and the challenges resulting therefrom.

Once, her doubts and feelings of the senselessness of it all had driven her to chuck everything and escape, as she herself described it, 'to the tower' on the summit of Praděd, where she spent a year working as a simple operator.

That place — a desolate plain, a transmission tower with the world off in the distant valleys — suited her somehow. Already on account of her height, which had once destined her for an unsuccessful career in volleyball, she seemed herself like a tower patiently stretching up towards the inimical heavens. Those feelings, unfortunately, could not simply be shooed away by well-aimed smashes and capably timed blocks. What kept her involved in sport and other such collective activities, more than her physique, was her skin-and-bones-emaciated, stubborn soul and the unconscious terror of her body, which remained incomprehensible to her for long years. Incomprehensible even to that little fellow whom she mistakenly married.

She came to realise that life at the tower was only possible if a person had somewhere to return to, from it. She had no such place, and so, after a year of Jeseníky winds, mountain tramping and lonely bottles of wine in high chalets she returned once more to the valley. This was all the more easy for her to do given the fact that, in an age of universal computer illiteracy, she was one of a mere handful of people truly learned in the field, and this opened doors for her everywhere. At the same time, it was all the more difficult in that, given the fact of her being practically without any personal ties, and rather prone to escape, she felt a strong repugnance for permanent residences. Who knows what it would be like if the world were actually as empty as it appeared to her to be? But the world is greater than our resistance to it, and it might turn out that the seeker will actually come across a sign, and the refugee might find a refuge after all. This sign and refuge, in Ester's case, became incarnate in her friend Pavla.

'What would have become of me, had we never met?' she once remarked to Pavla during a walk along the Laba in Pardubice.

'And of me?' replied the younger, dark-haired woman, so roundly adhering to Ester's emaciated lankiness. They strolled along the river together, not giving a fig for what anyone thought. At last, everything's in order, as Ester might have said, and indeed once had said.

But now that same Ester, whom nothing was really to knock off balance any more, was holding the strangest letter in her hand. Perhaps the only non-official correspondence she had received in many years. The character of the writing was not her mother's, but somewhat similar to it. Well, then? She slit open the envelope and read the salutation: *Dear sister!* The exclamation point was there, too. Here's that little Monika screeching like a bird in her orderly flowing heavens. Dear sister! That little slant-eyed brat, that little Chink, who expelled Ester from her maternal home and drove her father Alfréd Tomský out on the paths of melancholy alcoholism, where he stumbled about still from woman to woman, from one void to another. That little girl, who upturned their family, even when she was still at rest in her mother's womb, is writing here: *Dear…* Ester was suddenly knocked over by a wave of tenderness, a wave all the more strong, for communicating to her analytical mind that just a short while ago there would be no place for tenderness here at all, but rather tightly compressed lips, through which the slightest word would not pass.

'Little Monika,' she whispered, and read through the startling letter. Her analytical mind told her that, had it not been for Pavla, she wouldn't even have read it; but it also told her that, had it not been for that little creature, whom her mother had carried home beneath her heart from her last residency in America, Ester would never have set off on the road, at the end of which Pavla, her love, was waiting. Her analytical brain once again pulled up at the moment when her stubborn soul was wavering between anger and joy.

Without a word, she handed the letter to Pavla, who had been following the changes passing over her face for some time.

'You must call her,' Pavla said, once she read it through.

'I must?'

'We must.'

'And why, exactly?'

'Because, as the saying goes, the angel never knocks twice at your door.'

She unlocked the door. The lock was stubborn to the new-cut key, which Martin had her copy not too long ago, and which she was using for the first time. But it turned in the end. She entered, set her bag on the floor and looked around the room. Everything was different than before. Unbearably real and abandoned: the stacks of books on the floor, the dusty monitor and keyboard, on which someone had been writing, often, and long, with unwashed hands. The mirror, the comb and the shaving things on the writing table, Alpa francovka, the cooking pot she had given him, with dry coffee grounds on the bottom, shirts in varied degrees of cleanliness on hangers in the armoire, beer bottles arranged in a row along the wall. All of this smelt of Martin, like the unemptied ashtray on the windowsill at the head of the bed. She spilled it in the rubbish.

Martin's momentary rest now stretched out into a long unconsciousness, in which he had lain for five whole days since the accident. No one knew what had happened to him. It was unbearable. He lay there in the intensive care ward, enclosed within himself, as if he were never more to come round. Monika, a student of social medicine, was no expert on brain injuries, but she knew that a thing like this could either turn out well or completely dreadfully. And she'd rather not think of what Martin's father said, when she'd come across him in the hospital, both dressed in hospital whites, both of them feeling somehow to blame for Martin's collision with an unknown car. He was, after all, coming from his birthday celebration. He was, after all, coming over to see her. But why he should take a route across the railroad tracks on the very other side of town, no one had the foggiest. Monika gazed at him through the glass pane and asked, silently: Where are you? Where is a person's soul? Is there even such a thing? And will it be the same one, when it returns, if it does return at all?

And now she's standing here next to her bag as if she were on a railway platform, feeling that she ought to leave as soon as possible. That it might not have been the best idea to move into his flat, while he's not even in the world. She ought to go away from this world, which belongs to a stranger. She wasn't here for the first time, but actually she was, even if they'd made love back then on that bed, and over there, on the floor beneath the window. They had been drinking wine, and the dawn was coming up outside. She didn't go away. She lay down on his bed. After a moment, she even put on his big blue T-shirt, in which he often slept. She covered herself in his blanket, closed her eyes, and waited.

Suddenly, she realised that she was afraid of him. She wanted to be afraid for him, but she was afraid of him. With her eyes closed, she rolled over under his blanket and waited for him. For that dreadful man to come along and wound her. To throw her beneath the wheels of a car and then look on as her blood flowed, and then feel sorry for her and say that things like that can happen. She saw his dreadful hands, so often unwashed and with broken nails, his face, on which his beloved, boyish features gave way to hard, pitiless edges. His stomach, which would only swell larger with time, his sex, that weapon of his, with which he wounded other women, when, faithlessly, he procured himself pleasure and others — pain. He was unfaithful to his wife, unfaithful to that Eva of his, unfaithful to everybody. Ah, Martin, you're the guy who buttons his trousers and goes off on his own roguish way. Right now, in hospital, you have no feelings for anyone. You're a dreadful, dreadful person. What dreadfulness you carry around inside yourself! I can understand each and every woman who runs off as soon as she catches sight of you. I can understand each and every wife who runs off from her husband, who doesn't want anything to do with him, with that unshaven mug, scratchy beneath the neck, with those sly glances that pierce to the very heart.

She pulled her knees up to her chin and fell asleep like a child in her mother's womb. Such was her path, her struggle. When she was overcome, when she lost control of things that piled on her, she neither moaned nor sobbed — she was able to fall asleep. Up on the roof some pigeons were cooing. They entered Monika's dream and suddenly she felt good wrapped up in Martin's blanket. She awoke only to say to herself how good she suddenly felt. And that's how they began living together.

THE FORTY-FIFTH

They went on long walks under the great ash trees, the bark of which went green and black after a rain. Around the last cottages of Lomnice, and then further, along a sunken lane running between freshly ploughed fields, over the turned earth of which flocks of small birds fluttered. The mound called Klobouk shut the vista of the entire area before them. How simple and good, Alice said to herself. Just the arc of that mound and the blue-grey sky — what else could a person want from life? It was a precise image — her in a short black coat and a long woolen dress, her big flouncy hair pulled up into a careless bun, and alongside her, Kosinský in his old green army coat, in wildly coloured trousers, eternally stooped and eternally smoking. Their bundled-up figures at the base of Klobouk and the black dots of the birds in the cold autumn air. And the silence, a silence you have to learn how to hear, after which it feels so good.

Alice never believed that it would work out like this. Everything became real only after Kosinský learned of Figura's death. Suddenly, he was completely gone. Or, rather, he wanted to be gone. They sold their flat in Prague, piled computer, boxes of papers, and a few sacks of things into the car and they disappeared, as if from the face of the earth, as one of their friends put it. They really did settle down in Lomnice and Kosinský really did begin to work on that book. It was no simple affair. At first he was only interested in the cottage and didn't even want to hear of those papers. He crawled up on the roof, he repaired the floor, he put up a new fence, dug around the base of a wall that was always getting soaked. Who would've thought that the old bear knew how to do so many things? Sometimes, he went for a beer and chewed the fat with the local lads. He even started to think about farming.

'After what I've been through with people, it'd be better to spend my time among the cows and pigs. They, at least, are creatures of God,' he would say.

His old Catholic faith also came back to life, and quite regularly he practised his obligation, going to Mass each Sunday. Such a country boy I have, Alice said to herself, but she made no objections, and drove off to the district town to teach Czech at the local lyceum.

'All documents are repulsive,' Kosinský said to her one evening. 'I can't even look at those papers. I'd soonest toss them all into the stove.'

'And burn the house down while you're at it?'

He didn't burn down the house; he merely took his voluminous archive down into the cellar and shoved it in an old chest of drawers, which he locked. Then he went off to the tavern and got as drunk as a lord. Alice heard him stumbling through the house, bellowing about those Communist motherfuckers, the present government, the whole world and that idiotic shit called capitalism and democracy. Alice froze in fear of the bad old days returning, but she let him get it all out of him, as before. Some two days later they began to work on the book. All through the evenings he would fill up lined notebooks, without letting anyone read what he was writing. When she asked him why he wasn't writing on the computer, he said that writing was a personal thing and must be done by hand.

'So what are you writing about now?' she asked him as they slowly ascended Klobouk.

'About my childhood.'

'You were writing about your childhood back in the spring already.'

'One's childhood lasts a long time.'

'You're right about that. Childhood is the longest time of all.'

They found themselves on the bald brow of Klobouk, and before their eyes the pasturelands and woods spread out their green against the greyish blue. The ridge of the mountains was lost already in the coming darkness.

THE FORTY-SIXTH (AND LAST)

His keys, papers, telephone, money and bank cards had been stowed in the safe in the trauma unit. His clothes, soiled with dirt and blood, had been taken away by his mother to launder them. Just as she used to do, back when he still lived with his parents and brothers in a small two-plus-one. When they brought home a great brown crate with the logo Tatramat and extracted therefrom their first automatic washer with the glass door in the front and a programme panel allowing for various cleaning cycles for the laundry that would soon be tumbling behind that glass eye like some sort of cosmic phenomenon. His father and his technically adroit brother Petr hooked up the hoses and his mother began the first ever load. For her, laundering and ironing for a husband and three sons was merely the continuation of the destiny of an only sister of three brothers and a daughter of a strict mother. The laundering of men's clothes oppressed her all her life long, and it would be a lie to suggest that she always did it gladly. When she set the stained clothes of her youngest son to soak, she wept and asked herself... no, she didn't ask, it just occurred to her to ask, but such questions lead to nothing good. She treated the bloodstains with chemical agents and then put the clothes into the washer in hopes that soon she'd be ironing them, and soon Martin would be putting them on.

Martin, meanwhile, was lying in a hospital bed in a room filled with light and a silence that was wordlessly affecting his disconnected senses. Calmed to an almost deathly extent, he seems quite all right. The machines to which he was hooked up might suggest to the uninformed onlooker that it was they, actually, who were the cause of this unconscious peace of an otherwise living and healthy man. That the sensitive extremities of the probes and the mouths of the little hoses were what was holding the brain, otherwise ready to dawn, and the restless heart, in sleep. You only need unplug them all and he'd get up again; he'd be back to doing all those rash things.

This might last years, Mr Vrána, the retired physician, realised as he pulled a borrowed white coat on, over his civilian clothes, and went off to visit someone who could neither welcome, nor refuse, any visits. He recalled the case of a person whose head had been split open by the pole of a wagon pulled by spooked horses when it bashed through the windscreen of his car during a crash on a mountain road. He lay here for some years — three, as a matter of fact. A chain of relatives kept vigil by his bedside in shifts, beseeching the doctors all day long with their desperate arguments and God with their seething prayers. The reawakening of their son, father and husband had become the touchstone of their faith. But there had been happier cases too, Mr Vrána sighed to himself as he entered the room.

He bent down over Martin, stroked his head and spoke to him, as if his son were able to hear him. The ICU had a depressing effect on him. In these professional surroundings, where a doctor must always be ready with expert advice, a father's emotions only get in the way. He spoke with the attending physician and nurse. The cold terminology and assessment of the patient became a support for him in a situation which could not be solved by any further measures, or will. Everything possible has already been done; now it all depends on him. It was a fine phrase that; he'd used it many times himself, but only now did he understand how truly fine it was.

Night fell on the institute. A great cube set on a hill above the city, it shone through the night with the muted aquarium lights of its rooms. It might occur to a person passing by at night in a tram, whose eyes were drawn to those windows; or a person who hears from afar the siren of an ambulance speeding through the nocturnal streets; or a person who, in the middle of the night, rises, and, moved by an indefinable fear, paces through his dark flat to check on his sleeping family, that safety and security are never quite impregnable.

On the next day, Martin opened his eyes. The nurse was there. Her starched cap was whiter than snow in the mountains. Just an ordinary woman at work.

She said to him, 'So we're back, are we? We're back, Mr Vrána?'

He gazed up at her smiling face in that room full of the light of the rainy sky outside and everything, everything, came back to him, all the memories arose again from their shallow graves.

'We're here,' Martin said to the nurse.

Amended 17.03.2005

GLOSSARY

Agent assigned to Church matters. Církevní tajemník. A Communist official of the *Státní úřad pro věci církevní* (State Office for Ecclesial Matters) reporting on the doings of the clergy.

Alpa francovka. A Czech joint massage lotion.

Anatomy of Love. Anatomia Miłości (1972). Directed by Roman Załuski, screenplay by Ireniusz Iredyński. A Polish film starring Barbara Brylska and Jan Nowicki.

Babička, Barunka. References to the Czech Biedermeyer novel *Babička* [Grandma, 1855] by Božena Němcová (1820–1862), an idyll of the late 'national revival' period, in which the main character, the old 'Grandma' is an incarnation of the goodness and wisdom of the Czech people.

Bezruč, Petr (1867–1958). Czech poet, associated with the culture of Czech Silesia. Originally from Orava, which is about half an hour's train journey from Ostrava, where Balabán's novel is set. The citation is from his poem 'Maryčka Magdonová (Slezské písně)' [Maryčka Magdonová, a Silesian Song]. *'Šel starý Magdon z Ostravy domů, / v bartovské harendě večer se stavil, / s rozbitou lebkou do příkopy pad. / Plakala Maryčka Magdonova'* [Old Magdon was on his way home from Ostrava, / At evening he stopped at the Bartovice inn, / He fell in a ditch, with his skull smashed in, / And Maryčka, Magdon's wife, sobbed.']

Chartists. A reference to those who signed the Karta 77, a document of Czech and Slovak dissidents protesting the government's violations of civil rights in Czechoslovakia. Among the signatories was the author's uncle, noted Protestant theologian Milan Balabán (1929–2019).

Esmeralda. A Mexican re-make of a Venezuelan soap opera, starring Leticia Calderón and Fernando Colunga. It was popular in East-Central Europe in the 1990s.

General (Admiral) Nachymov. A Soviet liner, which sunk in the Black Sea near midnight on 31 August 1986, after being struck by another ship. Perhaps because of the proximity in time, the name of the ship is fresh in Martin's mind.

GSM. In the early days of mobiles, GSM was a European standard for 2G networks.

Hašler, Karel (1879–1941). Czech actor, director and songwriter. Author of patriotic songs, for which he was arrested by the Gestapo and murdered in Mauthausen. His works were suppressed by the Czechoslovak Communists after the war.

Holy Wednesday. Škaredá středa, literally 'ugly Wednesday,' is the Wednesday of Holy Week. In Czecho-Slovak regions, it is customary for boys to parade the streets making loud noises on wooden knockers — ironically, so as to 'chase Judas away.'

Hukvaldy. Town in Czech Silesia. Its most famous son is the composer Leoš Janáček, q.v.

Hunters of Mammoths. Historical novel by Eduard Štorch, first published in 1918 as *Lovci mamutů: Čtení o praobyvatelích země České* [Hunters of Mammoths: a Story of the Ancients Inhabiting the Czech Lands]. It was illustrated by Jaroslav Panuška and Zdeněk Burian.

Húsak, Gustav (1913–1991). The last first secretary of the Czechoslovak Communist Party; the last Communist President of Czechoslovakia before the Velvet Revolution of 1989, which, following the events in Poland, swept the Communists from power. He ruled Czechoslovakia for quite a long time, initiating in 1969 the period of 'normalisation' which began with the fall of the Prague Spring and reimposition of Soviet hegemony (after Alexander Dubček's experiment of 'Socialism with a human face.') For his docility towards the USSR, he won the unflattering nickname 'Húsak-Rusak.' A Slovak, it is rumoured that Húsak converted to Catholicism on his deathbed.

Janáček, Leoš (1854–1928). Czech composer, associated with Moravia, from which folklore he drew inspiration. *Jenůfa* (1904) is a work of his, and is often spoken of as the national opera of Moravia.

Kremlička, Rudolf (1886–1932). Czech modernist painter, member of the Tvrdošíjní (Hard-head) group, who favoured primitivism in art, but a sly primitivism, which betrays great skill and care in conception and execution. Many of his nudes and paintings of women in general are slightly abstract, soft, gentle and rounded female forms that seem to glow with a warm light.

Lahváč. A Czech pilsner brewed in Hanušovice, near Olomouc in Moravia.

Man on fire. This may refer to the death by self-immolation of Jan Palach (1948–1969), who set himself on fire protesting the Soviet occupation of Czechoslovakia following the suppression of the Prague Spring. He committed suicide on 16 January 1969 (dying three days later). On 25 February 1969, Jan Zajic (1950–1969) repeated the act, as did Evžen Plocek (1929–1969).

Mánes, Josef (1820–1871). Czech painter of the Romantic period.

Masaryk, Tomáš Garrigue (1850–1937). Czech philosopher and statesman, architect of the Czechoslovak Republic following the breakup of

the Austro-Hungarian Empire. He served as the first president of
Czechoslovakia, from its establishment in 1918 until 1935.

Novotný, Antonín (1904–1975). First Secretary of the Communist Party (and
thus head of state) of Czechoslovakia from 1953–1968. A blacksmith
by trade, he was a hardliner — replaced by Alexander Dubček during
the short-lived Prague Spring, which sought to relax the oppressive
policies of the Soviet-sponsored Communist regime and introduce
'socialism with a human face.'

Olaši Vlaši Laši. The names of various tribes of gypsies, or Roma, of which
there are many in Slovakia and Moravia.

Permon. A resort in Slovakia.

Preisler, Jan (1872–1918). Czech painter; a follower of Gaugin who evolved
towards a Klimt-like Art Nouveau expressiveness. The painting that
Martin is referring to is his *Black Lake* (1900).

Red Dragon. Červený drak. An Octoberfest-style lager brewed in Brno. It
has an ABV of 6%.

ROH — Revolučni Odborové Hnutí, or Revolutionary Trade Union
Movement, a Communist organisation in Czechoslovakia.

Soviet Army and the hooligans in Prague. The teacher (in both cases,
the word is *učitelka,* i.e. a female teacher) is toeing the Party line.
Unnerved at the loosening of totalitarian control in Czechoslovakia
during the so-called Prague Spring (5 January–21 August 1968)
ushered in by the reforming politician Alexander Dubček (1921–
1992), the Soviet Union invaded Czechoslovakia with military troops
in order to quash the liberalising movement, which was ardently,
and actively, supported by the people of Bohemia, Moravia and
Slovakia. Along with the Red Army, troops from Poland, Hungary
and Bulgaria invaded Czechoslovakia under the euphemistic slogan
of 'fraternal aid.'

StB — *Státní bezpečnost*, 'State Security' in English; the internal intelligence-gathering service of Communist Czechoslovakia; counterpart of the Soviet KGB.

Svoboda, Ludvík (1895–1979). Czechoslovak general, who served in both world wars, first as an Austro-Hungarian soldier, then a member of the Czechoslovak Legions, and finally in the forces of independent Czechoslovakia. President of Czechoslovakia from 1968 until 1975; a member of the short-lived reforming government of Alexander Dubček during the Prague Spring, as well as the harsher, Soviet-imposed government of Gustáv Husák, which succeeded it.

Šerák, Keprník, Vozka, Petrovy kameny. Mountains in the north-east of the Czech republic, in the Hrubý Jeseník range in Moravia/Silesia, near the Polish border.

Šumava. An unspoiled natural region of south-west Bohemia, on the border with Bavaria. Also known as the Bohemian Forest. Now a national park, the area was cleared of inhabitants following the Second World War (especially the Germans who lived there), and was a sort of no-man's land, patrolled by the border forces of the Communist Czechoslovak state — as it had become a popular, if difficult, area for attempted escapes across the Iron Curtain into West Germany.

Švanda. The name of Balabán's party hack is the same as that of a legendary bagpiper from the city of Strakonice. The Romantic poet and dramatic Josef Kajetán Tyl (1808–1856) dramatised the tale in his *Strakonický dudák anebo Hody divých žen* [The Strakonice Bagpiper, or the Feast of Wild Women, 1847].

Tatranka. Czech sweets made of layered wafers covered in chocolate. They were originally triangle-shaped, like the summits of mountains — hence the name (cf. Tatra Mountains).

Truth, which shall be victorious. Pravda vítězí — 'the truth prevails.' This, the Czech national motto, is derived from the words of Jan Hus (1369–

1415), a Czech priest burnt at the stake in Konstanz for preaching nationally-tinged theology, which would later embolden Martin Luther and set off the Protestant reformation a century after his death. Although a national hero to many Czechs in opposition to the Catholic Habsburgs who ruled Bohemia, Moravia and Slovakia for many centuries, he is especially dear to the hearts of the Protestant minority in the country — to which Martin and his family belong.

Třešňák, Vlastimil (born 1950). Czech musician. A signatory of the Charta 77, for which he was forced to emigrate to Sweden, from which he returned to Czechoslovakia only after the fall of Communism in the early 1990s. His name is somewhat homophonic with *třešňovice*, i.e. Kirsch.

Tunnellers — 'Barabové,' miners employed at the dangerous task of boring the deep tunnels that lead to the coal face. The Czech term derives from the patron saint of miners, St Barbara (sv. Barbora).

Tyger, tyger burning bright. The first line of the poem 'The Tyger' by the English Romantic William Blake (1757–1827). 'Tyger Tyger, burning bright, / In the forests of the night; /What immortal hand or eye, / Could frame thy fearful symmetry?'

Union of Socialist Youth. The Communist *Socjalistický sváz mládeže*, an organisation that ceased to exist with the fall of Communist rule in 1989.

Viktorka. A reference to a character from the the late Romantic novel *Babička, obrazy venkovského života* [Grandma, Scenes from Life in the Country], 1855, by Božena Němcová (1820–1862). Although the character of Viktorka has gone mad on account of an unhappy love, the fact that she inhabits the woodlands (becoming something of a forest nymph) fits with Mrs Vránová's nostalgic memories of a childhood spent amongst the elements of nature.

Voznesensky, Andrei Andreyevich (1933–2010). Russian poet, by turns persecuted and promoted by the Soviet government.

Vlčina. Vlčina Frenštát Pod Radhoštěm. A hotel south of Ostrava.

Women's League. Československý sváz žen (Czechoslovak Union of Women). A feminist organisation, it continues to exist to this day.

ABOUT THE AUTHOR

Jan Balabán was born in Šumperk, a town near the city of Olomouc in what was at the time Czechoslovakia, on 29 January 1961. He was raised in the city of Ostrava, which lies some 92 kilometres southwest of his birthplace. It is this city that forms the backdrop for most of his fiction.

He entered the University of Olomouc in the 1980s, where he studied Czech and English. Upon graduation, he began work as a technical translator in Ostrava. Up until the Velvet Revolution and the fall of Communism in 1989, his works were clandestinely published; like his brother the painter Daniel Balabán and so many other artists of his generation, he was a dissident.

Before his sudden and untimely death on 23 April 2010, he had published several books, mostly collections of short stories, in the now unfettered press of the free Czech Republic. These are: *Středověk* [Middle Age, 1995] *Boží lano* [The Rope of God, 1998], *Prázdniny* [Holidays, 1998], *Možná, že odcházíme* [Maybe We're Leaving, 2004 — available in English from Glagoslav], and *Jsme tady* [Here We Are, 2006]. He also published two novels, *Černý beran* [The Black Ram, 2000] and the book in hand *Kudy šel anděl* (Where was the Angel Going?, 2003], a screenplay *Srdce draka* [The Heart of a Dragon, 2001] and a stageplay entitled *Bezruč?!* [No Hands?!, 2009] in collaboration with Ivan Motýl. *Zeptej se táty* [Ask Dad], the manuscript of a novel that he was working on at his death, was posthumously published in 2010.

ABOUT THE TRANSLATOR

Charles S. Kraszewski (b. 1962) is a poet and translator, writing in both English and Polish. He is the author of three volumes of verse in English: *Beast, Diet of Nails, Chanameed*, and one in Polish, *Hallo Sztokholm*. He translates from Polish, Czech, and Slovak. Among his many translations published by Glagoslav may be found Jan Balabán's *Maybe We're Leaving*. He is a member of the Union of Polish Writers Abroad (London) and of the Association of Polish Writers (Kraków).

Maybe We're Leaving

by Jan Balaban

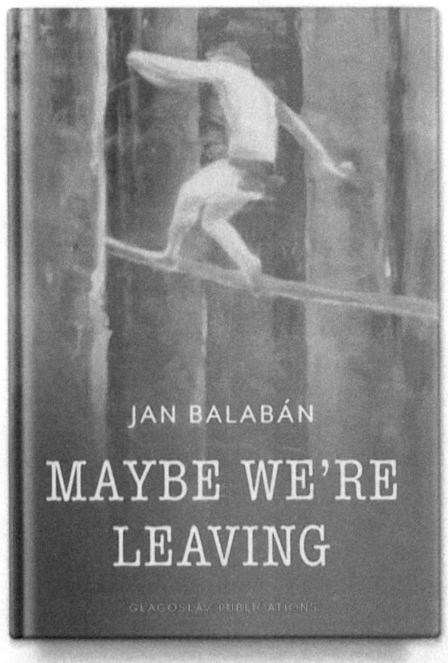

A young boy from the housing estates comes across a copse of old oaks to which he can escape, as to an oasis of calm. Although he may forget about it once he becomes an adult and "puts aside the things of childhood," it will remain a locus of balance, decades later, for a single mother struggling with the difficulties of raising the child she loves. A husband, on the lip of an ugly divorce, drives across town in the middle of the night to rescue his wife, abandoned by her lover, and then — as she falls asleep in the car — takes the long way home, to prolong a moment such as he has not experienced in years. An elderly doctor, self-diagnosed with Alzheimer's disease, makes use of the few precious moments of consciousness granted him each morning to pass on to his grandson what he has learned about life and living responsibly. Loss, and permanence, the ephemeral and the eternal, are common themes of Jan Balabán's collection of short stories *Maybe We're Leaving*, presented here in the English translation of Charles S. Kraszewski. With psychological insight that rivals the great novels of Fyodor Dostoevsky, the twenty-one linked narratives that make up the collection present us with everyday people, with everyday problems — and teach us to love and respect the former, and bear the latter.

Buy it > www.glagoslav.com

Forefathers' Eve

by Adam Mickiewicz

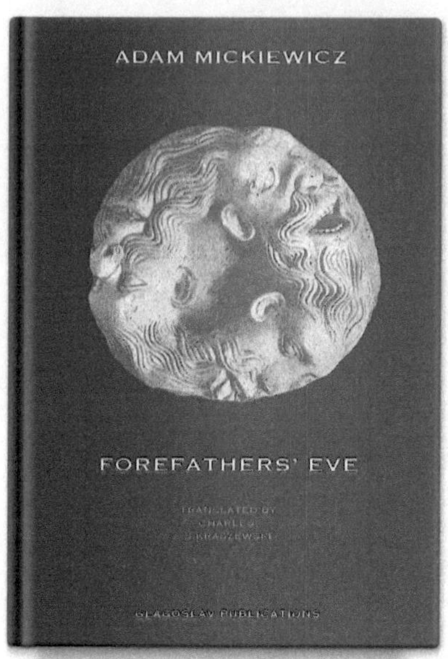

Forefathers' Eve [*Dziady*] is a four-part dramatic work begun circa 1820 and completed in 1832 – with Part I published only after the poet's death, in 1860. The drama's title refers to *Dziady*, an ancient Slavic and Lithuanian feast commemorating the dead. This is the grand work of Polish literature, and it is one that elevates Mickiewicz to a position among the "great Europeans" such as Dante and Goethe.

With its Christian background of the Communion of the Saints, revenant spirits, and the interpenetration of the worlds of time and eternity, *Forefathers' Eve* speaks to men and women of all times and places. While it is a truly Polish work – Polish actors covet the role of Gustaw/Konrad in the same way that Anglophone actors covet that of Hamlet – it is one of the most universal works of literature written during the nineteenth century. It has been compared to Goethe's Faust – and rightfully so...

Buy it > www.glagoslav.com

A Burglar of the Better Sort

by Tytus Czyżewski

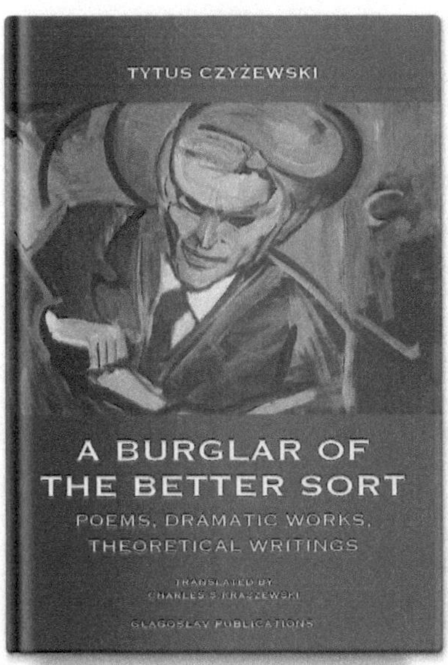

The history of Poland, since the eighteenth century, has been marked by an almost unending struggle for survival. From 1795 through 1945, she was partitioned four times by her stronger neighbours, most of whom were intent on suppressing if not eradicating Polish culture. It is not surprising, then, that much of the great literature written in modern Poland has been politically and patriotically engaged. Yet there is a second current as well, that of authors devoted above all to the craft of literary expression, creating 'art for art's sake,' and not as a didactic national service. Such a poet is Tytus Czyżewski, one of the chief, and most interesting, literary figures of the twentieth century. Growing to maturity in the benign Austrian partition of Poland, and creating most of his works in the twenty-year window of authentic Polish independence stretching between the two world wars, Czyżewski is an avant-garde poet, dramatist and painter who popularised the new approach to poetry established in France by Guillaume Apollinaire, and was to exert a marked influence on such multi-faceted artists as Tadeusz Kantor.

Buy it > www.glagoslav.com

The Door was Open

by Karine Khodikyan

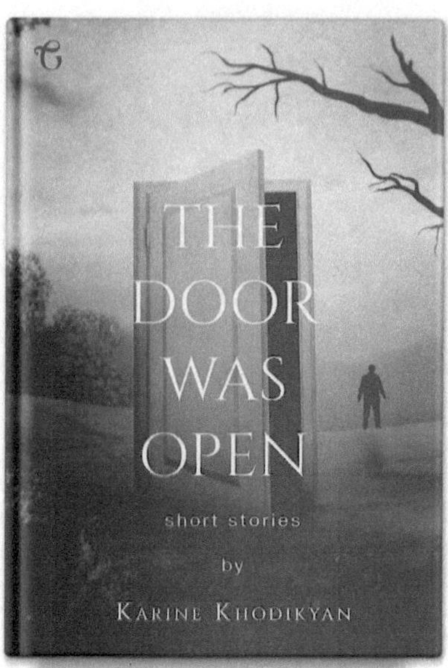

The short fiction of Karine Khodikyan can be described as intellectual fiction for women. These short stories with a "mystical touch" tell stories about women – young and old, happy and sad; even when the protagonist is not a woman, the story will immerse you into the life of a woman, revealing her role in anything and everything.

This book was published with the support of the Ministry of Culture of the Republic of Armenia under the "Armenian Literature in Translation" Program.

Buy it > www.glagoslav.com

The Frontier

28 Contemporary Ukrainian Poets - An Anthology

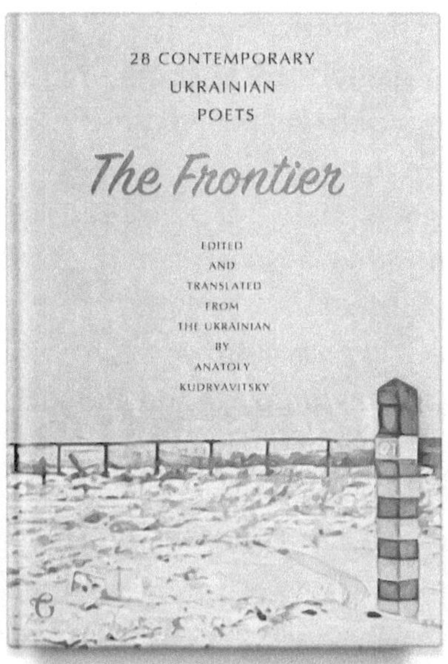

This anthology reflects a search of the Ukrainian nation for its identity, the roots of which lie deep inside Ukrainian-language poetry. Some of the included poets are well-known locally and internationally; among them are Serhiy Zhadan, Halyna Kruk, Ostap Slyvynsky, Marianna Kijanowska, Oleh Kotsarev, Anna Bagriana and, of course, the living legend of Ukrainian poetry, Vasyl Holoborodko. The next Ukrainian poetic generation also features prominently in the collection. Such poets as Les Beley, Olena Herasymyuk, Myroslav Laiuk, Hanna Malihon, Taras Malkovych, Julia Musakovska, Julia Stahivska and Lyuba Yakimchuk are the ones Ukrainians like to read today, and each of them already has an excellent reputation abroad due to festival appearances and translations to European languages. The work collected here documents poetry in Ukraine responding to challenges of the time by forging a radical new poetic, reconsidering writing techniques and language itself.

Edited and translated from the Ukrainian by Anatoly Kudryavitsky.

A Bilingual Edition.

Buy it > www.glagoslav.com

Glagoslav Publications Catalogue

- *The Time of Women* by Elena Chizhova
- *Andrei Tarkovsky: The Collector of Dreams* by Layla Alexander-Garrett
- *Andrei Tarkovsky - A Life on the Cross* by Lyudmila Boyadzhieva
- *Sin* by Zakhar Prilepin
- *Hardly Ever Otherwise* by Maria Matios
- *Khatyn* by Ales Adamovich
- *The Lost Button* by Irene Rozdobudko
- *Christened with Crosses* by Eduard Kochergin
- *The Vital Needs of the Dead* by Igor Sakhnovsky
- *The Sarabande of Sara's Band* by Larysa Denysenko
- *A Poet and Bin Laden* by Hamid Ismailov
- *Watching The Russians (Dutch Edition)* by Maria Konyukova
- *Kobzar* by Taras Shevchenko
- *The Stone Bridge* by Alexander Terekhov
- *Moryak* by Lee Mandel
- *King Stakh's Wild Hunt* by Uladzimir Karatkevich
- *The Hawks of Peace* by Dmitry Rogozin
- *Harlequin's Costume* by Leonid Yuzefovich
- *Depeche Mode* by Serhii Zhadan
- *The Grand Slam and other stories (Dutch Edition)* by Leonid Andreev
- *METRO 2033 (Dutch Edition)* by Dmitry Glukhovsky
- *METRO 2034 (Dutch Edition)* by Dmitry Glukhovsky
- *A Russian Story* by Eugenia Kononenko
- *Herstories, An Anthology of New Ukrainian Women Prose Writers*
- *The Battle of the Sexes Russian Style* by Nadezhda Ptushkina
- *A Book Without Photographs* by Sergey Shargunov
- *Down Among The Fishes* by Natalka Babina
- *disUNITY* by Anatoly Kudryavitsky
- *Sankya* by Zakhar Prilepin
- *Wolf Messing* by Tatiana Lungin
- *Good Stalin* by Victor Erofeyev
- *Solar Plexus* by Rustam Ibragimbekov

- *Don't Call me a Victim!* by Dina Yafasova
- *Poetin (Dutch Edition)* by Chris Hutchins and Alexander Korobko
- *A History of Belarus* by Lubov Bazan
- *Children's Fashion of the Russian Empire* by Alexander Vasiliev
- *Empire of Corruption - The Russian National Pastime* by Vladimir Soloviev
- *Heroes of the 90s: People and Money. The Modern History of Russian Capitalism*
- *Fifty Highlights from the Russian Literature (Dutch Edition)* by Maarten Tengbergen
- *Bajesvolk (Dutch Edition)* by Mikhail Khodorkovsky
- *Tsarina Alexandra's Diary (Dutch Edition)*
- *Myths about Russia* by Vladimir Medinskiy
- *Boris Yeltsin: The Decade that Shook the World* by Boris Minaev
- *A Man Of Change: A study of the political life of Boris Yeltsin*
- *Sberbank: The Rebirth of Russia's Financial Giant* by Evgeny Karasyuk
- *To Get Ukraine* by Oleksandr Shyshko
- *Asystole* by Oleg Pavlov
- *Gnedich* by Maria Rybakova
- *Marina Tsvetaeva: The Essential Poetry*
- *Multiple Personalities* by Tatyana Shcherbina
- *The Investigator* by Margarita Khemlin
- *The Exile* by Zinaida Tulub
- *Leo Tolstoy: Flight from paradise* by Pavel Basinsky
- *Moscow in the 1930* by Natalia Gromova
- *Laurus (Dutch edition)* by Evgenij Vodolazkin
- *Prisoner* by Anna Nemzer
- *The Crime of Chernobyl: The Nuclear Goulag* by Wladimir Tchertkoff
- *Alpine Ballad* by Vasil Bykau
- *The Complete Correspondence of Hryhory Skovoroda*
- *The Tale of Aypi* by Ak Welsapar
- *Selected Poems* by Lydia Grigorieva
- *The Fantastic Worlds of Yuri Vynnychuk*

- *The Garden of Divine Songs and Collected Poetry of Hryhory Skovoroda*
- *Adventures in the Slavic Kitchen: A Book of Essays with Recipes*
- *Seven Signs of the Lion* by Michael M. Naydan
- *Forefathers' Eve* by Adam Mickiewicz
- *One-Two* by Igor Eliseev
- *Girls, be Good* by Bojan Babić
- *Time of the Octopus* by Anatoly Kucherena
- *The Grand Harmony* by Bohdan Ihor Antonych
- *The Selected Lyric Poetry Of Maksym Rylsky*
- *The Shining Light* by Galymkair Mutanov
- *The Frontier: 28 Contemporary Ukrainian Poets - An Anthology*
- *Acropolis: The Wawel Plays* by Stanisław Wyspiański
- *Contours of the City* by Attyla Mohylny
- *Conversations Before Silence: The Selected Poetry of Oles Ilchenko*
- *The Secret History of my Sojourn in Russia* by Jaroslav Hašek
- *Mirror Sand: An Anthology of Russian Short Poems*
- *Maybe We're Leaving* by Jan Balaban
- *Death of the Snake Catcher* by Ak Welsapar
- *A Brown Man in Russia* by Vijay Menon
- *Hard Times* by Ostap Vyshnia
- *The Flying Dutchman* by Anatoly Kudryavitsky
- *Nikolai Gumilev's Africa* by Nikolai Gumilev
- *Combustions* by Srđan Srdić
- *The Sonnets* by Adam Mickiewicz
- *Dramatic Works* by Zygmunt Krasiński
- *Four Plays* by Juliusz Słowacki
- *Little Zinnobers* by Elena Chizhova
- *We Are Building Capitalism! Moscow in Transition 1992-1997*
- *The Nuremberg Trials* by Alexander Zvyagintsev
- *The Hemingway Game* by Evgeni Grishkovets
- *A Flame Out at Sea* by Dmitry Novikov
- *Jesus' Cat* by Grig
- *Want a Baby and Other Plays* by Sergei Tretyakov
- *I Mikhail Bulgakov: The Life and Times* by Marietta Chudakova
- *Leonardo's Handwriting* by Dina Rubina

- *A Burglar of the Better Sort* by Tytus Czyżewski
- *The Mouseiad and other Mock Epics* by Ignacy Krasicki
- *Ravens before Noah* by Susanna Harutyunyan
- *Duel* by Borys Antonenko-Davydovych
- *An English Queen and Stalingrad* by Natalia Kulishenko
- *Point Zero* by Narek Malian
- *Absolute Zero* by Artem Chekh
- *Olanda* by Rafał Wojasiński
- *Robinsons* by Aram Pachyan
- *The Monastery* by Zakhar Prilepin
- *The Selected Poetry of Bohdan Rubchak:*
  Songs of Love, Songs of Death, Songs of the Moon
- *Mebet* by Alexander Grigorenko
- *The Lawyer from Lychakiv* Street by Andriy Kokotiukha
- *Everyday Stories* by Mima Mihajlović
- *The Orchestra* by Vladimir Gonik

More coming soon...